Praise for BETH SHERMAN's JERSEY SHORE MYSTERIES

"Powerful, compelling, and riveting mystery."
Carolyn Hart

"Beth Sherman delivers a solid plot with
surprising twists that will fool even veteran
mystery readers."
Fort Lauderdale Sun-Sentinel

"Everything that Sherman writes
is right on target."
Asbury Park Press

"Ghostwriter Anne Hardaway is a delightful mix
of humor, pragmatism, and vulnerability."
Margaret Maron

"Beth Sherman tantalizes us with intrigue,
proving that even a tranquil town is capable of
canvassing and harboring its own brand of
mystifying danger."
Atlanticville

Other Jersey Shore Mysteries by Beth Sherman

DEAD MAN'S FLOAT
DEATH AT HIGH TIDE
DEATH'S A BEACH
THE DEVIL AND THE DEEP BLUE SEA

BETH SHERMAN

Murder Down the Shore

A JERSEY SHORE MYSTERY

AVON BOOKS

An Imprint of HarperCollinsPublishers

This is a work of fiction. Names, characters, places, and incidents are products of the author's imagination or are used fictitiously and are not to be construed as real. Any resemblance to actual events, locales, organizations, or persons, living or dead, is entirely coincidental.

AVON BOOKS
An Imprint of HarperCollins*Publishers*
10 East 53rd Street
New York, New York 10022-5299

Copyright © 2002 by Beth Sherman
ISBN: 0-380-81606-7
www.avonmystery.com

First Avon Books paperback printing: May 2002

Avon Trademark Reg. U.S. Pat. Off. and in Other Countries, Marca Registrada, Hecho en U.S.A.
HarperCollins ® is a registered trademark of HarperCollins Publishers Inc.

Printed in the U.S.A.

10 9 8 7 6 5 4 3 2 1

To Do:

1. Grocery Shopping
2. Laundry
3. Write Novel

Acknowledgments

As always, I'd like to thank Dominick Abel, Trish Lande Grader, Johanna Keller, and Andy, Jessie and Sam Edelstein. I'd also like to thank the many dog and cat owners who talked to me about their much beloved pets.

ACKNOWLEDGMENTS

Murder
Down the
Shore

Chapter 1

Cats, much like people, do not respond well to new, unusual, or unpredictable events. In fact, they get stressed out by them.

"Which do you think? Roses or hyacinths?"

Anne Hardaway turned to study the two flowers. The roses were pink and blowsy, like tissue-paper pompoms, the hyacinths striking yet understated, forming sprightly lavender towers.

She looked around the room again, at the bed with the curlicue wrought-iron headboard shaped like Venus on the half-shell, the dresser painted hot pink with its matching nightstand, the purple cheesecloth curtain swag blowing ever so slightly in the breeze.

"Could we do both?"

"Why not? Now if I just had more lilies, I'd . . ."

Patricia Mooney set a tin pitcher on the dresser and began interspersing the roses and hyacinths with black-eyed Susans, delphinium, and other flowers culled from her garden, creating an artful arrangement. She was a tall, slender

woman in her early forties with oval-shaped eyes, a perpetually distracted air, and a habit of starting projects that
never got finished. Her denim overalls were splattered with
dirt and paint, the result of gardening and home improve-
ment projects, and wisps of unevenly cut hair fell across
her face.

Anne smoothed the folds of the chenille bedspread, which
was covered with large appliquéd daisies, and watched the
midmorning sun dance across the pine plank floors. They
were on the second floor of the Laughing Gull, a small bed-
and-breakfast two blocks from the beach in Oceanside
Heights, New Jersey. There were five other rooms on this
level and six more below, all decorated with objects that had
been purchased for a song or rescued from the trash and re-
furbished—lamps made out of matchsticks and bottle caps,
pillows with silly sayings, mismatched teacups, Hummel
figurines, salt and pepper shakers from the 1950s—prompting *New Jersey* magazine to call the Laughing Gull "a
quirky little-known gem in the necklace of inns strung along
the Jersey Shore."

Anne glanced at her watch. Ten-thirty. In less than two
hours they'd be here.

"Stop worrying," Pat chided, sticking a blush-colored rose
next to a russet nasturtium.

"I just want everything to be perfect."

"It will be," said Pat. She had bought the Laughing Gull
two years ago when it was called the Dew Drop Inn and had
renovated it from top to bottom.

Anne smiled wanly. What if Pat was wrong? What if her
relatives took one look at the bed-and-breakfast and wished
they'd decided to hold the reunion someplace else—like
Disney World or Nashville or on one of those cruise ships to
nowhere that sailed one hundred miles into the Atlantic
Ocean, then turned around and came right back.

No, she argued, trying to play devil's advocate. This was their hometown where they'd grown up and lived for decades. They had roots here, memories. Even though, truth be told, every one of her relatives had left the Heights years ago. They rarely visited and seemed uninterested in what had changed in the intervening years and what had remained remarkably (at least to Anne) the same.

Of the twenty-nine people that she'd invited to the family reunion, only seven were returning. The others were too busy or had made other plans for this weekend or, it had seemed from the terse way they'd responded to the invite, simply didn't want to be bothered. But her second cousins were coming. Thank God for that. She was excited about seeing them again, especially Nora. It had been nearly a year since she'd last seen Nora.

She went into the hall, taking a quick inventory of each of the other rooms. Cece was to have the one with dozens of hats on the walls—bowlers, fedoras, ribbon-bedecked bonnets, straw boaters—right next to the small corner "suite" for Kimberly and Larry, which contained the only king-size bed in the house, as well as framed menus from 1950s Jersey diners, a collection of vintage waffle irons, and a wealth of bird-related knickknacks. Alex's room had a bug theme: dragonfly decals, an oval mirror shaped like a spider, ladybug Jell-O molds that doubled as candy jars, and a bumblebee bedspread. Henry was to occupy a corner room furnished with Pat's deceased grandparents' dark mahogany bedroom set, several silver candelabras, framed photos of Pat's relatives posing stiffly for the camera, and a stuffed rainbow trout, a room from which, at a certain angle, you could spot a slender ribbon of ocean.

Great-aunt Hannah was the only one not staying at the Laughing Gull. She was returning to Dovecote, the big gray house on Embury Street where Anne had spent so many holidays as a child, now dark and shuttered except on those rare occasions when Aunt Hannah returned to town.

Anne had briefly entertained the notion that Aunt Hannah would invite the others to stay with her. But her aunt was having none of it.

"What arrangements have you made for the family?" Aunt Hannah had asked in clipped tones on the phone.

"They'll stay with me," Anne had responded, instantly warming to the idea.

But her cousins had demurred, saying they didn't want to put Anne out, and Aunt Hannah's son, Henry, had suggested a bed-and-breakfast, something charming and cozy, near the beach.

In Henry's room, Anne caught a glimpse of her reflection in the mirror, which had hundreds of buttons pasted onto its frame. She was glad she still had a little time to get ready. Her long wavy red hair was pulled back in a ponytail, her face was smudged with dirt—the result of sweeping dust from under her living room sofa in anticipation of the Welcome Home lunch she planned to serve. She wore a man's work shirt over a pair of raggedy denim shorts, and there was a worried glint in her normally clear blue eyes. Still, she looked younger than forty-one. She rubbed a streak of dirt off her cheek and decided that with a little makeup and a blow-dryer, she could definitely pass for thirty-four or thirty-five.

She made a mental list of the things she had to do before the reunion lunch: Buy more diet soda and French bread at the Mini-Mart, stock up on film, pick up her dry cleaning, make sure there were enough clean beach towels.

She drifted back to the room she'd selected for Nora. It was bright and cheerful, a little sunnier than the others. (She hoped it wasn't too garish.) In the doorway, she stopped short. Pat had dumped the flowers onto the rag rug, where they drooped mournfully, and was starting to arrange them again from scratch.

"Colors clashed," Pat murmured, by way of explanation.

"I think it looked great," Anne protested. "Really."

She picked up a dripping rose and handed it to the frowning Pat. "My cousin Nora knows as much about flowers as I do about football. She'd be just as happy with an artificial wreath."

"You know what I've found?" Pat asked rhetorically. "It's the little touches that make a big impression and hook you right into a place."

"Thanks so much for fitting us in on such short notice."

Pat shrugged. "No problem-o. It's been a little slow this summer anyway. Especially after that brouhaha with the town council."

Pat was engaged in an ongoing battle with council members over whether she could legally sell self-published cookbooks, homemade sachets, painted trivets, "antique" small electrical appliances, and other notions displayed discreetly on the top shelf of a secondhand cupboard in the front parlor. According to council bylaws, zoning restrictions prohibited properties within a three-block radius of the boardwalk from "the buying or selling of goods." This was to ensure that the town's pristine beach didn't end up looking like Wildwood or Seaside Heights, where vendors hawked T-shirts and games of chance, and the scent of sausage and onions drifted down to the sand.

Pat had simply ignored the laws and shouted down the opposition, prompting her opponents to omit the Laughing Gull's name from all promotional brochures and maps touting the charms of Oceanside Heights.

That, coupled with Pat's personality, had sent the vacancy rate into overdrive, despite the brief plug from *New Jersey* magazine. It wasn't that Patricia Mooney was intentionally abrasive. But in Anne's opinion, Pat wasn't cut out to run a bed-and-breakfast. For starters, Pat wasn't a people person. She could be downright reclusive at times, retreating to her room at the back of the house and letting the teenagers she'd hired for the summer run the place.

At other times, Pat was practically in her guests' faces— fluffing pillows, rearranging knickknacks, chattering a mile a minute about whatever popped into her mind. She started projects but rarely finished them, threw money into improving the lavender turn-of-the-century bed-and-breakfast but rarely bothered to comb her prematurely gray hair or button her shirts correctly. She cooked elaborate breakfasts, but served wacky dishes like garlic-flavored flan and omelets laced with chives and sherry. Guests were either charmed or annoyed.

Anne hoped her relatives fit into the former camp. She'd tried to reserve rooms at six other places before settling on the Laughing Gull, but it was mid-August—the height of the tourist season—and all the inns she'd called were full. Now, as she gazed at the flowers strewn on the floor, she thought wistfully of the Early American antiques at the Royal Atlantic, overlooking the ocean, and of the charming afternoon teas served by the proprietor of the La-Dee-Da, on Abbott Avenue.

"So what do you have planned for the weekend?" Pat asked.

She'd shucked off her sandals and plopped down on the bed.

"The usual, I guess. We'll go to the beach, have a barbecue. Maybe drive down to Spring Lake or Barnegat Light. And, of course, there's the regatta on Sunday, followed by the concert."

"Who could forget that? Seems like the whole town's

turned upside down preparing for it. Sounds like you picked a good weekend for the reunion."

"I hope so."

Pat turned onto her side, propping herself up with one elbow. "You seem worried. What's the problem?"

Anne couldn't say, exactly. She and her cousins had been close in high school, but that was over twenty years ago. Apart from the occasional postcard or e-mail, she'd been woefully out of touch. She had only a dim idea of what their lives were like now and of the people they'd become. Then there was Aunt Hannah, who was as cranky and irascible as a grasshopper stuck inside a closed shoe box. The last Anne had heard, Aunt Hannah and her son, Henry, were no longer on speaking terms.

But Anne felt like now was the perfect time for a family reunion. Ever since her grandmother, Betty Hardaway, died four months ago, she'd been thinking about how cut off she felt from her family, how alone she was in the world. Of course, she had her boyfriend and her friends. But Grandma Betty had meant the world to her, and she'd lived on Cookman Street, only a few blocks away. Anne had thought briefly about having a Hardaway family reunion, then reconsidered. She'd seen the Hardaways at Grandma Betty's funeral. They were formal and remote. She remembered that she'd never been especially close to any of her father's relatives. Growing up, they'd been names tacked onto Christmas cards, staring out at her from old photographs, distant as the pale, far off constellations in the night sky.

Better to invite her mother's kin. They had been fixtures during her childhood, when the whole clan got together afternoons and weekends for cookouts and picnics, and she and her cousins would swim or ride bikes, or later, spend hours poring through teen magazines and doing each other's hair. When her mother developed Alzheimer's, her cousins had stood by her, offering support, distraction, and a sympathetic ear. She wished she'd kept in better touch these last few years.

Aloud, Anne said, "You know how families are. It can be hard for everyone to get along sometimes."

Pat let out a loud commiserating groan. "You're telling me. My mom's a royal pain in the behind." Pat rolled over onto her back and ticked off her mother's faults on her fingers. "She hates everything. She's too critical. She smokes too much. She's always feeling sorry for herself. I went over there a couple of months ago to help her clean out her attic and all she kept asking was when am I going to sell this 'dump' and find a man who'll take me off her hands."

Anne tried to imagine Pat cleaning out someone's attic. Pat was just about the messiest person she knew. While the public areas and guest rooms of the Laughing Gull were cleaned and swept each week by the hired help, Pat's private quarters were a regular pigsty. Stacks of old newspapers moldered in corners. Laundry was strewn about. Pat's various repair projects created a perpetual atmosphere of clutter. It was so dusty, you could see cobwebs on the windowsills. And if you opened one of Pat's closets, you'd better watch your head.

"Like I was ever a burden to Mother," Pat was saying sarcastically. "I've practically been on my own since I was twelve."

Anne nodded sympathetically. Her own mother had suffered from Alzheimer's for years before she died. Anne knew what it was like to take care of yourself at an impossibly young age, to assume the role of parent, caretaker, and watchdog when her mother could barely remember what year it was or the name of her only child.

"Family dynamics are never simple," Anne said, picking

up the soggy flowers and sticking them willy-nilly into the vase.

She wondered for the umpteenth time what her family's reaction to Mark Trasker would be. Trasker was a detective in the Neptune Township Sheriff's Office. He'd been her best friend and lover for over a year. He also happened to be black, a fact she hadn't shared with all her relatives.

Pat said, "It'll be interesting to see your cousins again. Especially Cecilia."

Anne remembered that Pat and Cece had been in the same class at school, two years ahead of her and Nora and a year behind Kimberly and Alex.

"Is Cecilia still a wild child?" Pat said, with a smirk. "Still painting those huge pictures of naked people doing the nasty?"

Anne blushed. "She works at California Pizza Kitchen, actually."

"In California?"

"San Francisco."

"She's a waitress?"

"I think she's the manager."

"Doesn't sound like the Cecilia I remember," Pat said. She peered out the window. It was a hot, humid morning. A band of low-lying clouds formed a raggedy gray line over the beach. "By the way, you might want to table those beach plans."

"Why?"

"Haven't you heard the latest forecast? Cloudy with scattered showers, all weekend long."

Chapter 2

Be patient with your cat. Don't be discouraged if it takes longer than expected to eliminate unwanted behaviors. If you're persistent, sincere, and vocal, you will prevail.

Oceanside Heights was unlike most towns on the Jersey Shore. Founded in 1896 by a crusading Methodist minister, it still retained a strong religious flavor. Each summer, more than one hundred tents were set up around the Church by the Sea and people from all over the country gathered for spirited camp revival meetings. In addition to services, there were gospel sings, organ recitals, and daily Bible hour. Restaurants and stores in the Heights were prohibited from selling alcohol, and on Sundays the beach didn't open until noon. Only a quarter of a mile wide, the Heights was known as "God's own acre," and was one of New Jersey's designated historic landmarks.

The Victorian houses, with their turrets, gingerbread, fret-work, and cupolas, were another draw for tourists, who some-times posed for snapshots in front of picturesque front porches. The Heights had a quaint, small-town flavor, still rare in the era of malls and superstores. But the town was also cranking up its marketing campaign, billing itself as "New Jersey's Best Kept Secret," and Anne wasn't so sure she liked the new and improved image.

There was a glossier look to Main Street these days, with many of the old shops and restaurants replaced by more up-scale stores. A fancy pizzeria had opened in what used to be a luncheonette; they didn't sell slices, you had to spring for a small pie. The shabby Advent Pharmacy had morphed into Ye Olde Soda Shop, designed to look like a 1950s soda shop, complete with cherry cokes and egg creams. An an-tiques "emporium" had opened near the corner of Main and Olin Street, with eighteen vendors selling everything from majolica to Mickey Mouse lunch boxes.

Oh, the hardware store was still there, as was Freedman's Bakery and Baby Face dolls. But the town was starting to look a little too cutesy and manicured for Anne's taste. She was shocked when a renovated five-bedroom house some blocks from the beach came on the market for $405,000, and secretly hoped the owners wouldn't get more than half of what they were asking. Her own house, a yellow Victorian cottage directly across from the beach, featured a wrap-around porch, bay windows, and gingerbread galore. Real estate agents were always sliding their cards into her mail-box, offering free estimates. But she wasn't interested.

She'd grown up in the house and still loved the view of the ocean from her living room and the way the waves rocked her to sleep at night. She'd kept the house looking much the way it had when her parents were still alive: same furniture, rugs, curtains, dishes. The familiarity was comforting, not to mention inexpensive. As a ghostwriter who worked from home, she tried to keep her overhead down. You didn't make a whole lot of money writing books on how to handle home repairs, or raise your kids right, or find a man, or dump the man you'd found, or any of the other myriad topics she'd covered in the last few years. But you did become an instant expert, with a wealth of trivia at your fingertips.

Her latest project—*The Pet Connection: How to Raise Well-adjusted, Nonneurotic Cats and Dogs*—was turning out to be fun. Unlike the prima donna authors Anne usually worked with, Edie Mintzler, a Los Angeles pet expert with a syndicated TV show, had a delightful sense of humor and boundless enthusiasm for her subject matter.

Anne had even started testing out what she'd learned on Harry, her one-eyed black-and-white cat, with mixed results. He'd gotten better at not climbing up her drapes since she'd invested in a tall scratching post with four "resting shelves." But Harry still refused to get into his carrier when it was time to go to the vet, and no amount of coaxing would convince him otherwise. Edie had told her to try taking the carrier apart, washing, it and placing a favorite blanket in the bottom half. Edie had also recommended giving Harry a special treat in the carrier bottom several times a day for a few days, gradually replacing the top, and making comforting, sympathetic noises.

Still no go. Harry had flatly refused to eat the strained jar of baby food chicken Anne had put in there to tempt him, shooting her a look that said, *You must be kidding!*

Anne knew when she was licked, even though Edie had told her to keep trying until it worked. Edie considered herself "bi-pet." She loved cats and dogs equally well and had genuine affection for hamsters, turtles, fish, rabbits, and garter snakes. Anne, she'd decided, was more of a cat person: independent, introspective, low-maintenance, a survivor.

Not that Anne wasn't happy. At the moment, work was good. Her health was fine. And her love life had taken a definite turn for the better, ever since she'd started dating Mark Trasker. They'd been seeing each other for nearly a year, and Anne found it was the first long-term relationship she'd been in that didn't seem like hard work. There were none of the stomach flips she'd experienced in the past, no tearful nights and anxious dawns, no analyzing every word he said, searching for hidden meanings and then repeating the conversations verbatim to her friends for further in-depth analysis.

Maybe it was because she and Trasker had started out as friends. Or maybe he was more together than the guys she'd dated in the past. Whatever the reason, Anne tried not to overanalyze their relationship. They were in sync and that's what mattered. They had fun together. They wanted the same things out of life. They enjoyed each other.

If there was a wrinkle in the fabric of their relationship, it had to do with the main difference between them, with race. Anne was white, Trasker was black. She'd gotten over feeling uncomfortable when they were in a store or on the beach and people stared at them a few beats too long, when his was the only black face at the movies or their favorite seafood joint. But skin color separated them in ways she couldn't entirely explain.

She felt that he experienced life differently than she did, that he detected wariness in a shopkeeper's "May I help you?" rage in a passing motorist's blaring car horn. The more time she spent with him, the more she realized that for Trasker each day presented a fresh series of potential land mines lurking beneath the placid surface of daily life.

At first, she thought he was overreacting. Then, after they'd been together for a little while, she thought, No, it's out there. She'd been naive to believe otherwise. Prejudice. Discrimination. Hatred. The looks, the stares, the unspoken relief when Trasker left a store or a restaurant where his was the only black face. It existed. It was constant. It informed Trasker's world and now her world, as well.

It seeped into the relationship, too, in ways she couldn't quite define. There was a part of him, the part having to do with his past, with growing up on welfare in the drug-soaked streets of Trenton, with having to put himself through college working the most menial jobs, with clawing his way through the predominantly white rank-and-file police force to make detective, that Trasker kept separate from her. Whenever she tried to draw him out further, he managed to change the subject.

Sometimes she tried to imagine what the future held. If she gave birth to a biracial child, would that child be teased and taunted growing up? Would she and Trasker ever get used to being viewed as, at best, a curiosity, at worst, an abomination in the natural order of things? Was she initially drawn to him because she, too, had always felt like an outsider? What would her family think? She'd told only Nora and Cece the truth. What would Kim or Alex or proper Aunt Hannah and Henry make of a black man in their midst? Would they accept him or would it only be a pretense, an excuse to criticize her values and the choices she'd made?

Anne placed her favorite blue ceramic salad bowl in the center of the dining table. She'd planned a cold buffet: gazpacho, three kinds of pasta salad, fresh greens, cold poached salmon with dill sauce, tomatoes and mozzarella cheese on squares of garlic toast, and a huge fruit platter, followed by apple crumb pie and ice cream. Invitations were prominently displayed in each of her relatives' rooms. *Welcome! Before you start unpacking, come to brunch chez Hardaway to kick off our Reunion Weekend at the Shore.*

She'd set the table with a peach-colored linen cloth, the

heavy silverplate flatware, and her mother's Lenox china, which almost never got used.

"Wow," Trasker had teased, when he'd stopped by on his way to work. "You're bringing out the heavy artillery."

"I want this to go well."

"How could it not? You've been planning these next few days as carefully and thoroughly as American soldiers about to storm the beaches of Normandy."

"True," Anne had countered playfully.

"Hey, they're going to enjoy every fun-filled minute. Once they get over the shock of meeting me, that is."

Anne had studied him carefully. She thought she'd seen concern behind his smiling brown eyes, the tension gathering on his usually smooth brow. Well, of course he was worried. He was meeting her family for the very first time. If only they could see him as she did, see how strong and caring and fine he was.

He'd come over and slid his arms around her. His mouth had moved down her neck and she'd shivered with pleasure. She loved when he touched her, loved the way his lips brushed her skin. He made her feel more sensuous than any man she'd ever known.

"Do you know how amazing you are?" he'd whispered, playing with her hair. "God, I love you."

She'd hugged him close, feeling how incredibly lucky she was to have found him. "I love you, too, T. You're the best."

Now, as she stood at the window and waited for her family to arrive, she realized she'd been harboring a secret agenda all along. If the weekend was a success, maybe Nora or Cece or Kim would want to get a summer place in the Heights. It would be just like old times. Shopping, hanging out, staying up and yakking until the wee hours of the morning. It'd be like having a sister, or sisters, if only for three months of the year.

She thought back to her childhood when her grandmother, Ruth, and Ruth's three sisters, Doris, Molly, and Hannah, had dominated the family. The four Rutter girls, as they'd been called well into their sixties, had grown up in the Heights and were as different from one another as four sisters could be. Grandma Ruth was the kind one, Molly the prettiest, Doris the quiet one, and Hannah . . . Well, Hannah was Hannah. Stern, overbearing, forceful, the family matriarch. Maybe that's why Hannah's two surviving sisters hadn't come to the reunion. Maybe they didn't want to be back under Hannah's thumb, even if it was only for a weekend.

Anne heard laughter outside and ran to the window. Her cousin Kimberly was coming up the front walk, looking not much different than she had at sixteen, in a calf-length denim skirt, a cap-sleeved cotton blouse, and low, sensible shoes. Her light brown hair was pulled back from her face with a paisley headband Anne could have sworn Kim had had in eleventh grade. Even her gold, wire-rimmed glasses looked the same. Next to Kim walked a woman with platinum-blond hair, cut in a short bob. The woman was fashionably thin, in a short black skirt and white cotton blouse that had yellowed with age. Over the blouse she wore a dirty gray baseball jersey with *Tigers* printed on the lapel. She had on brown army boots and thick white socks, and she carried a battered-looking gray duffel bag.

Anne threw open the front door and ran out to greet them.

"Hi guys. Welcome," she said, throwing her arms around her cousins. Then, to Cece: "I almost didn't recognize you at first."

"You like?" Cece said, pirouetting on the walkway. She raked the tips of her fingers through her hair. "It's a wig."

"It's fabulous," Anne said enthusiastically, feeling a surge of affection for her cousin. "You look like a movie star. And

I'm so glad you're both here. I didn't think you'd make it in time for lunch."

"I took the red-eye from the coast," Cece said. She bounded up the steps and sprawled in a wicker chair. "Let's porch sit for a while. Alex and Nora are right behind us. He's giving her a lift in his new 'Vette."

"Did he bring anyone with him?" Anne asked, suddenly worried. "I booked him a single room at the B&B."

"I believe Alex is between girlfriends right now," said Kim. "Though I wouldn't be surprised if he hooks up with one of his old flames here in town. Oh, and Larry said to tell you he's sorry he can't come to lunch. He brought his cell phone and all this boring work along so I don't think we'll be seeing much of him this weekend."

"But Aunt Hannah will be here," Cece added, with a sly wink.

Kim rolled her eyes. "Annie, wait till you hear who Aunt Hannah brought down. You'll never believe—"

She was interrupted by a soft scratching noise behind them.

"That must be Harry," Anne said.

She got up, opened the screen door, and the cat loped onto the porch. He eyed the visitors with suspicion, until Kim scooped him up in her arms and he let out a loud yelp of protest.

"He's darling," Kim exclaimed, petting him under the chin. "I hope Bootsie's okay. The girls promised they wouldn't let her starve, but you know how teenagers can be."

Harry wriggled uncomfortably. "It takes him a while to get used to people," Anne explained.

She sat down in the settee, opposite Kim, who had commandeered the wicker rocker and pulled the reluctant Harry into her lap.

"So what's this about Aunt Hannah?" Anne asked.

Cece started to giggle. "Hannah has a *boyfriend*," she said, in a stage whisper.

"You're kidding!"

"Well, a gentleman friend, at any rate," Kim corrected, stroking the fur between Harry's ears. "His name's Chase Merritt. He's in his mid-sixties, which would make him about twenty years younger than Hannah. She met him six weeks ago at the Gardner Museum and they've been inseparable ever since."

Anne's eyes widened in astonishment. "They're not . . . ?"

"Goodness, no," Kim shot back, coloring slightly. "He's staying at the Laughing Gull this weekend, not with Auntie. She made that very plain. But she's bought him some jewelry, including a big fat gold ring with an onyx stone that he wears all the time. And he does spend an awful lot of time at the Boston house. He's been over for dinner nearly every night."

"How's that going?" Cece interrupted. "Living in Aunt Hannah's oh-so-grand townhouse? I'd be afraid I'd use the wrong soup spoon or accidentally bump into one of those porcelain dogs that clutter up the place."

"It's only temporary," Kim said quickly. "Until the insurance money comes in and we can start the renovations on our place. The insurance company is giving us the runaround. They have some crazy idea it was arson. Of course, that's ridiculous. They just don't want to pay us the money."

Anne nodded sympathetically. A fire had broken out two months ago in Kim and Larry's four-bedroom center hall Colonial in Newton, Massachusetts. Luckily, the family had been at the movies when the fire broke out, the result of faulty wiring on the part of a careless electrician who'd been hired to install track lighting in the family room. Though the house hadn't burned down, it was temporarily unlivable.

Kim and Larry had taken the girls and their few possessions that hadn't been ruined and moved into Aunt Hannah's Beacon Hill townhouse.

"So how are your new digs?" Cece asked.

"It's actually not that bad," Kim amended. "There's a cook and a maid. I never even have to make the beds."

"Right," Cece said, and Anne thought she heard a trace of bitterness in her cousin's voice. "Must be nice to be filthy rich."

"I've been rich and I've been poor. Rich is better," Kim said, in a high falsetto, imitating their great-aunt.

Anne and Cece laughed. It had been one of Aunt Hannah's favorite bits of advice when they were younger. Not that they'd adhered to it. Nora, Alex, Cece, and Anne had never married. Kim had come closest, marrying Larry Ryerson, who parlayed a small family-owned shoe store into a chain called Trash Talk that catered to the changing tastes of teenagers. This year it was platform sneakers, iridescent sandals, and black leather shoes with chunky heels and boxy toes that looked like they'd be absolute hell on your feet.

Aunt Hannah herself had married into money, to an unassuming, gentle man who just happened to have founded the largest uniform supply company on the East Coast. They moved to Boston in 1984. When he died, three years later, she became the ninth wealthiest person in the state of Massachusetts, according to a business story in the *Boston Globe*, which Kim had dutifully clipped, Xeroxed, and mailed to each cousin.

"So what's going on in the Heights?" Kim asked Anne. "I barely recognize Main Street anymore."

"Never mind that," Cece said impatiently. "Give us the dirt. Did Isabel Covington ever get out of rehab? Has Dawn Arena gotten married yet? Is Teri Curley still with Bobby?"

For the next ten minutes Anne brought them up to date on the local gossip. It wasn't hard to do. The Heights was a small town. Everyone knew everybody else's business.

When she'd finished, she noticed that Harry had fallen asleep on Kim's lap and that the beach was pretty crowded for a cloudy Thursday afternoon. Colorful umbrellas had sprouted up like mushrooms; blankets lay end to end on the sand. The sky was hazy, but deceptive. You could still get a tan. Anne supposed that people were trying to get in a little last-minute sunbathing before the bad weather arrived.

"Hey," Cece cried out. "Here come Alex and Nora."

A green Corvette convertible came into view and eased into a parking space across the street. Alex was at the wheel. He and Nora were clearly brother and sister. Alex was muscular and tall, with deep blue eyes and an unruly shock of black hair. They each had the same prominent cheekbones, aquiline noses, and full lips, though Nora was sleeker-looking.

Back in high school, she'd done some catalog and runway modeling, and she still carried herself like a model, still possessed that same mixture of poise and nonchalance. Her skin was two or three shades darker than normal, as if she'd already spent lots of time in the sun this summer. Her hair was cut in wispy bangs and layered so that it just reached her shoulders.

Anne stood up and waved. Nora got out of the car and waved back excitedly.

She wore a sleeveless navy blue dress that showed off her legs and a pair of two-tone taupe and blue pumps. Nora loved to shop. As one of the partners in an up-and-coming Miami ad agency, she took clothes seriously and didn't own much that wasn't hand-sewn and expensive.

"She looks great," Anne said, to no one in particular.

"So what else is new?" Kim replied, with a grin.

They watched as Alex and Nora crossed the street and made their way to the porch.

"Hey, cuz," Alex said, crushing Anne in a bear hug.

"Hey yourself. I haven't seen you in ages."

Nora rushed forward and Anne was enveloped in a delicious cloud of perfume. She felt a wave of happiness. She couldn't help it. Nora had always been her favorite, though she tried not to let it show.

Nora took a step back. "God, it's great to see you," she said, her blue eyes dancing merrily, her laugh as musical as ever.

"Same here."

Anne looked around at her cousins. They were all smiling, and Anne thought they were pleased to be home at last, pleased at the chance to reconnect with one another after years of being apart. Alex got a camera out of his car and proceeded to snap a couple of photographs that were developed instantly, before their eyes. Cece took some pictures, so Alex could be in them, and then Anne grabbed the camera for a final shot.

Later she was to remember that moment: the steady crash of waves against the shoreline, the sky streaked with low white clouds, like a cream parfait, the joyful expressions on each of their faces, their smiles suffusing the instant photos. Her cousins. Her flesh and blood. She wanted to freeze time, to bottle this incredibly buoyant, wonderful feeling before everything went utterly and uncontrollably wrong.

Chapter 3

Cats are generally easier to take care of than dogs. They're more independent and don't require a tremendous amount of attention from their owners. Dogs, on the other hand, are more high maintenance. They eat more, crave affection, need regular exercise, and are more sociable creatures.

"You girls need to get a move on," Aunt Hannah remarked tartly.

They were midway through lunch. Aunt Hannah sat at one end of the table, opposite Anne. Chase Merritt was on Aunt Hannah's right, pouring her a second glass of iced tea.

He wasn't what Anne had expected. She'd been picturing a gentleman caller out of Tennessee Williams, someone who wore broad-brimmed felt hats and pulled a lady's chair out for her automatically, someone who waltzed effortlessly and knew the difference between a Beethoven concerto and a Bach sonata.

At first glance Chase Merritt was none of these things. A beefy, broad-shouldered man with shaggy eyebrows and deep jowls, Merritt gave the impression of being working class. His voice was gravelly. His hands were rough and thick. The beginnings of a beer belly sagged over his plaid Bermuda shorts. He looked like a plumber or a bit player in a third-rate gangster flick.

Yet his attitude was decidedly patrician, his table manners fastidious, and his Boston (pronounced Bah-ston) accent seemed exaggerated. He'd even brought a pretentious gift in an Isabella Stewart Gardner Museum tote bag—chocolate nut truffles dipped in brandy. He'd been condescendingly superior to Anne and her relatives from the minute he'd strolled through the door. *Wasn't the fish a tad undercooked? Didn't the Heights fairly ooze Victoriana? Wasn't it a shame that there was no world-class art museum in Jersey?*

His tone was so outraged, his face so stricken, that it sounded as if the state of New Jersey had offended him personally. When it came to Aunt Hannah, however, he couldn't have been more charming: soliciting her opinion on every topic raised at the table, complimenting her foregoing the garlic toast in favor of pita bread that Anne had put out at the last minute, addressing most of his remarks to Aunt Hannah alone, and gazing at Anne's aunt as if she were a spokesmodel for Victoria's Secret, instead of a wrinkled, silver-haired dowager.

Anne studied the gold and onyx ring on his pinkie finger. It looked like it had cost Aunt Hannah a bundle. Could she really care for him? Was it possible she'd fallen in love?

She certainly seemed to be savoring the attention. Short and plump, Aunt Hannah favored calf-length dresses with high collars, even in summer, like the pale gray, long-sleeved dress she had worn to the lunch. She had on sensible shoes with thick crepe soles. On formal occasions she donned elbow-length white kid gloves that buttoned up the side. Her collection of boxy patent leather handbags was so old they were now back in style. Her only concession to "fashion," as she called it, was her taste in jewelry, which was expensive and plentiful. Today she had on the large topaz ring she always wore, as well as a sapphire in a diamond setting and a pretty rectangular aquamarine ring. Sparkly earrings dangled from her ears, and each of her gold bracelets was an inch thick. Around her neck she wore a double string of pearls and a cameo on a gold chain.

Except for the jewelry, she was the sort of woman who didn't attract attention. Her features were plain. Square jaw, high forehead, thin lips. And she never seemed to fuss over her appearance. She wore very little makeup: pale lipstick, light blue eye shadow, some dusting powder that she hadn't completely rubbed in. Her thinning hair was dyed a champagne straw-colored shade and fashioned bouffant style. You might think she was the type of woman who in later life spent her free hours baking cookies for her grandchildren or handing out books and magazines as a hospital volunteer, but in this respect you'd be wrong. Hannah Rutter hated children and couldn't abide sick people.

Anne had seen photographs of Hannah as a young woman. Though her great-aunt had never been beautiful, she had exuded plenty of self confidence and superiority. Hannah had always set herself apart from the family. Anne suspected that at heart, she considered herself above the family, having had the smarts to marry into money and parlay her investments into a small fortune.

"In my day," she was saying, rapping her spoon sharply against her mug of tea to make her point, "if you weren't married by age twenty-one, your life, for all intent and purpose, was ruined."

Her dog—a black and tan pug named Bronte with droopy ears and a wrinkled, pushed-in face—barked in assent. The dog had a large mole on her left cheek, a flat nose, large protruding brown eyes, and skin that looked perpetually clenched and folded. Anne thought Bronte was just about the ugliest dog she'd ever seen.

She looked around the room for Harry and found him sitting in the far corner of the room, eyeing Bronte with a mixture of fear and dislike.

"Oh, I know times have changed since then," Aunt Hannah continued. "But aren't you girls tired of dating? Aren't you worried that by the time you've made up your minds to marry, all the eligible men will be taken?"

Nora speared a forkful of pasta salad. "Marriage doesn't guarantee happiness," she said lightly. "I'd rather be alone than saddled with a man I married because it no longer felt comfortable to be single. If you settle for less, you wind up with less."

Anne glanced at Kim, whose eyes were fixed on her plate. She'd sensed that Kim and Larry had their share of problems, a fact that was never mentioned in Kim's cheery Christmas newsletters. They'd married young, right after college, which many in the family had viewed as a mistake.

"Besides," Anne said, "women no longer need men to support them. We have our work, our friends. It's hard to be happily in love until you've shored up your own life first."

"Bosh," Aunt Hannah retorted. "Young people today are so bent on having careers." She waved her hand dismissively, as if to imply that all the books Anne had written and the advertisements Nora had created were no more significant than bits of dandelion fluff. "Can you honestly say you aren't happier now that you've found this detective of yours?"

Anne felt everyone's eyes boring down on her. "Of course I'm happy," she said carefully. "But it's not like I was miserable before I started dating Mark."

"When are we going to meet the young man?" Aunt Hannah asked pointedly. "I thought he'd want to join us for luncheon."

"He's at work," Anne said. "I'm not sure what time he's getting off tonight, but hopefully he can meet us for dinner."

The thought of that dinner made her palms sweat. What would Aunt Hannah do when she saw Trasker for the first time? How was she going to react?

"Well, dear, I trust he's more appropriate than some of your other beaux," Aunt Hannah chided.

Anne could feel herself blush. Several years ago she'd had a brief affair with a local married dentist named David Chilton, and news of this sorry transgression had reached Aunt Hannah in Boston. Her aunt managed to bring up Chilton's name whenever possible. If Hannah thought a married dentist was a problem, what would she make of Trasker?

Aunt Hannah turned back to Cece. "Cecilia, you haven't weighed in on this matter yet. As someone with a peripatetic work history, I'd like to hear your thoughts."

"I think you're right," Cece said quietly. "Being with a good man is infinitely more rewarding than any manner of work could be."

The cousins stared at her in amazement. Anne couldn't believe what she was hearing. Alex looked like he was trying hard not to burst out laughing. Nora gave Cece a disapproving look as if to say, *I can't believe you're being so disloyal.*

Alex raised his wineglass. "A toast," he proclaimed. "I do believe this is the first time that Cece and Aunt Hannah are on the same side of an argument."

"Oh, Alex, don't be so melodramatic," Cece chided. "I do

have a rather checkered employment history. I've tried my hand at practically everything—jewelry making, graphic design, word processing, reflexology—I could go on and on. Bottom line? Add them all up and what do you get? Not a heck of a lot."

Something in Cece's tone made Anne glance up. Cece seemed subdued, a paler, sadder version of her usual self. Her voice was husky, like she had a permanent sore throat. Anne wondered if she'd been ill.

"What about the job you have now?" Nora asked Cece, frowning.

Cece pushed her plate away and laid her napkin gently across the top as if she were covering a dead animal. Anne noticed she hadn't touched her food.

"It's okay," Cece said. "But I confess I don't really care about how to prepare and serve twenty-three kinds of pizza." She turned to Aunt Hannah and smiled shyly. "So if you know any nice, eligible young men, feel free to send them my way."

Aunt Hannah nodded approvingly, just as Alex nudged Anne under the table. Anne looked over at him and he lifted his eyebrows as if to say, *What's going on?*

Anne hadn't a clue. For as long as she could remember, Cece and Aunt Hannah had been battling it out. Cece was the only granddaughter of Hannah's brother, Thomas. Cece's mother had deserted the family when Cece was six and Hannah often said it was a shame Cecilia lacked a positive female role model. As far back as elementary school, Aunt Hannah had disapproved of Cece's clothes, friends, grades, deportment, and overall conduct. Even from Boston, Aunt Hannah weighed in on Cece's catch-as-catch-can life. Cece told Anne that she regularly received letters from Hannah, printed on engraved, pale blue stationery, chiding her on the way she changed jobs, apartments, men.

Anne had received similar notes. But instead of criticism they contained crisp acknowledgments of what Aunt Hannah referred to as Anne's "writing prowess." Each time Anne had sent Aunt Hannah one of her books, she'd received a blue letter in return. Anne had fancied she'd established a bond with her great-aunt, however tenuous and fragile it might be. Perhaps that's why Hannah had come to the reunion, out of a special feeling for Anne.

Cece, on the other hand, made no bones about the way she regarded Hannah. She'd always scoffed at her great-aunt's views and ignored the scolding stream of advice that came her way. "Hannah's an old crab," Cece used to say. "If she has nothing better to do than tear me down and carp at me, I feel sorry for her."

Anne had never felt particularly sorry for her great-aunt. It seemed to her as though Hannah took a singular pleasure in instructing members of the family on precisely how and why they'd gone wrong. Other people took up gardening or collected Depression glass; Aunt Hannah's favorite hobby was criticizing her relatives.

"One day," she was saying now, "I'll be gone from this world and you each shall be that much richer for it. I hope you deserve what I'm planning to leave you."

The people seated around the table heaved a collective sigh.

If Anne had a dime for every time she'd heard Hannah talk about their inheritance, she'd be rich. It was the old carrot-and-stick routine: I'll remember you in my will if you conform to my notion of how to live your lives.

True, Anne sometimes fantasized about what she'd do with her inheritance money. Travel to Fiji, get a master's degree, escape to a writers' colony and start penning that novel she was always putting off because work got in the way. Watching Aunt Hannah, she realized that people with money lived by a different set of rules. Not only did they get all the best toys but they could call the shots, take control. Most of all, they didn't have to make nice.

"Now, my dear," said Chase Merritt to Hannah. "We'll have no more morbid talk this afternoon. You are going to grace us with your lovely presence for many more years to come."

To Anne's astonishment, Aunt Hannah actually blushed. Her cheeks turned a faint shade of crimson and she bestowed on Chase Merritt what Anne rarely saw on her face—a broad, happy smile. Maybe she's in love with him, Anne thought. Maybe it's the real deal. After all, how many suitors had Aunt Hannah had over the years after Great-uncle Arnold died? Not a one before now.

The doorbell rang, interrupting Anne's reverie, and she excused herself to answer it. Henry Rutter stood on her front porch, perspiring heavily. He was attired as if for a day on the golf course: green short-sleeved polo shirt, checked slacks, white peaked cap. At fifty-one, he had a strong, muscular physique and straight, perfectly capped teeth. But his brow was lined, his skin seemed to sag, and his blue close-set eyes were bloodshot. Thin broken capillaries spilled across his nose and cheeks, giving his face an unnaturally ruddy hue.

Anne couldn't tell whether it was because he'd spent too much time in the sun or he'd been drinking. Henry drank too much. She'd been hoping he'd stay sober at the reunion.

"So sorry I'm late," he said, bending to kiss Anne's cheek. "I had a devil of a time fighting traffic on the turnpike."

Henry lived in north Jersey, in a one-bedroom condo that Anne had been in twice. She'd always been fond of Henry but saw him infrequently. He was a hard man to get to know. His drinking had created a wall of sorts around him. When he was drunk, he could be perfectly charming, but it usually didn't last long. Sober, he was quiet and wary, retreating into books and his work.

Trained as a lawyer, he had given up his practice to write legal thrillers in the manner of Scott Turow. But as far as Anne knew, his first novel had stalled, and he hadn't been able to stir up any interest among agents or editors in subsequent efforts. Women were drawn to him, but his romances never seemed to last very long. Anne had always thought of him as something of a loner.

"Come on in," she said. "I'm really glad you could make it this weekend."

"It was great of you to plan this, Annie. I hope I don't spoil things."

She studied his expression, which betrayed a certain nervousness. "What do you mean?"

He peered past her, down the long hallway. "It's just that things are somewhat strained between Mother and me. And they're about to get worse."

He pursed his lips, as though even her name tasted bad on his tongue, like rotten fruit. Henry and Aunt Hannah had never gotten along. Anne imagined how awkward it would be between mother and son and wondered why Henry had decided to come.

"Aunt Hannah's inside, eating lunch," Anne said. "If you'd rather not join us right now, I understand."

Henry shook his head. "Might as well get this over with," he said. "Shall we?"

Anne led the way. In the time it took to reach the dining room, she silently berated herself for inviting Aunt Hannah to the reunion weekend. Wouldn't it have been better for everyone if her great-aunt had stayed home? How was the family supposed to relax and enjoy themselves in the face of so much tension and ill feelings?

When they walked into the room, Henry was met by a chorus of greetings. The cousins got up to hug and kiss him and Alex clapped him on the back.

Aunt Hannah gazed stonily down at her plate, taking slow bites of her food, chewing it vigorously. Chase Merritt followed her lead, refusing to acknowledge the newcomer's presence. Even Bronte the dog growled at Henry, as though she could sense the invisible thread of dislike that connected her mistress and her mistress's only surviving child. Aunt Hannah had also had a daughter, but the girl, whose name was Jennie, had died young. No one in the family ever talked about her.

"Hello, Mother," Henry said stiffly, when they all were seated again.

Aunt Hannah reached for another piece of pita bread, pretending she hadn't heard the salutation. An awkward silence fell over the room.

"Well," Kim said brightly to no one in particular. "What's on the agenda today? Are we hitting the beach after lunch?"

"Excuse me for a moment, Kimmie," Henry interrupted. Turning to his mother, he said, "I take it you've received my letters."

For the first time Aunt Hannah turned her gaze on her son. Her eyes registered disapproval and annoyance and something else, something Anne could only think of as scorn. Henry looked away.

"This really isn't the time or the place," Aunt Hannah said tersely.

"Then when?" Henry asked petulantly. "You don't return my calls. You haven't answered my letters. What do I have to do? Get down on my knees and beg you to speak to me?"

Anne silently marveled at how parents had the power to turn adult children back into little kids. It was a gift of sorts.

"Really, Henderson," Aunt Hannah scolded. "Your manners are atrocious. To march in here and create a scene, in front of the family."

"Your mother's right," Chase Merritt chimed in. "This conversation should be conducted in private."

Henry shot him a withering look. "Is this your new beau?" he asked his mother sarcastically. "How kind of you to invite him to the reunion. If the rest of us had the temerity to show up with a new flame, I dare say our paramours would be skewered."

Anne would have felt bad for her great-aunt, if only the old lady didn't look as if she was enjoying herself so much. Aunt Hannah's eyes sparkled merrily and the corners of her mouth formed a Cheshire grin. She looked like she was spoiling for a good fight. Besides, what Henry had said was perfectly true.

"Please forgive my son," Aunt Hannah said to the others. "His father and I taught him manners though he doesn't see fit to use them."

She pulled her black leather handbag from under her napkin and extracted her wallet. Opening it, she reached inside and flung a handful of bills on the table. "You mentioned in your letters that you need money, Henderson. This ought to get you through the next chapter of that opus you're supposedly writing."

Henry winced, yet Anne couldn't help noticing how longingly he eyed the cash.

"I've given up asking you for help, Mother. It's useless and we both know it. That's what I came down here to say. I won't grovel and beg anymore. I'll leave that to Bronte." He looked around the table at the cousins. "But as long as I'm here, I might as well fill you in. Bet you can't guess what Mother's gone and done this time?" Henry announced to the group.

It was a rhetorical question. Anne could see he was hell-bent on filling them in.

"Mother is responsible for ending my engagement to the most wonderful woman in the world," Henry said bitterly. "Elise was my soul mate, the most beautiful, loving person I've ever known. And Mother made it her business to break us up."

The cousins exchanged glances. No one had heard about Henry's fiancée. This was getting interesting. Hannah sniffed in disgust.

"Mother really did a number on Elise," Henry continued. "Told her I'm an alcoholic who can't stay sober and can't hold down a job. But Mother didn't stop there. She informed Elise that if we got married, we wouldn't be getting a dime. And to top everything off, she gave Elise a list of my ex-girlfriends and explained in lavish detail why things didn't work out."

"Wow," Nora muttered under her breath.

"That young woman is a twenty-three-year-old gold digger who was only after your trust fund," Aunt Hannah said sharply.

"Which I can't get because of all the red tape you've created," Henry retorted. "Do you think I like asking you for an allowance? Do you think I like writing letters begging you for cash to pay the rent? Pleading for your help?"

"You should have thought of that when you sabotaged your law career, when you threw away years of hard work."

Henry turned a brighter shade of red. "You and Father pushed me into the law," he shouted. "It was never something I set out to do. But you didn't care. You wanted a lawyer in the family. Case closed."

It dawned on Anne why Henry had come to the reunion. To confront Aunt Hannah. To reopen old wounds and address old wrongs. To tell his mother off in spectacular fashion.

"Stop whining and act like a man," Aunt Hannah said coldly. "You could have earned a good living if you chose. And as for that strumpet you claim to love, if she really cared for you, she would never have allowed herself to be dissuaded."

Henry banged his fist against the table so hard the dishes rattled.

"My God, Mother," he shouted. "Can't you stand to see anyone happy?"

Aunt Hannah's eyes widened in disapproval. "You need to get hold of yourself, Henderson. You're three sheets to the wind already."

Henry drew himself up to his full height. "For your information, I haven't had a drink in six days. I've entered a new treatment program and it's working this time."

"Once a drunk, always a drunk," Aunt Hannah intoned.

"You're absolutely right, my dear," Chase Merritt echoed.

Kim clucked her tongue disapprovingly. "Really, Aunt Hannah," she said. "I think we ought to be supportive of Henry and—"

Aunt Hannah cut her off. "I've been down this road too many times before. He stays sober for a week or two and then it's back to the bottle."

Henry threw up his hands. "Fine," he said angrily. "I'm tired of fighting. Take your damn money. I don't want it. I'll manage without the trust somehow." He turned to the rest of the group. "I'm staying in town overnight but I'll be gone by tomorrow afternoon. I'm sorry if I've ruined the reunion. It was nice seeing you all. I only wish it could have been under more pleasant circumstances."

Rising to his feet, he began walking out of the room. In the doorway, he turned back and his gaze rested on Aunt Hannah.

"I'm sick of you playing God, Mother. It's got to stop.

You have the upper hand now. But you'll be sorry for the rotten way you've treated me. I promise."

With that he stormed out of the house, slamming the front door behind him.

For a few stunned seconds, no one spoke. Anne felt the tension leak from the room, like helium leaving a balloon.

"Well," said Chase Merritt, helping himself to another bowl of pasta. "You folks really know how to throw a party."

Chapter 4

Most cats love to play. Pouncing, chasing, and batting inanimate objects around the house are fun activities that stimulate cats and often serve to echo their natural hunting activities.

Salt air drifted over the boardwalk like mist. It was late afternoon and the ocean churned and swirled. The water had turned greenish-gray. Waves beat against the shoreline, sending up feathery plumes of spray. The sky was bloated with clouds, heavy with the promise of rain.

Anne, Cece, and Nora had driven to Seaside Heights, which was about forty minutes away from Oceanside Heights in terms of miles—and light years away in terms of everything else. The boardwalk in Anne's hometown was a slender expanse of wood, with old-fashioned Victorian houses on one side and a strip of pristine white beach on the other. Here in Seaside Heights, the wide boardwalk was packed with arcades and games that dared you to try your luck and win a giant stuffed panda, a Betty Boop doll, a TV, a basket of groceries.

Roller coaster cars hurtled through space, whirling and looping and turning, ascending to dizzying heights, then plummeting rapidly down slopes as steep and sheer as cliffs. Screams split the air at such regular intervals that after a while they became background music, as innocuous as the calls of the arcade barkers or the keening of the gulls. The cousins had screamed themselves hoarse on the Zipper, gotten motion sickness on the Gravitron, played Skee-Ball at Lucky Leo's, ridden the carousel, and wandered into shops selling tacky souvenirs and hundreds of different T-shirts.

Now they were back on the boardwalk, amid throngs of people. Overhead, the giant tubes and slides of the waterworks looked like a gigantic slimy insect. The Ferris wheel lurched to a stop, the cars rocking crazily before tracing another loop in the sky. The breeze smelled of sausage and onions. Anne was glad they'd come. Especially after the Henry debacle. She'd invited her other two cousins to come along, but Alex had said he planned to visit an old friend and Kim begged off to run an errand.

"I feel like we're seventeen again," said Cece, pulling a handful of caramel popcorn out of a cardboard box.

"You think?" asked Nora, eyeing the teenage girls on the beach in their teensy string bikinis.

Anne suddenly saw herself as a nervous high school kid, standing outside a dark, smoky bar in the mid-seventies, trying to get past the bouncers with the one fake ID card they'd managed to cadge from a friend of a friend's older brother.

"Remember the firemen?" Anne said, with a giggle.

Nora whooped with laughter. "I bet Cece does. She kissed hers for so long I thought we'd have to use a crowbar to pry them apart."

"Well, he *was* awfully cute," Cece said, smiling.

Anne licked her blueberry ripple frozen custard. "Who wants to go on the Himalaya?"

"No, the Bobsled first. My treat," Nora said.

Cece groaned. "You've paid for everything, all afternoon."

"Hey, business is good. You guys saw my ad. We have more high-profile clients now, like the tourism board."

On the way down the shore in Anne's Mustang, they'd passed a billboard created by Nora's advertising company. It showed a beautiful woman emerging from the bluest strip of ocean Anne had ever seen. A glittering city skyline rose up behind Beauty while a waiter in a white jacket stood nearby holding a tropical drink. *Pack a swimsuit, not an agenda*, the billboard advised. *Florida! Where the lush life is only a plane ride away.*

"That's great," Cece said enthusiastically. "To have your own successful business. Wow! Way to go."

Anne studied Cece carefully. It seemed to her that Cece sounded a little *too* enthusiastic. Her two cousins had always been competitive, though it was hard to compete with Nora and win. Nora had an edge over most people when it came to looks, brains, and talent.

They walked past stalls selling meatball sandwiches and cheese steaks, past booths where people lined up to shoot small spongy balls into baskets or hit moving metal ducks with toy guns.

"What was going on at lunch today between you and Aunt Hannah?" Nora asked Cece.

Cece smiled and skipped a few steps ahead of them on the boardwalk.

"Just trying to be accommodating," she sang out.

But her face gave her away. Her eyes had narrowed and she was biting the inside of her lower lip.

Anne recognized that look. She'd seen it many times in

the past: when Cece had gotten caught shoplifting lipstick back in tenth grade, when she'd flunked geometry and had to go to summer school, when she'd been forced to tell her parents she'd sideswiped a jeep and wrecked the family station wagon, in short whenever Cece found herself in a jam.

"What's up with you?" Nora asked.

Cece took a deep breath and exhaled dramatically. "Okay, I might as well come clean with you guys. I'm not working at the restaurant anymore."

"Did you quit?" Anne said.

"Not exactly," Cece said, finishing off the last of her popcorn and tossing the box in the trash. "I got fired—again. And I was hoping to convince our sanctimonious auntie to give me a loan."

"By buttering her up?" Anne teased.

"Yup. I've decided to apply to business school. It's really tough in California. Unless you're in Silicion Valley or the entertainment industry, you can't find a decent job. I'm tired of reinventing myself. I need to be taken seriously this time."

Nora said, "How about student loans? That's how I put myself through school."

Cece frowned. "They'll do a credit check, right? They'll find out I'm so heavily in debt it's pathetic."

"How much do you need?" Nora asked.

"B-school costs about twenty grand a year, for two years. Plus meal money, rent money. I'm figuring it'll run me at least sixty thousand."

Nora stopped in her tracks and two teenage boys with big biceps and small bathing trunks eyed her appraisingly.

"You can't snow Aunt Hannah," Nora said, sounding annoyed. "The old bird's too smart for that."

"Hope springs eternal," Cece sang out. "I'm going to ask her right after dinner tonight. Unless *you* feel like lending me the money, that is."

Nora looked away, gazing at the ocean as if it were some rare and wondrous phenomenon she'd never encountered before. *No way*, Anne thought. *Not now. Not for Cece.*

"You know I'd love to help out," Nora said gently. "But all my money's tied up in the business. It isn't possible to . . ."

"Never mind," Cece said, obviously peeved. "That's why I didn't come to you in the first place."

"Hey, look over there," Anne interrupted, trying to forestall an argument. "Let's get our fortunes told."

She steered her cousins over to an arcade lined with antique games and amusements, a collection of early Wurlitzer jukeboxes, old-fashioned pinball machines, and vintage signs. Against one wall stood a life-size porcelain woman in a glass box. Above her head, a sign said: *Madame Zita Tells Your Fortune—10 Cents.*

"Cool," Nora said. "I have some change."

Anne reached inside her handbag, but Cece was quicker.

"Not this time," Cece said, fumbling for her wallet. "As broke as I am, I think I can afford thirty cents."

She yanked a worn leather wallet free from the clutter of her purse and its contents went flying, spilling onto the floor of the arcade. Anne and Nora knelt down to help retrieve Cece's stuff: a driver's license, lipstick, blush, eye shadow, comb, tissues, and other assorted detritus, which had scattered all over the floor of the arcade.

"Guess I should clean out my bag one of these days, huh?" Cece joked, grabbing a pen, which had landed near a pinball machine.

Anne reached for a date book lying facedown. When she picked it up, a picture slid out, a wallet-size color photograph of a baby who looked to be about six months old. The child was wearing a pink romper over a puffy white blouse.

She had large blue eyes and wispy tufts of black hair on her head.

"Who's this?" Anne said, holding up the photo. The baby looked like she had just woken up from a nap. Her cheeks were puffed out; her rosebud mouth formed the beginnings of a yawn.

Cece snatched the picture back. She looked uncomfortable. "My neighbor's kid. Sweet girl. I baby-sit for her now and then."

"Oh, she's darling," Nora said, and Anne heard a note of longing in her voice.

Nora had always wanted children. It was just a matter of finding the right guy and settling down. But with the business doing so well, she'd told Anne she didn't have much time for men. Dating was hard work, she'd said to Anne, in their last marathon phone conversation. She was too busy to kiss a lot of frogs in search of Prince Charming.

Still, men were constantly attracted to Nora. It had irked Anne, once upon a time. How she and Nora could walk into a bar and it was like she didn't exist. The guys in the room were all over Nora, trying to get Nora's attention, and ultimately her phone number. Anne had resented it until she figured out it didn't mean anything to Nora. Her cousin had evaded the admiring throng of men and downplayed the compliments. Nora didn't believe a word of it anyway. She was hyper-critical of herself. And Anne had finally realized that underneath the beautiful, polished exterior, Nora was as insecure and self-conscious as a self-effacing wallflower.

Cece took the child's photograph back and stuck it in her wallet. Then she checked to make sure she had everything.

"Okay," she announced, brandishing three dimes. "I'm going first."

She walked up to Madame Zita's booth and dropped the

coin in the slot. Immediately they heard the sound of tinny carousel music. Red lights flashed. The fortune-teller's head bobbed up and her shoulders swiveled around to face front. She winked one eye and her mouth twisted into a leer. There was something simultaneously garish and ghastly about the performance. Madame Zita's movements were jerky, forced. It reminded Anne of a *Twilight Zone* episode set in a department store where the painted mannequins came to life and glided through the dark, empty store, haunted and lost.

A white card shot through a slot in the booth.

"Here goes nothing," Cece said. She reached for the card and read it aloud: *"Beware the smiling serpent."*

"Pretty cryptic," Anne commented.

"Just my luck," Cece complained. "I get one that sounds like a lousy fortune cookie."

"Have you come across any snakes lately?" Nora teased.

"Only on blind dates. My last several have been from the sub-basement of hell."

Anne rolled her eyes sympathetically. "If there is a God, I hope he sees to it that I never have to go on another blind date again."

"Seems like a safe bet," Cece said. "Especially if you stick with that detective of yours."

Anne smiled. She wished Trasker could have come along. He would have gotten a kick out of the hokey fortune-teller.

Nora stepped up to the booth. "My turn," she announced, taking a coin from Cece and inserting it in the machine. Madame Zita went through her routine again. A second card dropped out of the slot.

Nora cleared her throat dramatically and read the message: *"You will be unlucky in love."*

For a second, her face appeared to crumple. But in the

next instant, she smiled and tossed back her shining dark hair.

"What do *you* know?" Nora said to the fortune-teller. "You only cost a dime."

"Aren't there any positive fortunes in this thing?" Cece asked, giving the machine a quick kick.

Anne walked over to Madame Zita. "We'll soon find out," she said, with a grin.

She collected her dime and dropped it in the slot with a flourish.

The music played. Madame Z did her thing again, weaving and bobbing like a giant puppet.

"Here goes nothing," Anne said, plucking out the card.

"You go girl," Cece shouted. "Make it a good one."

Anne looked at the card, then grimaced. "Oh, brother," she joked. "Now I'm really in trouble. It says, '*Danger will befall you.*' "

Her cousins started to laugh. Anne joined in, but just as she did she felt a sudden fierce internal chill, like someone was walking over her grave.

Chapter 5

Cats seem to loathe water and won't go near a lake, river, or swimming pool for fear of falling in. As for stormy weather, your kitty would much prefer to watch the raindrops fall from a cozy perch indoors than to suffer the indignity of actually getting wet.

It was after five when Anne got home. She fed Harry, sorted the mail, washed the lunch dishes, and cleaned up the house. Then she sat down at her computer to work on the pet book. She was up to chapter three, titled "How to Train Kitty." She looked over Edie Mintzler's notes and began to write:

A sharp clap surprises your cat into stopping what he's doing. You can also try hissing at kitty to let her

*know she has seriously violated your rules. If this fails
to work, hold a lightweight magazine by the spine and
toss it so it lands near the cat. Another option is to fill
an aluminum can with a few pieces of gravel; when
rolled or dropped, the can makes a frightening noise
and is a good tool for scaring puss away from places
that are off-limits.*

Anne looked up from the screen and stared off into
space. Why hadn't any of these things worked with Harry?
Edie had explained they were most effective when training
kittens, and Harry was twelve years old. But Anne had a
different theory. Harry was a tough customer. He didn't
scare easy. Still, there had to be a way to get him to stop
clawing the furniture. Maybe she could talk Edie into doing a chapter geared to older cats, who were more set in
their ways.

The phone interrupted her reverie. It was Trasker, calling
to say he wouldn't be able to join her family for dinner at the
Pelican Café.

"I'm sorry, Annie," he said. "But the Hughes case is heat-
ing up and I'm pulling a double shift tonight. I'll swing by
tomorrow and make my apologies to everyone in person. I
promise."

Anne had mixed feelings. She'd been looking forward to
having Trasker meet her cousins, especially Nora and Cece.
She knew they'd like him. And she wanted so much for him
to like them, too. But a part of her was relieved. It meant she
could postpone the whole race issue for one more day.
Maybe she should tell everyone else about Trasker in advance, rather than springing him on them cold. Maybe that
way everything would go smoothly.

"That's okay," she said aloud. "There'll be plenty of time
over the weekend. I'm glad the case is going well."

"It would be even better if I was teamed with another partner."

"Is Burns making you crazy again?"

Trasker laughed. "That's putting it mildly."

He and his partner, Detective Ed Burns, didn't get along. Trasker believed that Burns was a bigot, that Burns deeply resented being teamed with a black man. There were subtle signs—a roll of the eyes, whispered phone conversations, the occasional snide put-down—but nothing overt enough to include in a written report.

"So how did lunch go?" Trasker asked, changing the subject.

"Okay, up to a point. Then fireworks broke out."

He chuckled. "Uh oh."

"Could you come over after you get through?"

"Sure. It shouldn't be later than eleven."

After she hung up, she got back to work. A few minutes later, the phone rang again. She picked it up, hoping it was Trasker calling back to say he was coming earlier.

"Hello," said a faint, quavering voice.

"Yes," Anne said, thinking it was a wrong number.

"This is your Aunt Hannah."

"Oh, hi."

It was the last person Anne expected to hear from. Aunt Hannah almost never used the telephone, relying instead on short, curt notes, like the one notifying Anne that she would be attending the reunion.

"I need some information about a matter that has come to my attention."

Anne waited, feeling perplexed. Her aunt sounded agitated.

"You'll have to do some research, make certain inquiries on my behalf."

"What's wrong?" Anne said, feeling her stomach tighten.

Her aunt's strange tone of voice was making her nervous. "Has something happened?"

Before her aunt could answer, Anne heard a sharp, high trill.

"Hold on," Aunt Hannah said. "There's someone at my door."

Anne looked out her office window. The beach had emptied. Though it hadn't started raining, the sky looked ominous, the dark clouds tinged with a faint wash of yellow, like a bruise.

On the other end of the line, she heard Aunt Hannah's voice, then a man's voice. Anne couldn't be sure, but she thought it sounded like Alex.

Though she couldn't make out all the words, she could hear them arguing. She thought she heard him say, "Need it right away . . . begging you."

Aunt Hannah raised her voice. "Not now. I want you to leave."

Anne heard a door slam. She pictured Aunt Hannah crossing the hall, her shoes clacking against the polished oak floor, then going over to the round mahogany end table by the sofa, where the old-fashioned black dial telephone rested on a crocheted doily.

"Anne," her aunt gasped into the phone. She sounded out of breath, even panicky. "Are you still there?"

"Yes. What's going on?"

"You wrote a book a few years back, on adoption."

Anne immediately thought of the book in question: *And Baby Makes Three: Your A to Z Guide to Quick, Easy Adoptions*, ghostwritten for Andrea Klores Edelman, Ph.D., a psychologist specializing in helping couples navigate the red tape, emotional uncertainty, and outright stress of the adoption process.

"There was a review in the *Boston Globe*," Aunt Hannah

said hurriedly. "The lady you wrote it with was interviewed on TV."

That sounded right, Anne thought. Andrea Klores Edelman was a consummate self-promoter. When Triple Star Publishing refused to pay for a book tour, the psychologist had hired her own publicist and traveled to more than a dozen cities, talking about everything from the pros and cons of meeting the birth mother to finding an adoption agency you could trust.

"You must help me. It's very important," Aunt Hannah said, and now mixed with the agitation, Anne heard the petulant, imperious tone her aunt often used when talking to hired help or insignificant shop girls. The grand dame used to getting her own way.

"Are you thinking of adopting?" Anne asked. She couldn't imagine Hannah caring for a child. But maybe it was lonely in the big old house in Boston. Maybe Hannah had a private benevolent side. Or perhaps she liked the idea of a young ward she could mold and influence . . .

"I don't want to go into it over the phone and I don't want you to mention this to anyone. Be at my house at nine A.M. tomorrow morning. I'll explain everything then."

Anne said, "Are you coming to dinner tonight?"

"I'm dining in. I'll see you tomorrow at nine sharp."

She hung up abruptly, leaving Anne to ponder the heretofore unheard-of fact that her aunt had actually asked for her help.

Dinner that evening was a strained affair. Cece showed up. And Kim came with her husband, Larry. But everyone else was a no-show, which contributed to the unpleasantness. Larry and Cece had never gotten along. Not that Larry had an especially warm relationship with anyone in Kim's family. He was a boorish, overbearing man, who talked at people, instead of to them, and who believed himself to be an expert on practically everything.

Anne always wondered why Kim had married Larry. It certainly wasn't a physical attraction. Larry was five feet, three inches tall, balding and overweight, with badly pock-marked skin. He alternately bullied his wife or treated her condescendingly, and was so immersed in his business that he barely had time for his two daughters. It pained Anne to watch the way Kim seemed to shrink in his presence and tried so hard to please him, to smooth the way and act agree-able. It was as though with Larry, Kim became her worst self—insecure, artificial, pleading.

They'd been married for twenty-three years, and in all that time Anne had never seen them exchange a single kind word or endearment. She'd never heard them joke around or noticed any hint of friendship between them. Kim seemed trapped within the confines of her marriage, but then, Anne would remind herself, Kim must have been getting some-thing out of the relationship. No one was putting a gun to her head and forcing her to stay married to Larry. There must have been an upside, only Anne was damned if she knew what it was.

Anne, Cece, and Kim made small talk at dinner, most of it centered around the town—the soaring price of real estate, the influx of tourists from outside the United States, whether the new antiques emporium would flourish. But the conver-sation was stilted, with long, uncomfortable pauses. It was clear that Larry looked down at Cece, while she treated him with contempt. Kim chattered away, trying to ease the ten-sion and failing miserably. It was like a live version of her newsletter, complete with the most minute details of her bridge lessons, her daughters' busy social lives, the art history class she was auditing at Holy Cross, the calligraphy she'd learned in order to create a family tree she was working on, made with parchment paper and genuine India ink, the stacks of documents and memorabilia she'd poured through to research the family tree.

Larry was sullen, distracted, and even more hostile than usual, berating the waiters for taking too long, ignoring his wife, baiting Cece. Several times during the meal, Larry received calls on his cell phone and left the table to talk. Anne saw him through the restaurant's plate-glass window, gesticulating with his free hand and yelling into the phone.

After dessert, at Kim's suggestion, they took a walk around the Heights. The sky was still overcast, but daylight hadn't yet faded into night, and the residential blocks looked more or less the same as they had when Anne and her cousins were growing up. Small bungalows and campground cottages, with jigsaw scrollwork on the eaves and second-story balconies, were interspersed with larger houses: Eastlake and Colonial Revival homes and sprawling Victorian Gothic buildings, many of which had been converted into inns and painted in fetching, historically correct shades of seafoam green, powder-puff pink, and robin's-egg blue.

Anne's favorite were the Stick Style houses, characterized by the decorative stickwork applied to the outside clapboard walls in a pattern of vertical, horizontal, and diagonal boards. Their broad overhanging eaves and encircling verandas had a welcoming, homey look she especially liked.

They stopped in front of one such house, with a white gingerbread porch festooned with baskets of geraniums and hydrangeas. "Oh, I just love it here," Kim enthused. "Wouldn't it be wonderful to spend a few hours on that porch, drinking in the ocean air?"

"No thanks," Larry commented acidly. "There's nothing to do in this one-horse burg except go to church and spy on the neighbors."

He took yet another call on his cell phone, speaking three words before hanging up, which seemed to put him in an even fouler mood.

"So Boston's more to your liking?" Cece asked snidely, as they walked along.

"It's better than Graveside Heights."

"I don't think you'd be happy living anywhere," Cece commented. "You know what they say: 'Wherever you go, there you are.'"

"Spare me the New Age platitudes," Larry barked. "I'd rather sweep coals in hell than take advice from a washed up ex-hippy."

"Be careful what you wish for," Cece said sweetly.

"You know what I wish? That you'd go back to painting soft-core porn or peddling wheatgrass or whatever it is you do on the Left Coast."

Cece glared at him. "Actually, right now, I'm more concerned with pest control." She turned to Kim. "Have you ever considered getting one of those zappers to keep small, annoying bugs away?"

Larry scowled. "Good idea, Kim. And while you're at it, how about buying Cecilia a padlock for that big fat mouth of hers?"

"Listen, you two," Anne broke in hurriedly. "Why don't we call a cease-fire until I can send for reinforcements?"

Larry and Cece ignored her entreaty, trading insults for the next few minutes until nature put an end to their bickering. The sky opened up and it began to rain, a torrential downpour that left the four of them thoroughly soaked with only one goal—getting indoors. After a hasty good-bye, the others sprinted toward the Laughing Gull while Anne ran the five blocks home, her clothes plastered to her skin, her sandals slapping against the wet pavement. It felt strangely exhilarating to be out in the storm alone. Thunder crashed overhead; jagged lightning bolts sliced the clouds over the Atlantic only to vanish in a flash. It seemed as though the temperature had dropped twenty degrees in mere seconds. The rain formed a dense, cold curtain obscuring the familiar streets, cloaking the houses, cars, and lawns in a mantle of gray.

By the time she got home, Anne was drenched. She padded up the stairs, dripping as she went, and peeled off her soggy clothes in the bathroom. Then she took a long, hot shower and put on sweatpants and a sweatshirt, which passed for pajamas on cool summer nights. Trasker arrived as she was curled up on the window seat in the living room, drinking a glass of white wine.

"What a day," he said, removing his shoes and his rain slicker. "I am so glad to be here."

"Not half as glad as I am," she smiled.

He came over and kissed her lightly on the mouth, running his fingers idly through her hair. "How's the reunion going?" he asked.

Anne let out a mock groan. As he dried off and poured himself a glass of wine, she proceeded to fill him in on the day's events.

"Pretty tough stuff," he said, when she'd finished. "But that happens when families get together. Wait till you meet mine."

Trasker's parents were dead. He had several siblings in various cities across the country, none of whom he seemed especially close to.

"You know," he continued. "It was great that you took the initiative and organized this shindig in the first place. It

shows you care, for one thing. That you're interested in con-
necting with these people. And they came because they want
to reconnect with you, too. The rest of the weekend will
probably be a breeze."

She stared into the darkness, watching dimly lit waves
crash heavily against the beach. "I hope so, T. Henry is leaving tomorrow, so there shouldn't be any more showdowns
between him and Aunt Hannah. What do you think she
wants from me?"

"Sounds like she's planning to adopt and she'd like you to
steer her in the right direction."

Anne sat up and stretched. The wine had made her a little
sleepy. She could almost feel disappointment wash over her,
as palpable and steady as rain. Despite what Trasker had
said, it looked like the reunion wasn't going to bring her
family closer together. Her cousins probably couldn't wait
to go home.

Trasker came over and rubbed her shoulders. "I know
what you need," he said gently.

She felt herself start to relax under his touch. Trasker's
massages were a little slice of heaven. She liked to joke that
if he ever left the sheriff's office, he could become a professional masseur. His strong, sure hands kneaded the muscles
in her neck and back, easing away the tensions of the day.
Her body felt warm all over; her skin seemed to tingle.

He turned her around and gave her a deep, passionate kiss
on the mouth. "Want to have a sleep-over tonight? I packed
my toothbrush."

She smiled in anticipation. "I'd love to."

He kissed her again, harder this time, as the rain drummed
against the roof and the ocean pounded the shore.

Being with her family was like getting swept up in a
melodrama: the pent-up hostilities, the petty jealousies, the

constant Sturm und Drang. But with Trasker, life was so
easy. There were all kinds of family ties in this world, she
thought, as they climbed the stairs to the bedroom. The kind
you were born into and the kind you created on your own.

Chapter 6

> *A dog's anxiety can be*
> *relieved by touch, such*
> *as petting and hugging,*
> *and by discipline, a return*
> *to clearly discernible*
> *rules and regulations.*

Aunt Hannah's house was a sprawling three-story Queen Anne on the corner of Webb and Pennsylvania avenues, painted a deep gray color with sapphire-blue shutters. Gingerbread and intricately turned spindles adorned the facade, wrapping the turn-of-the-century house in what looked like a creamy, lace scarf to protect it from the blustery ocean breeze. Shingles were laid in wavy patterns so that the whole surface seemed to undulate, an impression further accentuated by asymmetrical turrets, balconies, and projecting bays. The house had two gabled roofs, one on the north side and one on the east, flanking an octagonal brick tower with a ruby glass window. A wide wraparound porch encircled the first floor, enlivened by arched columns and fanciful scrollwork. There was a second smaller balcony above the porch, and above that, a band of patterned bricks that wound around the house like a delicate ribbon.

It was a beautiful old home, and even though Aunt Hannah was rarely in residence, she made sure the exterior was painted every six years and that the lawn and garden were well tended. Anne had many memories of playing there as a child, mostly in wintertime: running up and down the back stairs with her cousins, watching the cook prepare the Christmas goose, sipping tea in the parlor while her mother inquired about Aunt Hannah's health. Her legs had itched in the heavy wool tights her mother had made her wear under her best wool dress, as she studied the row of portraits that seemed to follow her with their eyes and the jeweled Easter eggs arrayed like royalty in a mirrored, gilt case.

Henry was always at the edges of these gatherings, studying in his room or sitting in a corner with his nose stuck in a book. Often he was away at school. Pursuing his undergraduate degree at the University of Virginia, attending Oxford on a fellowship, getting a law degree from Duke. Excellent schools all. But Aunt Hannah never seemed satisfied. She liked to maintain that Henry didn't live up to his potential, that he could have gotten better grades, a better clerkship, a greater salary, if he applied himself more. Anne had felt the tension stretched between them like a wire, the sense that Henry was being forced into a mold and labeled the black sheep of the family, deservedly or not.

Anne and her cousins had empathized with him. They'd always looked up to Henry because he was older and because he seemed to travel in wider, more glamorous circles. But secretly she felt they'd been glad it was Henry Aunt Hannah singled out for criticism and not them. And that feeling created a certain distance between him and them, one that grew harder to bridge as the years went by.

In the summer the cousins—with their muddy feet and

sticky fingers—were not permitted inside Dovecote. Aunt
Hannah had entertained on the "veranda," and the house was
subject to frequent airings—the rugs shaken and beaten with
whisk brooms, the slipcovers changed to breezy white linen,
the windows thrown open while the bees droned lazily amid
the lush garden roses.

Anne and her cousins had mocked Aunt Hannah's fastidi-
ousness and had dared one another to sneak inside the house
and wreak havoc on their great-aunt's housekeeping. Anne
seemed to recall that on one occasion Cece had done just
that, secreting a frog in the linen closet, which, much to the
children's disappointment, must have hopped to safety before being discovered, since they'd heard nothing more
about the incident.

Looking back, Anne wondered what her parents had
thought of Aunt Hannah. They'd treated her great-aunt with
the deference usually reserved for ministers and movie stars.
They'd ignored Hannah's eccentricities, tolerated her steady
stream of unwanted advice, and listened with rapt attention
as she'd picked apart every denizen of the Heights. Was it
possible her parents had respected Hannah's opinion? Or
were they merely cowed by her immense wealth, unable to
fault anyone whose riches insulated her from the standards
of behavior expected from everyone else?

Now as Anne approached the house, it seemed less im-
posing than in her memories. A pretty Queen Anne with
none of the homey touches belonging to the other homes
surrounding it. No flags or pots of geraniums hanging from
the porch, no bicycles leaning against the gate, no sign that
anyone lived there at all. The house was dark, the drapes
drawn, adding to the deserted, quiet atmosphere on the
block.

Normally at nine A.M. on a Friday morning in August,
there would be plenty of people on the streets. But it was

still raining heavily, an angry, insistent rain with intermittent downpours that kept most folks indoors.

Anne was therefore surprised to see Kim hurrying down the front porch steps. Her cousin was wearing a long yellow slicker over a white cotton blouse and a green-and-blue-plaid pleated skirt. The sight of Kim running, with her hair streaming wildly behind her and her stockings splattered with mud, made her look for all the world like an overage Catholic schoolgirl who'd managed to piss off the nuns.

"Kim," Anne called out.

Her cousin glanced up, startled, a panic-stricken expression in her eyes. "Oh . . . you scared me."

"What's up?" Anne extended her large umbrella so Kim could take shelter, but her cousin just stood there in the rain, a terrified expression on her face.

"I . . . I came by to see Auntie," she said haltingly.

Anne gestured toward the porch. "Come on," she said, taking Kim's arm.

She steered Kim up the steps. The first thing she noticed was that the front door to Dovecote was slightly ajar. The second was a plaid umbrella on the welcome mat that Anne recognized as Kim's.

"Is Aunt Hannah home?" Anne asked.

Kim sat down heavily in a white wicker porch chair with a floral cushion. Her eyes were glazed, unfocused. Bending forward, she wrapped her hands around her knees and dropped her head. Her face was ashen. She looked like she was going to be sick.

"Kim, what's wrong?"

A low moan escaped Kim's lips. Anne felt a sliver of fear shoot through her. She'd never seen Kim act this way before. Kim was usually so capable and controlled, so unfailingly cheerful.

"I can't go back in there," Kim whispered hoarsely. "Please don't make me."

"Why? What's happened? Did Aunt Hannah say something to you? Did she do something?"

Instead of responding, Kim rocked back and forth, her head cradled between her knees. "See for yourself," she managed to rasp.

Slowly, Anne got up and walked over to the door. Opening it wider, she peered inside. The house was silent except for the ticking of the grandfather clock in the hall and a faint whimpering sound. She stepped into the hallway, conscious in her confusion that she was dripping profusely onto her great-aunt's oak floor.

"Aunt Hannah," she called out. "It's Anne. Are you here?"

She walked into the living room, which looked much as it had the last time she'd visited, nearly ten years ago. The plump camelback sofa and overstuffed armchairs were slip-covered in their customary summer whites. In the far corner stood the black Knabe baby grand piano that no one ever played, opposite two ornate gold chairs with embroidered seat cushions, in the style of Louis XIV or Louis XV—Anne never could keep her Louis straight. In the cherrywood bookshelves, leather-bound volumes were arranged alphabetically by color, from a set of periwinkle Balzac to a half-dozen scarlet tomes by Poe. The mahogany coffee table sported several covered silver boxes, which Anne knew contained an assortment of wrapped peppermints and chocolates.

It was a tastefully decorated room, though perhaps a little too grand for a small seaside town. Aunt Hannah's one concession to the locale was an oil seascape of fishing boats on the sand at sunrise, which hung over the sofa and was completely at odds with the rest of the paintings in the room—dark Italianate landscapes, peasant girls drinking from a fountain, deer wandering in a forest, and glistening bowls of fruit.

Crossing the room, Anne noticed that the summer carpets, with their floral design and ivy borders, were streaked with mud. The whimpering was coming from the back parlor, a smallish room near the kitchen that served as a study. Entering, Anne pulled up abruptly, stunned by what she saw. Her great-aunt was lying facedown on the Aubusson rug, next to an overturned ottoman and a broken lamp. Her quilted white bathrobe, decorated with tiny pink rosebuds, was covered with brownish-red blood. There was blood everywhere. It had soaked into the carpet, stained the ottoman, splattered onto the walls and the furniture.

Anne felt horror wash over her. Her heart began thudding so hard she could practically feel it pulsating in her ears. For a moment the shock was so great that she had trouble catching her breath and had to lean against the doorway for support. This couldn't be happening. Couldn't be. No. But it was.

"Aunt Hannah?"

Only silence.

Kneeling beside the body, she placed her fingers on Aunt Hannah's left wrist, hopelessly searching for a pulse. Nothing. Her aunt's skin felt cold to the touch, cold and papery like the skin of a reptile. Aunt Hannah's head was turned to the side, her facial muscles tense, her mouth forming a grimace as though dying had come hard. Her hair was disheveled, her hands clenched into fists.

The dog, Bronte, continued to whimper from under the delicate rosewood desk where she lay cowering in fright, her muzzle streaked with dried blood. Anne wondered how long the pug had been there, if she had seen whoever did this monstrous thing. "Here, Bronte," she called. "Here, girl."

But the dog refused to come out from under the desk and

began to let out a series of high-pitched, nervous yelps that were worse than the whimpering.

Anne glanced around, searching for the murder weapon. The room was a mess: papers scattered about, a teacup smashed to bits in a puddle of tea, an afghan and pillows strewn on the floor.

She went over to the desk, picked up the phone, and dialed 911, although the emergency was clearly over, the body cold. She was aware that she was in shock, that she was speaking slowly and woodenly, as if she were on auto pilot. She called Trasker's number at work, pressed 0 when she reached his voice mail, and explained to the desk clerk on duty that she needed to get a message to Mark Trasker as soon as possible.

After she'd hung up, she continued to stare at the body as the rain beat against the window pane and Bronte yelped her distress. Under her robe, Aunt Hannah was wearing a white flannel nightgown. Her slippers, old-fashioned pink ones with open toes and quilted soles, looked as if they'd been kicked off during the struggle and lay at right angles in the far corner of the room.

Only then did Anne realize something was missing. Not in the room, but on Aunt Hannah's person. And suddenly Anne realized what it was: jewelry. Her aunt's hands, usually adorned with several rings, were completely bare. No bangles or charm bracelets. No earrings. No pendants hanging from gold chains. But that was to be expected, was it not? It looked as if before Aunt Hannah was killed, she had probably been preparing to go to sleep or just waking up, and who wore jewelry to bed? Did Hannah?

Anne walked over to the desk. Had Aunt Hannah been sitting there before she'd been killed? Or had she been curled up in the armchair, sipping tea? Anne knew she shouldn't touch anything, but she leafed through the papers lying on the desktop and the floor anyway: assorted bills, a warranty for a new refrigerator, a few estimates on what it would cost to build a new roof.

Aunt Hannah's checkbook was lying near the sofa. It was the kind of book where, when you tore off a check, a narrow stub at the top was left attached to the book to record the date, the amount, and the reason for the payment.

The last check Aunt Hannah had written was six days before, made out to the Preservation League of Greater Boston, in the amount of $250. Prior to that, she'd written checks to her cleaners, a Talbot's clothing store, the Gardner Museum, and a place called Pet-sations.

Anne was about to close the book when she noticed there was writing on the topmost, unused check. In her small, spidery script, Aunt Hannah had filled out the date: August 18, 2000, nothing more. It was today's date, and it set Anne to wondering. Had Aunt Hannah filled the date out incorrectly and then stopped, realizing her error? Or had she started to write the check last night, before she'd been killed? And, if so, was she making it out to her murderer?

Anne looked at the wastebasket, which was on its side, surrounded by a half-dozen balled-up tissues, a couple of candy wrappers, a pen that had run out of ink, and a crumpled piece of paper. Anne smoothed the paper out. It had come from a notepad that said, *From the desk of Hannah G. Rutter*. Underneath that, Aunt Hannah had scrawled a word in her bad handwriting. *Greenly* or *Greeley*, Anne couldn't tell which, surrounded by a series of squares, triangles, and wavy lines that looked like doodling.

Nothing about adoption. But then what had Aunt Hannah wanted to talk about this morning? Why had she summoned Anne to Dovecote?

With a final uneasy glance at the body, Anne left the room and entered the kitchen, a country-style room that was as tidy and ordered as the study was disheveled. The cupboards had been stenciled with flowers and stained with a pale white wash. Their glass-paned fronts revealed a set of blue and white Delft china, mixing bowls, a tea set, jelly jars, and canisters. The countertop and backsplash consisted of pale ivory and blue tiles; copper pots and wooden spoons hung from hooks on the walls. On the kitchen table, a large dried flower arrangement rested atop a lace cloth. No dishes in the sink, no indication that Aunt Hannah had eaten breakfast.

The back door was slightly ajar and the bay window above the sink was open. Was this how the killer had entered, catching Aunt Hannah by surprise in the study, then leaving via the back door? If so, then he or she had been careful to replace the coffeemaker, the basket of fruit, and the decorative wooden rooster on the countertop beneath the window. Again, no visible sign of an intruder. The terracotta floor looked swept clean, as if it hadn't been walked on in weeks. And as far as she knew, Dovecote didn't have an alarm system.

Anne gazed out the window at the small garden beyond, still feeling numb. Dovecote's caretaker had planted giant sunflowers and tall stately gladiolas, which appeared to be weeping in the driving rain. How could this be happening? How could Aunt Hannah be dead? Hearing the steady bleat of a siren, Anne retraced her steps to the front of the house. Walking outside, she saw the ambulance rounding the corner at breakneck speed. It was only after it had pulled up to the curb, after the technicians had gotten out and steered their stretcher up the porch steps in the rain, that she realized Kim was gone.

Chapter 7

> *When you become a dog owner, it's important to get to know your dog. Is he a wise guy or overly submissive? Does he behave differently with women than with men? Is he an easygoing slob, happy to do what you say? Is he standoffish? Pushy? Extroverted? Knowing your dog's personality will help you understand and train him properly.*

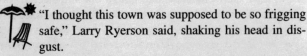 "I thought this town was supposed to be so frigging safe," Larry Ryerson said, shaking his head in disgust.

Chase Merritt banged his cup down and sloshed coffee onto a pine cocktail table laden with muffins, scones, cookies, and rolls. "Indeed," he echoed crossly. "The very idea that an upstanding woman like Hannah could be attacked in such a vile, heinous manner makes my blood boil."

I bet it does, Anne thought. *It must be vexing to have your meal ticket unceremoniously dispatched.* She wondered whether Aunt Hannah had prepaid Merritt's bill.

Pat Mooney ran to mop up the coffee, which was threatening to leak onto several copies of *Martha Stewart Living* that Pat had placed on the table for the reading pleasure of her guests, six of whom were now being interrogated by detectives in the small adjoining breakfast nook where three kinds of juice, hot coffee, tea, cocoa and assorted baked goods were customarily served between the hours of eight and eleven A.M.

It was now twenty past eleven. Anne could tell Pat was itching to clear the food away and get back to her own quarters in the bed-and-breakfast—a small bedroom and sitting room in the rear of the house, where she could watch TV or eat in private. Pat seemed upset. And why not? It wasn't every day someone was killed in the Heights. Pat couldn't stand the sight of cops swarming through her B&B. But Pat was also the type of person who really couldn't bear any stress well. When she got overly tense (like the time last winter when the boiler broke down or the time she fell in love with the substitute mailman) her eye began to twitch and her skin broke out in hives.

Anne could relate to what Pat was experiencing. She felt awful herself. She'd come to the Laughing Gull in search of Kim, only to be told by Larry that Kim had taken to bed, overwhelmed by discovering the body and by the worst migraine she'd ever had. A half-hour later, Ed Burns and another detective whom Anne had never seen before had arrived and began to question them, one by one. They were talking to Cece now. Anne heard the steady patter of their questions and Cece's monosyllabic responses through the thin wall that separated the parlor from the breakfast nook.

Nora sat by the window, staring out at the rain, her face pale and drawn. Henry loitered by the door, looking as if he'd love to bolt, if he could. Chase Merritt and Larry were at opposite ends of the small game table, where a heated Scrabble game had been played by two boys from Allentown, Pennsylvania, who had relocated upstairs with their parents and several of the other guests, no doubt to gossip over the murder.

Murder. The word left Anne feeling numb. The sight of Aunt Hannah, cold and dead, her robe caked with dried blood, made Anne sick. She looked around for Alex and found him standing by the cupboard, pretending to examine vintage toasters and blenders.

Anne and the others had compared notes. It turned out that Chase Merritt had been the last one of them to see Hannah alive. He said he'd gone to Dovecote at seven o'clock, enjoyed two glasses of sherry and some pimento-stuffed olives with Aunt Hannah, and then left when Hannah had insisted she was feeling poorly. She was uncharacteristically morose, Merritt said, though she'd refused to tell him why. At that point in his narrative, Merritt had stared at Henry accusingly, as though it were obvious Hannah's son had caused her great unhappiness.

Anne was both relieved and dismayed that Trasker was nowhere in sight. She wanted him there to comfort her and to provide whatever insights he could into the investigation. But she didn't want her family's first impressions of Trasker to be formed while he was on the job. When she'd first met Trasker she'd been a suspect in the murder of a prima donna actress whose memoirs she just happened to be ghostwriting. She knew firsthand how off-putting and frightening it was to be grilled by him, to look into those cool, impassive eyes and feel the firm, inviolable grip of the law closing in on you.

She'd spent many hours envisioning the initial meeting between Trasker and her relatives, how he'd charm them with his warmth and easy humor, how they'd come across as quirky, but lovable. How the race issue would melt into the background as everyone got to know one another.

But it was peculiar that Trasker hadn't been at the crime scene and wasn't there now. Where was he? What was going on?

As if reading her mind, Alex said, "Where's that detective friend of yours?"

"He's probably on his way," Anne replied. She tried to muster up a smile and couldn't quite pull it off. "Hey, you want to go outside for a while? I could use some air."

"Sure."

They stepped out onto the porch, where a row of empty rocking chairs shifted back and forth in the wind. The street was slick with rain, the beach sodden and brown, with the sand a flat spit of mud. Waves broke on the pilings of the fishing pier and dashed against the shoreline like a string of broken promises.

Anne looked over at Alex. He pulled out a cigarette, cupped it with his hand to light it, and inhaled deeply, blowing a series of smoke rings that were instantly whisked away by the ocean breeze. He wore chinos, loafers, a 1950's-style short-sleeve navy shirt that buttoned down the front, and a slouchy hat that made Anne think of Sinatra and the Rat Pack and Vegas lounge lizards. The clothes fit Alex to a tee, although he looked more like an actor or a musician than the salesman that he was. Over the years Alex had sold men's sportswear, vacuum cleaners, deck furniture, travel packages, and plumbing supplies. But what he sold best was himself.

Back when they were growing up, half the girls in town had been wild about him, hanging around his house, inscribing his name in the inside covers of their schoolbooks. The more daring among them had slipped notes into his locker, inviting him to meet them under the bleachers or on the fishing pier late at night. Sometimes he went, sometimes not. The thrill of the chase appealed to Alex. Once he got the girl, he usually lost interest and moved on.

Back then he was the sort of boy who normally wouldn't have looked twice at Anne. But because they were related, because Anne and his sister, Nora, were so close, Anne got to flutter around the edges of his circle of friends—boys who were athletic and handsome, girls who were cheerleaders and drove their own cars.

Alex had treated Anne with affection, as though she were another sister. She, in turn, had looked up to him, admiring his carefree nature, his ability to make people like him, the way he commanded attention without seeming to desire it.

The fact that he was her cousin prevented her from entertaining any romantic notions about him that she otherwise might have indulged in. As they grew older, she continued to be charmed by him, but also bemused, and she sometimes wondered if her cousin had succumbed to the Peter Pan syndrome and had simply refused to grow up.

From what she could gather, he still liked fast cars, loose women, and what he himself referred to as toys—the newest, most expensive phones, computers, home electronic devices, and exercise equipment, all designed to make his life easier. As a salesman, he had a knack for putting people at ease, for winning them over, which was part of why Anne was reluctant to quiz him about Aunt Hannah.

"This is really rough," he said, gazing down at her with those deep blue eyes that were so like his sister's. "I hope Hannah didn't suffer much. It sounded like there was so much blood. Is it possible to die like that without being in excruciating pain?"

"I don't know. I don't think so."

Alex blew another smoke ring. The temperature had dropped about fifteen degrees, and Anne found she was shivering.

"Who would want to hurt a poor defenseless old lady?" Alex asked.

It was a question Anne had been considering all morning. The Heights was a small, relatively safe town, the kind of place where neighbors looked out for one another and the crime blotter in the local paper detailed the rescue of cats stuck in trees and the return of missing trash cans that had strayed in high winds.

Aunt Hannah had been a fixture of sorts in the Heights. Though she spent most of her time up in Boston now, nearly everyone knew who she was. It was hard to believe she was murdered by someone from town, harder still to think a stranger—one of the sunburned tourists who descended on the Heights each summer—had done it.

Anne turned to Alex. He was staring at the ocean, which was choppy and gray, studded with whitecaps.

She said, "Remember earlier when I told everyone how Aunt Hannah called me yesterday to ask for my help with adoption?"

"That is so weird. I can't imagine what she had in mind." Alex crushed his cigarette out against the sole of his shoe and tossed the butt into the grass. "Though I confess there were times I used to wish she'd adopt me. I could use a fairy godmother to help me out of a jam now and then."

"Are you in trouble?"

"No more than usual," he said, with a grin.

"Anything I can do to help?"

"Not this time, Annie. But thanks for asking."

She nodded, wondering if it was women trouble or money problems. He'd been known to suffer from both in the past. As Nora was fond of saying: "Hell hath no fury like a woman scorned by my fickle brother."

Aloud, Anne said, "Anyway, about yesterday. When I was on the phone with Aunt Hannah, her doorbell rang. She went to answer it and I thought I could hear a man's voice talking to her. They were arguing." Anne caught her breath. She realized she'd been speaking too fast, nearly tripping over the words. "I thought it was you, actually. It sounded like you. This would have been around six o'clock." She hated that she was nervous, but she plunged ahead. "Because you didn't mention it, mention seeing Aunt Hannah again, when we were all comparing notes before."

Alex fixed his gaze on her and she was reminded of the time back in high school when she'd seen him get beaten up in a fight for stealing another boy's girlfriend. His eyes had the same blank expression now, like every trace of emotion had been erased.

"Wasn't me," he said evenly. "I was with Heather Vance yesterday afternoon. You know Heather, don't you? We were catching up on old times."

Sure, she knew Heather Vance. Heather and Alex had been an item for a while during his senior year. She worked for her father over at the drugstore, and Anne had heard she was currently between boyfriends.

Alex smiled ruefully. "It's odd how life works out, don't you think? Seeing Heather again after all these years, coming down here to hook up with you guys, and then out of the blue Aunt Hannah is murdered."

Had Alex quarreled with Hannah yesterday? Impossible to know. Anne had seen her cousin talk his way out of many difficult situations with the ease of a man to whom lying came naturally. Still, Alex was more of a lover than a fighter. She couldn't picture him engaged in a shouting match with an eighty-four-year-old woman. It would be more Alex's style to sweet-talk his auntie into doing what he wanted.

"You're frowning, cuz," Alex said.

So she was. But before she could reply, Detective Ed Burns opened the door leading to the porch and informed them that their presence was requested inside.

"During the first few days of our investigation," said Detective Burns, addressing the group assembled in the front parlor of the Laughing Gull, "I'd like all of you to remain here in the Heights. The sheriff's office will be working with the state police and other local law-enforcement agents to try to solve this terrible crime. We'll probably be interviewing each of you again as more information comes to light."

Burns was short and stocky, with eyes that bulged slightly, a scruffy brown beard and a big hook nose that looked as though it had been broken more than once. He usually wore a harsh, stern, expression, which matched his hard-as-nails personality. He swaggered when he walked and had a reputation for being a bully. Trasker didn't like Burns much. He'd told Anne there had been lots of guys like Burns at the police academy. Too quick on the trigger, too skittish and rash to make a good partner. Burns had a history of racial profiling—pulling black men out of their cars or off the streets to search for guns, drugs, anything incriminating, solely on the basis of their skin color.

Burns had made detective a year ago, been brought up on assault charges filed by a black prostitute (that were later dropped), and transferred from the hardscrabble streets of Newark to the Neptune Township Sheriff's Office, where it was Trasker's misfortune to be assigned to work with him.

Though Anne had met Burns only a couple of times, she didn't like him.

Now he was passing his business cards around, telling them to call him if they had any information that might be relevant to this case.

Pat, who'd brought out a fresh tray of muffins and replenished the silver coffee urn twice, looked up from sweeping crumbs off the floor and said, "Mrs. Rutter was a rich woman and everyone knew it. Was somebody trying to steal from her?"

"That's unclear at this time, ma'am," Burns responded.

Anne heard something in his voice—a certainty, a smoothness—that led her to believe Neptune's finest knew more than Burns was letting on.

Chase Merritt rose to his feet. His face was flushed, his paunchy belly protruded over the waistband of his polyester pants. "Of course she was robbed," he shouted, in his patrician Boston accent. "Her jewelry's missing. Her rings. Her bracelets. They're gone." He shook his fist angrily at Ed Burns. "I told you they'd been stolen. Some lowlife drifter is probably pawning them right now."

The cousins glared at him, as though he were the man in question.

Burns said, "We're pursuing several leads at the moment." Then he stared straight at Anne.

Her heart sank. It felt as though he were training his gun on her, as though he had her squarely in his sights. *He knows something, all right*, she thought. *Something bad*.

It didn't take long to find out what. Shortly after Anne got home, the doorbell rang and there stood Detective Ed Burns in his official sheriff's office rain slicker, dripping water onto the wood plank floor. From behind Anne's legs, Harry eyed the detective warily.

"I'd like to take a look around your kitchen," Burns informed Anne briskly, clearly pleased she was puzzled by the odd request.

"Sure. Right this way."

She wondered why Trasker wasn't there himself to bring her up to speed on the investigation. Or was that a gross conflict of interest, considering that she and her family were involved?

It didn't take Burns long to find what he was after.

On her counter, half-hidden by a white Braun coffeemaker, was a square piece of butcher block, which held her new steak knives, purchased last spring on sale at Linens 'n Things in the Freehold Mall. They were top-of-the-line German high-carbon stainless-steel knives, guaranteed not to rust or stain, and sold in a set of seven. Henckels. That was the name of the manufacturer. She remembered standing in the store and marveling at their feel, at the weight of the blade against the mass of the wood handles, envisioning the steaks she would grill, the roasts she would learn to cook, but never had.

She saw in an instant that the eight-inch chef's knife was missing.

Slipping on a pair of latex gloves, Burns took out what looked like the world's largest heavy-duty baggie. He picked up the set and gently eased it into the bag. "May I borrow these?" he said, his eyes twinkling. He was enjoying this, enjoying the chance to exercise his authority, to let her know who was boss.

And why not, she thought. Ed Burns had as much regard for Trasker as Trasker had for him. He must have recoiled when he found out his new partner was black, and involved with a white woman, to boot. Burns was probably salivating at the chance to implicate her in Aunt Hannah's death.

"I take it you've located the murder weapon," Anne said

lightly, trying not to reveal how scared she felt. Her mouth had gone dry. Her legs felt slightly rubbery. Why would they look here for the knife?

"Could be," Burns said, cracking his knuckles. "In the meantime, you need to answer a few questions for me."

He sat down at her kitchen table and motioned for her to do likewise, acting like he owned the joint. Then he pulled a notebook and pen from the breast pocket of his gray suit.

"There's a knife missing from this set," he said slowly, as though he were explaining a math problem to a dull-witted third-grader. "When's the last time you used it?"

Anne honestly couldn't remember. She'd bought the set in April, had used a few of the knives once or twice to cut cheese and vegetables—including the chef's knife to cut up a whole chicken—and then had pushed the block to the back of the counter and hadn't reached for them again. She still used the knives in her silverware drawer, out of habit.

Aloud, she said, "I don't know. I haven't even noticed the knives for several months."

"What was your relationship with the deceased?"

Anne felt her mouth grow dry. "She was my great-aunt."

"We know that," Burns said impatiently. "I'm talking about what you felt toward the deceased. A lot of people in this town couldn't stand her. Were you one of them?"

"Hannah was a difficult woman," Anne began, then stopped short. Questions flitted through her mind like wayward sparrows. If she was a suspect in a murder investigation, shouldn't she have a lawyer present? Did calling a lawyer make you look guilty? Where could you find a lawyer on such short notice? If they were planning to arrest her, wouldn't they have taken her directly to the sheriff's office?

Ed Burns appeared pleased by her confusion. He hammered her with questions over and over again until she was physically exhausted and the rain beating against the windowpanes began to give her a headache. They went over the same ground again and again: why she'd organized the reunion weekend, where she bought the knives, what Hannah had said about adoption on the phone.

When Burns finally stood up to go, she felt a palpable sense of relief. She walked him to the door, trailed by Harry. She'd never been so glad to get rid of anyone in her life. The minute he left, she'd call Trasker and find out what was going on.

Ed Burns had one hand on the front doorknob when he turned back. "Oh, yes," he announced. "There's one more thing."

Anne saw he'd been building up to this all along, waiting to spring it on her. He stared at her with his bulging frog's eyes and said, "Your aunt's lawyer turned over a copy of her will to us. She was worth $250 million and she divided her estate five ways, between you and your cousins. Congratulations, little lady. You hit the jackpot."

Anne was so stunned she could barely think straight. It was so much money, more than Lotto, more than she'd ever dreamed of, and she burst out laughing.

Burns looked at her as if she'd lost her mind. "You don't seem all that surprised," he commented dryly. "But you probably knew about the money. You've known for a while."

"Oh, give it a rest," Anne said, finally losing patience with being bullied. "Why don't you concentrate on finding the killer instead of playing these silly mind games with me?"

Ed Burns glared at her. "Watch your tongue, missy. Or you'll be sorry."

He opened the door, letting in a blast of sea air. The next thing Anne knew, something small and wet had bounded into the hallway. She stepped back in surprise. Harry let out a wail, then ran upstairs, faster than Anne had ever seen him move. Aunt Hannah's dog, Bronte, shook herself off, spraying muddy water all over Anne. Then the dog settled into a crouch and began to yip and yelp at the top of her lungs.

"There was a codicil in the will," Ed Burns said, shouting to be heard above the yelping, "that you were to look after her pooch." He placed a small trunk on the floor that looked as if it was covered in dyed red crocodile skin. " 'Course it'll take a month or so for the will to be probated, but you wouldn't want Fido here languishing in a kennel, now would you?"

For the first time during their meeting, Anne was speechless.

"We'll talk again soon," Ed Burns said. "You have a nice day."

Chapter 8

> *Growling, crying, hissing,*
> *or snarling means your*
> *cat is really ticked off.*

Trasker wasn't in his office, so Anne left a message on his answering machine asking that he call her right away. She'd managed to placate the dog temporarily with bologna and roast beef and some leftover pasta salad, but she still wouldn't stop barking. She had no idea what dogs ate or if it was okay to serve them cat food. Harry, meanwhile, had gone into hiding, from whence he could not be coaxed, no matter how long Anne spent calling him or how much Cat Chow she put out.

She went into her office and e-mailed Edie Mintzler a brief message:

> *Help! I've temporarily inherited a female pug who*
> *didn't come with an instruction manual. What do I do?*

Then she picked up the phone and dialed.

"This is Tina," answered the perky voice on the other end. "How can I help you?"

Tina Lassell was a systems analyst with the phone company, as well as a sci-fi enthusiast. They'd met when Anne was ghosting *The Unofficial Guide to the X-Files*. At the time, Tina had been planning to create an *X-Files* museum in Camden, but plans for the museum had since fallen through, due to lack of funds and interest.

"Tina, hi. This is Anne Hardaway."

"Wow, this is cosmic. I was just thinking about you."

Anne couldn't help smiling. "Do you have a new book idea?"

"Wait till you hear," Tina said excitedly. "What do you think about a book on sci-fi actors? Like you could interview people on *Star Trek* and *Mystery Science Theater* to find out if they've ever had extraterrestrial encounters or what they think about UFOs."

Anne suppressed a chuckle. People were always trying to give her book ideas. She even had a couple of projects of her own on the back burner. The most recent one was a book about teens and witchcraft, which her publisher, Triple Star, had turned down and which was probably sitting atop slush piles on the desks of various editors she'd sent it to at a half-dozen other publishing houses.

"I'll give it some thought," Anne said, not wanting to hurt Tina's feelings. "Meantime, I have a favor to ask."

She briefly described the circumstances of her aunt's death.

"God, that's awful," Tina sympathized. "What can I do to help?"

"I need to know the phone numbers of all the people Hannah called and the people who called her since she arrived in the Heights yesterday."

"No problem. I just need her phone number and I should have it for you in a little while."

"Thanks, Tina. I really appreciate your help."

After she hung up, Anne sat at her desk, staring out the window at the gray, rainy afternoon. Ocean Avenue was practically deserted. Even the gulls had disappeared. The rain pattered against the roof like a series of exclamation points. The air smelled briny. On the dunes, the sea grass tossed restlessly in the wind.

Of course, the cops would be getting the same phone information through official channels. But she needed to be one step ahead of them if someone was trying to frame her for murder. Who could have taken the steak knife? Anybody at the reunion lunch. The knives had been sitting out on the counter for all the world to see. She felt nauseous thinking about it.

She picked up the phone to call Trasker again and hung up halfway through his recorded message.

As soon as the will was probated, she'd be $50 million richer. She'd never had to work another day in her life. She could move to Paris, buy a Cessna, raise Thoroughbreds.

Only she didn't want the money. Not this way. It felt all wrong. Too many of her relatives had died. Her parents. Her grandmother. Now this. It was like her family was made up of this great big quilt and the squares of fabric were being snipped away, one by one. It didn't matter that Aunt Hannah was difficult to get along with. Hannah Rutter had been bound to Anne by blood and now, as Anne watched the raindrops slide down the windowpanes like a trail of tears, she felt more alone than ever.

The Hanley-Britt adoption agency was sandwiched between a Sir Speedy copy shop and the Dance Connection ballet academy on a ramshackle street in Red Bank that, unlike most of the town, had not yet been gentrified by antiques shops, coffee bars, and art galleries. Housed in a tan brick two-story building, the agency looked as if it had seen better days. Paint was flaking off the front door, the windows were coated with a thick layer of grime, and the lettering on the sign out front was fading away, so that it spelled Hany-Bit.

Inside, an elderly receptionist sat at a battered desk, leafing through a copy of *Good Housekeeping* magazine. Anne stuck her sopping wet umbrella in a garbage can underneath the coat tree that had been placed by the door expressly for that purpose.

"Excuse me," she said to the receptionist. "I wonder if you could help me?"

The woman glanced up. Her eyes were a milky gray. Her thin white hair had been dyed a coppery gold. "Yes," she chirped.

"A woman named Hannah Rutter called here yesterday afternoon at around four-thirty." Four thirty-nine to be exact, according to Tina Lassell, an hour and a half before she called Anne, a conversation that lasted for three minutes and seventeen seconds. "I'd like to know who she spoke to and what—"

"Are you with the police, miss?" the receptionist inquired. "A detective was here earlier and he said someone from his office might be coming back."

"That's right," Anne said.

She hadn't been planning to lie, but she'd probably get more information as a duly deputized officer of the law than she would as a well-intentioned niece.

The receptionist waved Anne toward the back of the office, which was decorated in 1950s ugly: fake dark wood paneling, two sofas upholstered in olive-green corduroy, a glass boomerang-shaped coffee table, rust-colored shag carpeting, a few black filing cabinets, and a couple of dusty-looking potted palms.

The walls were bare except for several identical black-and-white posters showing head shots of children photographed against a pale gray background. The kids appeared to range between one and eight years of age. Most did not smile for the camera. Instead, they had serious, grave expressions, as if their worries and cares far surpassed their years. But what struck Anne most were their eyes, which were expressionless and flat, failing to reflect any trace of warmth or joy.

As Anne walked by, two young women sitting at desks glanced up.

"Sherry," the receptionist called out. "Someone's here to see you about that lady who got killed."

Another woman emerged from a doorway on the left.

"Sherry Marcus," the woman said, extending her hand for Anne to shake. She was in her mid- to late forties, with close-cropped frosted blond hair and wire-rimmed aviator glasses, and she wore a long purple chenille sweater over tight black pants. The sweater had little purple pompoms on it that shook when she moved. "I'm the agency's director," she said, "and you are—?"

"Lynnette Quigley," Anne said, using the name of one of the cashiers at the Mini-Mart in the Heights, then compounding the lie. "With the Neptune Township Sheriff's Office."

Hopefully, by the time the cops got back here, this whole mess would be resolved.

"Won't you sit down?" asked Sherry, ushering Anne into a small room that was barely large enough to contain a desk, a swivel chair, and an uncomfortable ladderback chair with a rush seat, upon which Anne sat.

On the wall behind Sherry's desk was another adoption poster of the children Anne had seen in the outer room. Next to it was a Far Side wall calendar. The illustration for the month of August showed a bunch of cows cavorting in a field. "Car!" one of the cows warned, sighting an approaching vehicle, prompting several of the animals nearest him to stop dancing and begin contentedly chewing grass.

"What can I do for you?" Sherry asked.

"You were the one who spoke to Mrs. Rutter, right?" It was an easy assumption. Anne couldn't imagine Aunt Hannah dealing with anyone other than the person in charge.

After Sherry nodded her assent, Anne took a small notebook and pen out of her pocketbook. It was her idea book, which she used to jot down thoughts, questions, and observations on her book projects. She flipped past a page on why cats crave privacy and turned to a blank sheet. "I'd like to review the conversation you had with Mrs. Rutter," she said.

Sherry Marcus shrugged. Her desk was obsessively neat—paperweight, stapler, and framed photos lined up in descending height order, yellow legal pads stacked to one side, correspondence on the other, pencils sharpened to fine lead points. A half-dozen photo albums with gold and maroon covers were wedged between wooden bookends.

"Like I told the detective earlier," Sherry said, "there's not much to tell. The lady had some questions and was put through to me. She sounded very upset, very agitated. She primarily wanted to know if adoption records are sealed or if we're allowed to release them to the public after a certain number of years have elapsed. I explained that we're a small, privately run agency and it is our policy not to release confidential information.

"If you came in here trying to track down your birth parents, knowing you've been adopted through our agency, we couldn't help you. Unlike some other states, New Jersey doesn't have a mutual consent registry or a voluntary consent registry, where identifying information can be released to both parties. You would have to obtain a court order and convince a judge that the records needed to be opened, which is usually only done because of medical necessity. Or you could hire a private investigator to conduct a search, which is costly and time-consuming and doesn't always produce results."

A phone rang in the outer office and Anne realized how quiet the agency was, how airless and still. She scribbled *sealed records, confidential, consent registry* in the notebook, then looked up at Sherry.

"How far back do the records go?" she asked.

"We were founded in 1912 by the wives of two wealthy philanthropists, Mrs. Dorothea Hanley and Mrs. Iris Britt."

"And how long have *you* been here?"

Sherry Marcus blinked, thrown off balance by the question. "About a year and a half."

"So you're used to dealing with these types of inquiries."

"I suppose."

"And you were able to relieve Mrs. Rutter's anxiety."

Sherry ran her fingers through her short hair and frowned. "Actually, no. She still sounded very upset about the possibility of the records being made public. Her voice was trembling, like nothing I'd said had convinced her."

Anne decided to shift gears. "Are your records kept here, in this office?"

"Why yes," Sherry said, sounding surprised.

"It seems that they'd take up a lot of space and I didn't see many filing cabinets."

"We transferred everything to computer in March. It was a slow, painstaking job, but well worth the effort."

Anne thought a moment. "Would it be possible for someone to hack their way into the system?"

"I can't see how. The data is only accessible with a password, which we change each time someone is hired or leaves the agency."

"Did Mrs. Rutter give any indication that she'd used your agency before?"

"No. I asked her that very question, but she didn't answer me."

Anne indicated the poster on the wall. "Are those children that are waiting to be adopted?"

"No. The poster's old. From the 1960s. Those kids would be grown by now."

"I see. Could I have your number, in case I need to call you during the course of the investigation?"

"Certainly."

Sherry reached inside her desk and took out a buttercup-yellow card. She scribbled something on the bottom and handed the card to Anne. "My home number," she explained. "In case you need to reach me after business hours."

"Thanks," Anne said, studying the card. In the top left corner was a drawing of a child's smiling face.

"You know," said Sherry, "the system has changed dramatically in the last two decades. The children we place now are mostly of color—blacks, Latinos, Asians." Sherry pulled one of the photo albums out from between the bookends and pushed it across the desk. It was a portfolio of kids, Anne saw. Each page had a picture of a child and a brief bio: height, weight, color of hair and eyes, birthplace, favorite things. Hardly any of the children were white, unlike the kids in the poster, who were all Caucasian.

"If you want a white baby," Sherry was saying, "you need to go out of state, to Texas or Kentucky. And so many people are forgoing domestic adoptions altogether these days and traveling overseas, to China or Russia."

Anne nodded politely. Did she look like she was interested in adopting? A cat was about all she could handle at this point.

"Do you have children, Miss Quigley?" Sherry asked.

"I'm not even married."

"It really doesn't matter in this day and age. Nearly half our clients are single women who are sick and tired of waiting for Mr. Right to show up."

Anne thought of Trasker. Would they have children together some day? Biracial children?

"I'll be in touch," Anne said, rising.

On her way out, she passed the poster of the children waiting to be adopted. They seemed to watch her as she walked by, following her with their blank, lifeless eyes.

Chapter 9

Cats and dogs don't speak the same language. For instance, when a dog wags its tail, it usually means, "Hi. I'm happy to see you." But when a cat's tail wags, it means, "I'm worried and mad as hell." A dog who misinterprets the signal as "Let's be friends" is in for an unpleasant surprise.

Anne sat in her car outside the adoption agency. It was pouring so hard she couldn't see a thing through the windshield. Rain drummed against the roof of the Mustang, sounding oddly soothing. Sitting there was like being in a cocoon, closed off from the outside world.

From the glove compartment she retrieved her cell phone, a birthday gift from Trasker that she rarely used. Now she punched in her own number.

Nora picked up the phone. "Hi," she said, sounding frazzled. "When are you coming home? I don't think I'm cut out to be a pet-sitter. Harry's been arching his back and wagging his tail a lot. I thought only dogs did that."

"I'll be back as soon as I can. In the meantime, could you try to separate them?"

"I'll do my best. Oh, you had a couple of messages. Helen called from Virginia to offer her condolences. And someone named Edie called from California."

"Anyone else?"

"Nope."

Anne heard staccato barking, followed by a crash and a loud shriek that sounded disturbingly like Harry. "Oh, shit," Nora said. "Gotta go."

After she got off the phone, Anne dialed Trasker's number at work. "Hey," she said, raising her voice to be heard over the driving rain. "It's me. Call me as soon as you can, okay?" There was a short beep on his machine. Did that mean he'd picked up the three other messages she'd left for him that day? What was going on?

She took two Tylenol from her handbag and swallowed them without water, gagging a little. Her head was pounding and she felt slightly feverish. She glanced at her watch. Five-thirty. God, this nightmarish day was never going to end.

Leaning back against the headrest, she closed her eyes. *Focus*, she told herself. *Try to concentrate.*

Aunt Hannah had made three phone calls yesterday from Dovecote. One to Hanley-Britt. One to Anne. And one to the Laughing Gull at three-thirty P.M. Between five-fifteen and eleven, Hannah had received four phone calls, all placed from the Laughing Gull. Anne knew how the bed-and-breakfast operated. None of the rooms had phones. Adjacent to the front parlor was a small anteroom that contained a pay phone, a soda machine, and a trunk filled with extra beach towels. All of the calls from the B&B had been placed from the pay phone; the call Aunt Hannah had made went directly to the main number, which rang at the telephone atop the reception desk.

This information was leading Anne exactly nowhere. She didn't know what she'd been expecting—that Hannah would contact some unknown person, a ne'er-do-well who'd turn out to be the killer. No, Hannah had probably called Chase Merritt about when to come over for cocktails. Or maybe one of her cousins, maybe Kim, in fact, to . . . what? Run an errand? Pick up a bottle of sherry or those olives Merritt had said they'd eaten?

As for who had called Hannah from the B&B, that would be fairly easy to check out. Alex was the most obvious choice. Alex wanting to come over, to ask his auntie to bail him out of his latest jam. Had Alex been at Dovecote yesterday afternoon? She tried to picture Alex slipping one of the kitchen knives into his pocket. *I'll get another bottle of wine*, he'd said to Anne during lunch. *You sit.*

But Chase Merritt and each of her relatives—with the exception of Henry—had been in the kitchen alone at some point. Drifting in and out to get fresh bread and more napkins, refilling water glasses, fetching dessert plates, helping to clear the table. But none of them would . . . Oh, she didn't want to think about it anymore.

She started the car, turned her windshield wipers on the highest setting, and drove back toward the Heights. There was so much rainfall on the roads that the Mustang was nearly hydroplaning. Plumes of water shot up on either side of the car, like dirty fountains. She turned on her favorite oldies station and listened to the Foundations croon "Build Me Up, Buttercup."

It was one of the songs they'd played at the first boy-girl party she'd ever gone to, in fifth grade. She remembered huddling in a corner with Cece, Nora, and Kim, pretending not to care if anyone asked her to dance.

Please, she begged silently, although to whom she couldn't say, since she no longer believed in God. *Don't let it be one of my cousins. Not that.* She saw Aunt Hannah lying facedown on the floor, her bathrobe matted with dried blood, and she started to cry, her tears mingling with the rain pelting the windshield until the road ahead grew blurry. A car in back of her honked and she wiped her tears away, willing herself to focus on driving.

She realized she was starving. She hadn't eaten breakfast, and her stomach was making "feed me" noises. The Ocean Diner was a few miles away, and she decided to head there. She hadn't been to the diner in weeks. The last time was with Trasker, when they realized at one in the morning on a Sunday night that they had to have cheese steaks and home fries. For some reason the memory saddened her and she flicked off the radio and drove for a while with only the *whoosh* of the wipers for company.

The Ocean Diner was a landmark of sorts on the Jersey Shore. Built during the Depression, it advertised itself as the oldest establishment of its kind in the state, a claim hotly disputed by a diner in Trenton. Anne had eaten in both places, and no matter who was right historically, she would swear to the fact that the Ocean had the best donuts in the Garden State—light, not too sugary, melt-in-your-mouth delicious.

She parked near the entrance and got a window booth, overlooking Route 35. It had a maroon vinyl banquette and paper placemats with pictures of cocktails no one ordered anymore: Mai Tai, Grasshopper, Pink Lady, Gimlet. It might be nice to sip a Mai Tai with a little pink umbrella in it. She could stare out the window and pretend she was in Barbados, watching a tropical storm.

"You ready, hon?" asked the plump waitress in the faded gray uniform.

"I'll have a short stack of pancakes, bacon, and tea with lemon," Anne said.

There was something comforting about eating breakfast foods at dinnertime.

"Coming right up," said the waitress, heading for the kitchen.

Anne took a sip of icewater and looked around. Usually if she were by herself at a restaurant, she killed time by eavesdropping on people seated closest to her. It was amazing what you ended up overhearing—tales of adultery, greed, chicanery, lust. The seven deadly sins, sandwiched between the appetizer and dessert.

Today, however, the diner was only half-full and no one was seated within earshot. Anne got up and walked to the front of the restaurant. Across from the cashier was a small table on which lay three or four newspapers. This was one of the Ocean Diner's amenities. Each day the owner bought the papers, which circulated among his customers.

Anne took two—the *Landsdown Park Press* and the *Star-Ledger*—and returned to the booth. She opened the *Press* first, flipping through the arts section. A couple new movies looked promising and a jazz trio was playing at Jason's in Belmar. If things were different, she would have organized a group outing to the club tonight with her cousins and Trasker in tow. It would have been so great, so relaxing and fun. She wondered if she'd ever feel normal again or if, no matter how things turned out, her relationship with the people closest to her would be permanently and disturbingly altered.

Pushing the thought from her mind, she turned to the business pages. For months there'd been rumors in the press that Triple Star Publishing would be sold. Though her editor, Phil Smedley, maintained it would never happen, Anne knew that publishing conglomerates were swallowing up little companies left and right. If Triple Star were sold, the new owner might decide the books Anne wrote weren't earning a big enough return and she'd be out of luck, not to mention out of work.

But all thoughts of Triple Star were immediately forgotten when she saw the lead story in the business section. SHOE MAGNATE FAILS TO TOE THE LINE, blared the headline. TRASH TALK ON VERGE OF BANKRUPTCY. It was a wire story, Anne noted, written by a reporter for the Associated Press. She read it straight through, without stopping:

Just a year ago, Lawrence T. Ryerson was receiving the highest accolade the footwear industry bestows on its own. Amid thunderous cheers, Ryerson stepped up to the podium at New York's Plaza Hotel to accept the Golden Slipper award, bestowed each September on the industry's best and brightest stars. His company, LTR, Inc., was racking up $650 million in annual sales. His chain of Trash Talk shoe stores, catering to teen and preteen girls, had expanded to a record 87 stores nationwide. And his designs, encompassing platform sandals, platform sneakers, and platform square-toed shoes in suede, leather, and polyester, were being hailed as nothing short of revolutionary.

But the buzz has faded to an unpleasant sting. Today Ryerson is reportedly on the verge of bankruptcy and is considering closing all but a handful of stores. The stock price of LTR, which reached a high of $53 a share last November is down to $9. First quarter earnings were down 40 percent. And the company has reportedly racked up an outstanding debt of $400 million.

"Teenage girls are notoriously fickle," said William

Boyle, an analyst with Goldman Sachs, who recommended selling the stock back in January. "They don't stay loyal to products for long."

Still, industry observers note that the problems at LTR, Inc. extend beyond the uncertainties of the teen market. Ryerson has been criticized for overexpanding the Trash Talk chain, opening too many new stores in too short a period of time, sometimes only miles apart. Several competitors are producing lower-priced variations of his signature line, which in the past Ryerson has termed "cheap knockoffs." (He was unavailable for comment for this article.)

In the spring the company was shaken by reports that overseas workers in the Dominican Republic were being paid the U.S. equivalent of 8 cents an hour and were subject to harsh, unfair working conditions, prompting such teen pop stars as Britney Spears and Christina Aguilera to spearhead a widespread boycott of Trash Talk products. The shoes sell for $45 and up in the States.

In addition, the shoes themselves have lately come under fire. "They're seventies retreads, only clunkier, bigger and uglier," said Lindsey Falk Dutton, editor of *Footwear Today*, an industry trade journal. "The pendulum in girls' fashion has swung back to prettier, more romantic styles that make these shoes look 'out.' Frankly, I don't think anyone will miss them."

If Ryerson can't stop the downward spiral, the same could be said about Trash Talk.

Anne looked through the *Star-Ledger*, but could find no mention of Larry's company. The *Press* was an afternoon paper. Maybe the story had just broken.

She pushed the papers away from her and sat staring into

space. When the waitress returned with her dinner, she picked at her food, barely touching the pancakes and bacon. No wonder Larry had seemed so frantic last night. His company was going down the tubes. He needed money. Lots of money. Fast.

Anne would bet that Aunt Hannah wouldn't have floated Larry a loan or agreed to invest in his company, no matter how much he begged and pleaded. It was no secret that Aunt Hannah hadn't approved of Larry. He's a sharpie, she used to say. Low-class. No manners. Not nearly good enough for our Kim.

On that score, Anne would have to agree. Apart from his ability to provide lavishly for his family, Larry was a washout in Anne's book. An abrasive, argumentative know-it-all who didn't seem to appreciate or even tolerate his devoted wife. Anne pictured Larry and Kim's two teenage daughters, pale, willowy Marisa, and wisecracking, studious Leigh. Anne had visited Kim in the hospital the day after each of the girls was born. Thinking of that made her wonder again what Aunt Hannah's interest in adoption had been.

She thought of the picture of the baby in Cece's wallet. Had that little girl been adopted by Cece? And if so, what possible interest would it be to Hannah?

Anne remembered how her great-aunt's voice had sounded on the phone when she'd called about adoption. Frightened mostly. But of what? Or whom? She tried to imagine Larry rapping brusquely on the brass knocker adorning the front door of Dovecote, demanding that Aunt Hannah let him in, demanding money.

As soon as Anne had summoned the image, she dismissed it. Larry might be obnoxious, but he wasn't stupid. He'd never ask for money himself. Not when he could send Kim.

Chapter 10

*For dogs and cats, steal-
ing is often a bid for
attention, not a spiteful
act. Even the negative attention that results from
swiping socks or food
may be worth it to a frus-
trated pet. One solution:
Whenever possible,
replace what your pet
steals with something it's
all right for him to have.*

Kim wasn't at the Laughing Gull. Neither was
Larry. In fact, the B&B was unusually quiet. Anne
wondered if the other guests had packed up and
gone home.

Pat was in the kitchen, tossing ingredients furiously into
assorted pots and pans. Uh oh, Anne thought. Pat was in one
of her manic phases. The fake marble counters were littered
with mixing bowls, measuring spoons, eggs, milk, pints of
ripe blueberries and strawberries, zucchini, broccoli, and a

dozen other assorted fruits and vegetables. The seafoam-green cabinets were thrown open, revealing a jumble of dried and canned food. When Pat opened the refrigerator, Anne could see that it was packed. Cube steak rested precariously on a package of chicken breasts; seltzer and wine bottles were scattered like bowling pins on a bottom shelf.

"My new omelet," Pat explained, pitching sunflower seeds into a gloppy-looking batter. "It's kind of a summer medley."

"Did Kim say where she was going or when she'd be back?"

"Nope. But your cousin Cecilia told me to tell you she'd be back around nine. She wants to talk to you."

Anne nodded, distracted. Where could Kim be? Larry's white Lexus was parked out front, so she couldn't have gone far.

"Hey, Annie," Pat said, stirring the mixture so vigorously that it sloshed over the sides of the bowl. "I didn't get a chance to tell you before, but I'm real sorry about your aunt." Pat wiped her face with the back of her hand and got butter all over her hair. "I didn't know Mrs. Rutter that well, but I've always loved that house. I wish I could get my roses to bloom as nicely as she did." Pat offered the spoon to Anne. "Want a taste? It's pretty good. Don't you think?"

She was talking so fast Anne could barely understand her.

"No, thanks. I'm not hungry," Anne said, declining the tasting offer. "Listen, Pat. I'm sure the police have been over this with you. But did you notice anything unusual last night? I mean—" Anne stopped, unsure how to proceed. "You and I have known each other a long time and I need to know . . . well, I need to find out my relatives' whereabouts last night and early this morning. It's very important."

Pat stopped stirring the batter and studied Anne's face. "I'll tell you what I told the cops. Far as I know, everyone was tucked in by eleven. That's when I lock the front door each night. House rules and all. The back door is kept locked all the time after eight P.M."

"Could someone have sneaked out in the middle of the night and gotten back in?"

"I don't see how without waking everyone up and borrowing an awfully tall ladder to climb to the second floor. Besides, all the windows have screens that are bolted from the inside. They're double hung, with heavy sashes. Hard to open from the outside."

"It was raining pretty heavily last night. Maybe the storm drowned out the noise. Where do you keep the key to the front door?"

"In a drawer at the desk."

"So it's possible someone could have borrowed it and let themselves back in here without anyone being the wiser."

Pat narrowed her eyes. "I suppose. But the alarm system was turned on." Pat hesitated. "Anyway, do you actually think a member of your family could be capable of murder?"

Anne felt a sudden burst of shame. Her suspicions were awful. But someone had taken the knife from her kitchen and she had to find out who it was. "What about this morning?" she persisted. "What time did you wake up?"

Pat poured some of the egg mixture into a skillet on the stove. "I'm usually up by five. I unlock the front door at six." She turned the flame up and the skillet emitted a soft hiss. "Like I told the police, your cousin Kim left the house at 7:08 A.M. I know the exact time because I was listening to the radio and they always do traffic and weather on the eights."

"What about the others?"

"I didn't see anyone else until breakfast."

Anne said, "I'm not sure if you've heard or not, but I seem to be the chief suspect."

"What?" Pat exclaimed, slamming the eggs against the side of the pan.

Anne recounted what had transpired earlier with Ed Burns and the missing chef's knife.

"But someone else must have taken that knife from your kitchen," Pat said indignantly.

"Apparently so. Which is why if you saw anything—anything at all, I need to know about it."

Anne was sure there was something else. It wasn't so much what Pat had told her just now, but the way Pat had said it. Like she'd been reciting a speech she'd rehearsed in front of the mirror. It sounded too practiced, and she'd spoken a little too quickly.

Pat looked wildly around the room. Her hands were trembling. Her eye had begun to twitch. Oh, God. Anne thought. Something's really wrong and she knows it.

"Pat?" Anne said. "What is it?"

Pat bit down on her lip and the fine lines by her eyes deepened. She looked nervous and edgy, like she wanted to jump out of her skin.

"Pat," Anne repeated, suddenly feeling the way she did when she went fishing off the pier by the ocean and there was that first gentle tug on her line.

She looked over at Pat and was surprised to find that Pat was blushing.

"It's not like I still care about him anymore," Pat said softly, still not meeting Anne's gaze.

The omelet in the skillet was starting to take shape and Pat folded it over expertly.

Alex, Anne thought. *Of course. Why didn't I remember until now?* Pat used to have quite a thing for Alex, and anything to do with romance always threw her into a tizzy.

"He went out at about, oh, maybe eleven forty-five P.M.

and came back a little after one." Pat nervously licked her lips. "I wasn't spying on him or anything," she added defensively. "Everybody knows I lock the door between eleven P.M. and seven A.M., but there's a key on the hook."

They'd dated for a brief time during Alex's senior year of high school, and Pat had mooned after him for months after he'd broken things off. It all came rushing back to Anne as she watched Pat idly prod the omelet with a fork. The kitchen smelled like roasted fruit.

"I've been having trouble sleeping," Pat continued, stirring the batter like it was stew. "And the storm made it worse. All that water pounding against my poor roof. I kept thinking there'd be leaks, which I can't afford just now, so I went to get a glass of wine and I saw Alex go out. I couldn't help wondering where he was going on a night like that, and as I said I couldn't sleep, so I . . . I waited up."

Pat finally lifted her face and looked Anne in the eye. She still seemed embarrassed, but she was smiling bashfully and Anne knew that if Alex could somehow bottle his charm, his magnetism, whatever he had that made women fall for him, he'd never have money troubles again.

"I threw on some clothes and waited for him in the parlor. I was going to pretend to be reading a magazine and act all surprised when he came in. But when I heard him coming up the walk, I lost my nerve. Why would he be interested in starting up again after all these years? He doesn't even live here anymore and I know myself, Annie. A one-night stand would just about break my heart. It didn't really matter because he must have seen the light; he practically ran up the stairs to his room."

"What about the alarm system?"

Pat hung her head sheepishly. "Sometimes I forget to turn it on."

"Why didn't you tell this to the police?"

Pat sighed heavily. "What would be the point? I didn't want to get Alex in trouble. I know him better than the cops ever could. Alex would never harm poor Mrs. Rutter, so what's the sense of pointing them his way?"

Anne's thoughts were spinning in a half dozen directions. Should she tell Trasker about Alex herself? Where had he gone on such a rainy, storm-tossed night? What was troubling him?

Pat gave a sudden start. "Oh, cripes," she cried out. "My omelet."

It was burning noiselessly, filling the air with a pungent, acrid odor. While Pat turned off the flame, Anne grabbed the skillet. She dumped the charred remains in the trash, then ran cold water over the inside of the pan. It was a mess, much like what her life had become in just two short days.

Dovecote looked less impressive at night. Without daylight to illuminate the rambling garden, the stained glass panels, and all the architectural ornaments and doodads that made the house one of the Heights' landmark jewels, it could have been merely another seaside cottage, albeit larger and slightly taller than its neighbors.

Anne lingered in front of the house, staring up at the turrets and balconies. It was ten o'clock, still raining steadily. She'd given up trying to locate Kim, and she hadn't the foggiest notion of where Alex could be. After looking in all their old haunts—the fishing pier, the gazebo on Pilgrim Pathway, the south end of the boardwalk overlooking Fletcher Lake, the ice cream parlor, the tiny patch of land that was Liberty Park—Anne had decided to call it a night. She was on her way home by way of Webb Avenue, not the shortest route, and now, gazing up at Dovecote, Anne realized she had gone this way deliberately, that she needed to see the house.

Yellow police tape was plastered across the front door. Anne crept around to the back. The ground was so muddy her feet squished with every step. Someone had stuck police tape across the back door, too. Anne tried the knob. Locked. The light from the old-fashioned streetlamps on Webb barely reached the rear garden and Anne had to strain her eyes to see. In the rainy dark, she could just make out the three steep steps that led to the kitchen. On either side of the top step sat two baskets of impatiens, amid dozens of scattered petals torn loose by the wind and rain.

In the wet, dark night, the garden looked like a small patch of jungle, a tangled sea of drooping, sodden vegetation gone wild. In one corner was a small gray eight-by-twelve-foot shed where tools, paint, and odds and ends were stored. Anne entered it, grateful to be out of the rain temporarily. She hadn't set foot inside the shed for thirty-odd years, ever since the hot summer day she and Cece had entered to do some "exploring" and had accidentally tipped over two cans of paint thinner, incurring Aunt Hannah's and their parents' wrath, and inadvertently suffusing the garden with the unpleasant odor of turpentine for several days.

Spying a small flashlight on one of the shelves, Anne flicked it on and looked around. The shed was arranged with the same neatness and attention to order that characterized Dovecote. Gardening equipment—a rake, spades, watering cans, bags of potting soil, hoses—were arrayed along one wall, opposite plain wooden shelves lined with toolboxes, fertilizer, pruning shears, and cans and bottles containing various pesticides. Anne trained her flashlight on the latter group. One by one, she picked up the containers and gave each a little shake. Some were nearly empty; others emitted a sloshing sound as the liquid inside was jiggled. Toward the back sat what appeared to be an aerosol can with the words *Bug Off* spelled out in black letters above a picture of a beetle on its back, its legs waving helplessly in the air.

When Anne shook the *Bug Off*, she heard a dry rattle. Turning the can upside down, she unscrewed the bottom, which came off easily in her hand. Inside were two keys attached to a simple silver ring. One for the front door, one for the back. Anne remembered her mother telling her father about this trick of Aunt Hannah's, a far better plan, her mother had said, than hiding keys beneath the doormat or secreting them in one of those magnetic boxes that were then affixed beneath patio tables or flower pots. In fact, Anne's mother had been so struck by the scheme that she'd gone out and purchased a plastic head of lettuce, which she'd placed in the refrigerator for the sole purpose of storing her engagement ring and wedding band in when she wasn't wearing them, the only unfortunate consequence being that they were quite cold whenever she'd slip them on her finger.

Anne wondered which of her relatives knew about the hidden keys. Perhaps all of them did. Stories about Aunt Hannah tended to be apocryphal and were told and retold, with wry shakes of the head.

Anne left the shed, taking the flashlight with her. Pulling on a pair of gloves she'd brought with her, she easily opened the back door with the key. She placed her umbrella outside on the mat and took her shoes off in the kitchen, to track in as little mud as possible. The last thing she wanted was to leave any trace that she'd been there.

Passing through the kitchen, she entered Aunt Hannah's study, which looked almost as she had left it that morning, except for the chalk outline on the floor, where the Aubusson carpet had been, tracing the contours of how her great-aunt's body had lain. Anne sat down at the desk and took a second look at Hannah's papers. Most of the documents dated back a few years, which made sense, considering Dovecote was a vacation home, not a primary residence. There were various receipts describing work done on the house—chimney cleaning, roof repairs, the installation of a new boiler, new weather stripping on the doors and windows. Anne also found a pile of old tax returns, a brochure from a dog show in which Bronte had apparently competed, two expired driver's licenses, a flyer describing the properties, including Dovecote, on last summer's annual house tour, and a worn-looking address book with a pink leather cover. Someone had flung Hannah's checkbook on the desk. Anne flipped it open and rechecked the date on the stub of the first unused check: August 18, 2000. Why was that there? What did it mean?

Moving quickly and noiselessly, Anne left the study and walked through the living room, careful to keep her flashlight low to the ground and away from the windows, so as not to arouse the neighbors' suspicions.

It didn't appear as though the police had disturbed anything in there; the room had the orderly, pristine appearance that Anne always associated with Aunt Hannah. She tiptoed past the baby grand piano and the bookshelves, stopping briefly in front of the vitrine containing the jewel-encrusted eggs. Her favorite had always been the gold egg, inlaid with rubies and sapphires, from which a miniature bunny, fashioned out of what looked like spun sugar, popped up, smiling rakishly. Anne scanned the glass shelves, searching for the egg. But the place where it normally sat was bare.

On a whim, Anne crossed the room and climbed up onto the sofa. Her feet sank into the soft, plump cushions as she rested the flashlight on the back of the couch and reached for the oil painting hanging above, a nineteenth-century seascape of fishing boats moored on the beach at dawn, done in luminous shades of pale silver and rose.

The canvas swung forward easily as if it were a cabinet door on hinges, revealing a wall safe behind it. Anne had been prepared to try a variety of random numerical combinations—Aunt Hannah's birthday, phone number, or address with the letters transposed into numbers—but she saw at once there was no need. The safe was ajar, and reaching her hand inside the wall cavity, Anne found that it was empty.

Hard to believe that Aunt Hannah would leave the safe that way. Had the police figured out the combination? Or was this the work of the murderer, who knew the combination because he or she knew Hannah?

It was rumored within the family that Hannah, who had lived through the Great Depression, was not especially keen on banks and had kept large amounts of cash squirreled at Dovecote and at her Boston townhouse. Anne thought back to the first time she'd found out what was stored behind the fishing boats. It was the summer she'd turned ten, on the Fourth of July. The family had gathered in Aunt Hannah's living room—her cousins, aunts and uncles, her parents—for cocktails and hors d'oeuvres, before heading down to the ocean to watch the fireworks.

Anne remembered that Aunt Hannah had worn a long white dress with puffy sleeves, large navy buttons down the front, and a red sash at the waist. An Independence Day dress. It needed extra special jewelry, Aunt Hannah had said, and she'd opened the wall safe right there in front of everybody and pulled out a necklace so glittering and sparkly that it almost hurt Anne's eyes to look at it. It was made of rubies, a dark lipstick red, cut in perfect small rectangles like blocks of red ice.

Later that night, as they watched the fireworks explode

over the beach, Anne and Cece and Nora had talked about how beautiful the necklace was, how they couldn't wait until they were old enough to deck themselves out in diamonds, emeralds, and pearls. "Exquisite," Nora had said, pronouncing the word like it was a foreign language she was speaking for the first time.

Anne supposed it was possible that Aunt Hannah had left most of her good jewelry in Boston. She didn't spend much time in the Heights anymore and was rarely invited to social events in New Jersey that called for expensive clothes and jewels. But it was odd to find the safe open. Aunt Hannah would never have left it unlocked, of that Anne was sure.

Leaving the safe as she found it, Anne got down from the sofa and headed upstairs. The second floor was laid out like a T, with several bedrooms, bathrooms, and sitting rooms branching off a central hallway and a large master bedroom at the very end. It was a charming, airy space. White high-pile carpeting covered the floor. Along one wall, opposite a big bay window, stood a four-poster bed with a gauzy white canopy that reminded Anne of mosquito netting, and a comforter, bolsters, and pillows in a pink and lavender floral print. The bed was made up, and Anne saw that alongside it stood a dog-size bed adorned with what looked like lavender silk cushions and Bronte's name embroidered in gold thread. There was also a white eight-drawer bureau, a chaise longue upholstered in the same fabric as the comforter, and a diminutive, pricy-looking antique desk, fashioned from a light wood and inlaid with swags and flowers.

Anne sat down at the desk and ran the flashlight over its surface. In a leather monogrammed box she found nearly a dozen letters from Henry, all with their envelopes slit open. Anne picked up the top one. It was postmarked two weeks earlier and addressed to the house in Boston. She slid the stationery out and read through it quickly:

Dear Mother,

I shall never know how you managed to learn of my disbarment and the unfortunate events leading up to it. Despite what you may think, the incident has changed my life in profound and unforeseen ways, and I am doing everything in my power to "make it right." Were it not for Elise's love, I do not think I could go on. From a more practical standpoint, I have been besieged by constant legal bills and an enormous debt that has all but left me penniless. Does it please you to know that I have been served with eviction notices, that the electricity and phone service have been shut off because I cannot pay the bills, that I am reduced to taking my midday meal at a soup kitchen in a neighboring town, from whence I arrive and depart by bus because my car has been repossessed? I can only hope that this news is in some small measure disturbing to you, enough to find it in your heart to loan me the money I need so that I may make reparations to all parties involved. I know it is a large sum, but I am begging you to help me as I have nowhere else to turn.

Your son,

Henderson

Disbarment, Anne thought. Wow. That sounded serious.

She shone her flashlight over the desktop. There was less stuff there than on the desk in Aunt Hannah's study. A heart-shaped box filled with paper clips, a tape dispenser, a paperweight of a flower encased in glass, and a leather cup for pens and pencils. On the left side of the desk were three small drawers. Anne opened the top one, which revealed a half-dozen boxes of stationery and rolls of return address labels. The middle drawer contained an unopened box of nut fudge, a Bible, and a package of Eyes Tea, tea bags designed to be placed on the eyes for "soothing relief from eye strain and mild headaches."

The bottom drawer contained assorted memorabilia: old black-and-white photographs, postcards showing the beach and the boardwalk and inns in the Heights that had shut down long ago, old theater programs, menus from shipboard cruises, pamphlets describing the various ministers who'd spoken at the Church by the Sea over the years, matchbooks from now defunct restaurants. She recognized herself in a couple of the pictures. There was one of her and Nora as children, wearing frilly party dresses, standing stiffly on the front porch, gazing solemnly into the camera. Another of her and her mother in the garden on Ocean Avenue, flanking a three-foot-high sunflower.

Anne was about to put everything back when she noticed a slim packet in the back of the drawer, tied with a pink satin ribbon. Unwrapping the package, Anne found a pink envelope with a half-dozen photos of a pretty blond child and a shy-looking blond teenage girl. *Jennie at three*, Aunt Hannah had written on the back of one picture of the girl dressed as a ballerina in a gauzy tutu.

Anne stared hard at the photograph. So this was Jennie, Aunt Hannah's eldest child, who'd died in her early twenties. No one in the family ever spoke about Jennie and there were no photos of her displayed at Dovecote or in the Boston house. Though Anne was sure she'd never seen Jennie's face before, the girl looked familiar. Gray almond-shaped eyes, snub nose, thin lips. Anne examined the other pictures, each of which was carefully labeled: Jennie astride a bicycle; Jennie playing the piano; fourteen-year-old Jennie, wearing a cardigan sweater, plaid skirt, bobby socks, and saddle shoes, sitting demurely on a swing, ankles crossed, holding a bouquet of roses, her expression at once tremulous and longing. But then all these pictures seemed sad somehow. Anne couldn't say why exactly. Maybe because in each one, Jennie was alone, and seemed to derive no pleasure from whatever it was she was doing. Her expression was vacant, almost dazed. The photographs themselves looked staged, the girl in the spotlight a reluctant actress.

Anne tried to recall how Jennie had died. A sudden illness? An accident? But nothing came to mind. Maybe one of the cousins remembered. Surely Henry knew.

She put the pictures aside and examined what else was in the envelope, feeling a twinge of guilt as she did so. Going through Hannah's desk and wall safe in search of clues was one thing, but these objects were more personal, and Anne knew how very angry Hannah would be if she knew.

There were three small objects in the envelope: a lock of blond hair, a faded business card, and a tiny gold charm bracelet. Anne studied the card, which had been printed on stiff creamy paper stock, in formal gold script. *The Greeley House*, it said, listing an address in Point Pleasant Beach. Then, underneath, in smaller type, *We Are Fair, And We Care*.

Greeley again. Well, it should be easy enough to check out. Anne held the charm bracelet up to the light. This must have belonged to Jennie, she thought, slipping the bracelet and the card in the pocket of her jeans and putting everything else back where she'd found it.

She left the room and padded noiselessly into the hallway. At the top of the stairs she paused, caught off-guard by a noise outside, the sound of a car horn bleating down the street. Grasping the polished mahogany banister, she descended the stairs, anxious to be out of this house, to detach herself from the stale remains of Aunt Hannah's life and death. She'd reached the landing between the two floors when she heard a key turn in the lock.

After that, everything happened fast. The lights went on. Two policemen appeared at the foot of the stairs, waving their service revolvers at her chest. Before she had a chance to react or flee or even panic, Detective Edward Burns stepped forward and in a clear, loud voice announced: "Anne Hardaway, you are under arrest for the murder of Hannah Rutter."

Chapter 11

*Cats need more space
than dogs. If a dog zooms
up to a cat, he'll more
than likely encounter a
series of paw smacks and
hisses.*

Later, Anne would come to regard what followed as
the worst night of her life. When she recalled the police questioning her for what seemed like hours,
confronting her with the "evidence"—her fingerprints on the
knife, Aunt Hannah's jewelry—a topaz, sapphire, and aquamarine ring, plus a cameo on a gold chain—tucked beneath
the cotton sweaters in her bedroom bureau drawer, she wondered how she'd gotten through it at all. The small, dirty jail
cell with its cot, toilet, and sink, the smell of disinfectant and
sweat, her stomach clenched in tight, anxious knots. But at
the time she simply felt numb and exhausted, like she'd been
trapped under water and couldn't come up for air.

When the blue light of dawn crept through the bars on the
window, she awoke with a start, disoriented and dazed, and
it took a few moments to realize where she was and how

she'd come to be there. It had finally stopped raining and the birds were chirping wildly. She could see five other cells, all empty except for the wild-eyed incoherent female drug addict directly across the way who spent half the night ranting and the other half begging for a fix, before collapsing in a heap like a pile of dirty laundry, her streaked purple hair flopping across her face. Anne went to the sink and splashed tepid water on her face. Then she sat on the edge of the lumpy cot and tried to connect the dots.

Someone had broken into her house and planted Aunt Hannah's jewelry in her bedroom. Someone had stolen her chef's knife and used it to stab Hannah to death. This last was especially puzzling. How had the killer managed to leave Anne's fingerprints on the knife while obscuring his own? Wouldn't both sets of prints have surfaced? Or wouldn't the stabbing have erased Anne's prints entirely? As for the jewelry, it was probably planted while Anne was at Dovecote discovering the body. Or sometime yesterday afternoon.

But why would anyone go to all that trouble? She wasn't exactly the most popular person in the Heights, but she couldn't imagine who would hate her enough to frame her for murder. She had a sudden image of the reunion lunch, her cousins seated around the dining room table, eating and laughing, the closest thing to a brother and sisters that she'd ever known. It couldn't have been one of them.

But who else had access to the knife? Who else stood to benefit from Hannah's death?

At nine o'clock, Anne and her court-appointed lawyer were standing before a silver-haired judge in a black robe, who spoke at length of "this heinous crime" and the "overwhelming number of stab wounds" before announcing to the packed courtroom that bail was set at $250,000. Anne felt as if someone had struck her. Weeks, maybe months of sitting in that cell or a worse one like it lay ahead before the case would even come to trial.

She hung her head in defeat and then yanked it up again at the sound of a dog barking in the courtroom. Bronte stood squarely before the judge's bench, with her head cocked, yipping in righteous indignation. Anne couldn't have been more relieved if Lassie had marched in and staged a jail break. Nora, who held the dog's leash, handed something to the judge, and then Anne was free to go, and Nora was leading her and Bronte down the courthouse steps, past a throng of reporters and photographers.

They took the Corvette, with Nora driving and Bronte sprawled on the backseat. Anne thought she'd never seen such a beautiful morning. The sun was shining, the air was sweet and warm, even the fast-food joints along the road seemed bright and newly minted. She munched the box of Cap'n Crunch cereal Nora had brought and swigged hot coffee from a thermos. It tasted grand.

"Thanks for bailing me out," Anne said.

"No problem," Nora replied. "Cece and Alex wanted to come, but I thought it'd be better if we didn't attract too much attention. Cece found a bail bondsman in Lakewood who was happy to loan us the money, so long as you don't skip town, that is."

"Where would I flee to?" Anne asked wryly. "The way things are going, I'd wind up on *America's Most Wanted* before I got to Newark Airport. Listen, who put up the collateral?"

"I did. Business has never been better."

"I really owe you one."

"Don't sweat it, cuz. You'd do the same for me."

They'd passed the exit for the Heights and kept driving south on Route 35. Anne didn't care where they were headed. She felt like she never wanted to leave this car, like she'd rather drive around Jersey all day than face the herd of reporters who were probably camped outside her doorstep.

"What happened yesterday?" she asked. "With the cops, I mean."

Nora laughed her musical laugh. She looked stunning, as usual. For her day in court, she'd worn a short white cotton sundress, with a square neckline and a cinched waist, along with strappy white sandals and a tiny silver Kate Spade bag. Her hair was fashioned in a French twist and she wore heart-shaped diamond earrings that glinted in the light.

"Yesterday I put Harry in your bedroom and I kept Bronte with me, in your office," said Nora, settling into her story. "Right after you called, the doorbell rang. It was a detective and two police officers. The detective had a search warrant and they spent about forty minutes turning the house upside down. I couldn't imagine what they were looking for and none of them would tell me a thing. It upset Harry no end. In fact, I thought my biggest problem yesterday was going to be stopping Harry and Bronte from killing each other."

Anne glanced at the backseat, where Bronte was content-edly drooling on the upholstery, a dreamy expression on the black mask of her face.

"Before I finally separated them," Nora continued, as Route 35 narrowed down to two lanes, "Harry would arch his back and spit and hiss and Bronte would snarl and growl and bare her teeth. It's a good thing they're both afraid of each other or they'd tear each other to pieces. By the way, I hope you don't mind that I didn't bring Harry with me this morning. I figured he needed some down time without the pug princess in his face."

The car turned onto Bridge Avenue in Bay Head and Anne realized immediately where they were going. Good, she thought. It's about time.

"When they finally found Auntie's jewelry in your sweater drawer," Nora noted, "it was like they'd unearthed the prize in a box of Cracker Jack. Smiles all around. One of the cops even high-fived the other one. Real professional, right?"

"Did you leave the house at any point yesterday?"

"I tried to take Bronte for a walk, but she refused to go out in the rain. She had a couple of accidents, once in your office and twice in the living room, but I think I managed to clean everything up."

"So you didn't go out at all before the police found the jewelry?"

"No."

Despite the coffee, Anne felt incredibly tired. She rested her head against the seat back and closed her eyes. Almost against her will, she pictured someone kneeling over Hannah's body and plucking bracelets, rings, and necklaces from the corpse. It was a ghoulish image, and Anne tried not to think about it.

"Why do the cops have your fingerprints on file in the first place?" Nora asked.

"Remember when I was ghostwriting the autobiography of Mallory Loving?"

"The actress?"

"Yes. For a while there, I was suspected of doing away with her. Mark Trasker got hold of my fingerprints then, when someone broke into my house and. . . . Anyway, it's a long story."

The car passed a cheese shop, a liquor store, and an ice cream parlor, before turning and pulling up in front of a gray three-story apartment building.

It was a modest-looking structure, part Victorian, part Cape Cod, designed to accentuate its proximity to the seaside. The exterior was constructed of faded gray planks, complete with knotholes and striations, reminiscent of the boardwalk. Each level was set back from the one below it and featured a series of decks separated from the inside by sliding glass doors. The builder had also added several small round windows that brought to mind portholes on board ship.

"I'll take Bronte for a walk on the beach," Nora said. "She could probably use the exercise."

"Okay, thanks."

"We'll be back in about a half an hour or so."

Anne nodded and got out of the car. On the wall at the front of the building was a list of tenants. Anne pressed the buzzer for 3D. After a few moments, a second buzzer sounded and Anne opened the front door. She trotted up three flights of stairs and arrived on the third floor slightly out of breath.

The door to apartment 3D was ajar and when she stepped inside, she was immediately enfolded in a big bear hug.

"How are you, babe?" Trasker asked, as he stroked her hair and rubbed the small of her back.

"Where the hell have you been?"

She took a step back and surveyed him. He was dressed in weekend casual attire: jeans, gray T-shirt, Nike high-tops. He looked tired, especially around the eyes.

"You didn't answer any of my calls," she said, suddenly feeling angry at him, almost wishing she hadn't come.

"I'm sorry, Annie. It's just that I wanted to have something to tell you when I called. Something positive. I had myself recused from the case right away because of my connection to you and your family. I'm doing everything I can, but I have to stay in the background on this one. I had no idea they were planning to arrest you. Otherwise I'd have been at your house in a heartbeat." He closed the door behind him and ushered her into the living room. "I just made a fresh pot of coffee."

Trasker had recently moved to Bay Head and still hadn't

unpacked all his stuff. The room was messier than usual. Textbooks and manuals were piled willy-nilly on the glass coffee table. The black leather sofa was littered with reams of computer printouts, and a fax machine in the corner whirred noisily as it spit out more paper. In the galley kitchen off the entrance hall, the counter was strewn with half-opened cartons of Chinese food and a couple empty beer bottles. A wobbly mound of dishes poked out of the sink.

"I didn't get much shuteye last night," Trasker said, crossing to the fax machine and scanning the pages it had emitted. "But then you probably didn't sleep so well either."

"Back up for a second," Anne said, taking a seat on the couch. "You took yourself off the case?"

Trasker had put on his reading glasses and was studying the fax with interest.

"It's a conflict of interest, Annie. I can't be impartial. And I didn't want to jeopardize the investigation. Evans thought it was the right move."

"I didn't think he knew about us."

"He didn't. Not until that snake-in-the-grass partner of mine gave him an earful. A prince among men, that one," Trasker said sarcastically. "Luckily it doesn't matter all that much because I have lots of contacts and I was able to call in a few favors."

Anne poured herself a cup of coffee. It was strong and hot. She felt as though she needed to drink a gallon or two if she wanted to make it through the rest of the day.

"You know what I can't figure out," she said. "Why the cops would think of searching my house for the knife?"

"I'll tell you why," Trasker said. "A man by the name of Chase Merritt told them he'd seen a set of steak knives in your kitchen."

"How very helpful of him," Anne commented wryly.

Trasker came over and sat beside her. Putting down the fax, he took hold of her hand. "I ran a background check on Merritt. And I hope you don't mind that I've run similar checks on your relatives who came to the reunion. I've been a detective long enough to know that money is a powerful motivator, especially if you're desperately in need of it. Everyone at your lunch had motive and opportunity to spare."

"I don't want to believe any of them could have done it."

"I know," Trasker said gently. "But I'm approaching this the way a doctor would approach a patient whose symptoms don't add up to any known disease. We have to go down the list and rule out each suspect, one by one, just like a doctor rules out various maladies until he comes up with the right diagnosis."

Anne settled back against the sofa cushions. The morning sun was streaming through the skylights and the apartment had a warm, drowsy air. Anne felt the same way she had in the car, that she wanted to stay there all day, in this warm pleasant cocoon, and never reenter her life. She pictured Trasker making love to her, his lips brushing against her skin, his hands tenderly exploring her body. Then the fax machine whirred anew and she was jolted out of her fantasy.

"What did you find out so far?" she asked him.

"Well, for starters, your cousin Cecilia has a pretty lengthy arrest record."

"You mean penny-ante stuff like shoplifting, right?"

Trasker picked up the fax and handed it to Anne. She scanned the piece of paper quickly, feeling a sudden tightness in her chest.

"Oh, my God," she said softly, staring at the fax until the words began to blur. It said that in the last six months

Cecilia Jamison had been arrested six times on prostitution charges. The last time was in the middle of June, when she spent three weeks in a county jail.

Anne couldn't believe it. Her beautiful, talented cousin performing sexual acts with strangers. "Why?" she said, her voice cracking on the word.

Trasker said, "Apparently, Cecilia is flat broke. She was living in a brothel in San Francisco and turning tricks to survive. Before that she was literally homeless, picked up by the cops twice and deposited in a city shelter."

"I had no idea," Anne whispered.

Why hadn't Cece confided in any of them? Why hadn't she asked for help?

Trasker slipped an arm around Anne's shoulder. "I'm sorry, honey. I know this is hard."

Anne gazed into his deep brown eyes. "Just because Cece needs money, it doesn't make her a murderer."

"Of course not," Trasker said kindly. "I'm only trying to get a clearer picture of what's been happening in your family."

Anne sighed. "Then you better hear what I've found out."

She told him everything she'd discovered at Aunt Hannah's the night before, along with her visit to the adoption agency and Alex's late-night disappearance from the Laughing Gull.

When she'd finished, Trasker said, "According to the police report, your aunt was stabbed between midnight and two A.M. Do you think it's possible Alex used the key to enter Dovecote, stole the jeweled egg and whatever was in the wall safe, and then killed your aunt in a panic when she woke up and confronted him?"

"No," Anne blurted out.

She got up and began pacing the length of the living

room. There had to be another explanation. Though what it could be, she didn't know. She started to have the panicky drowning feeling in her chest again and suddenly needed fresh air. The news about Cece had upset her a great deal.

"Could we go out on the deck?" she asked Trasker.

"Sure."

He followed her outside to where two striped green-and-white lounge chairs had been set up next to a green plastic table and a small gas grill. From this vantage point, you could see a strip of beach and the ocean, which was a deep bluish-green, the water choppy and flecked with foam. People had already begun to lay out towels and chairs.

Anne perched on one of the chaises. There was a brisk wind blowing and the bracing salt air soothed her nerves.

"What about Larry?" she mused. "He's in big financial trouble. He could certainly use a share of Aunt Hannah's inheritance."

"Absolutely. It's beginning to look like the fire that broke out at his home in Massachusetts was arson."

"Kim mentioned something about that. But she didn't believe it could be true."

"Well, Kim's been acting quite peculiar lately. For one thing, she never adequately explained what she was doing when you ran into her at Dovecote. And she appeared nervous and upset when Burns questioned her. I got hold of a copy of his report. He had the feeling she was hiding something. Maybe she'll open up to you."

"Maybe."

But even as she spoke, Anne felt doubtful. She couldn't be sure of anything anymore. Except that she was in deep, deep trouble.

"I came up empty on Henry. But perhaps your aunt managed to have whatever he did covered up."

"How is that possible?"

"You'd be surprised what money can buy."

"Isn't Henry in the clear? After all, he never went into my kitchen, so he didn't have access to the knife."

"He could have arrived earlier than he said he did, while you were at the Laughing Gull, and taken the knife then."

"That applies to anyone."

"I suppose so. But I think I'll drive up to Bergen County this morning anyway and do some nosing around. There's something I've been meaning to ask you: Who besides you has a key to your house?"

Anne thought a moment. "Well, you do. And Helen, of course. And Delia."

Helen Passelbessy and Delia Graustark were Anne's two closest friends. But they were both away this weekend.

"Do you always lock your doors when you go out?" Trasker asked. "Even if you're just running over to the Mini-Mart or something?"

Anne nodded. Oceanside Heights was generally a safe shore town, but you could never be too careful.

"Have you made spare keys for any of your cousins over the years?"

"No. They never stick around long enough to need one."

"Then that brings us back to the reunion lunch."

Anne watched a flock of seagulls skim low over the sand, then turn and soar above the ocean. It was a lousy beach day, but people were already splashing around in the churning surf. The very ordinariness of this scene struck her as strange. Waves crashed against the shoreline, just like always, except now she was facing a murder charge. In the distance, she spotted Nora and the dog leaving the beach and heading back toward the apartment.

Turning to Trasker, she said, "What about Chase Merritt? Anything shady in his past?"

"Plenty," Trasker replied. "The man's a grifter, with a

habit of preying on elderly women. I've got a pal in the Boston PD who's checking Merritt out. We should know more by this afternoon."

Trasker's expression was grave. He was gazing at Anne, but not really seeming to see her, as though his thoughts were sprinting ahead of him. His mouth formed a thin, tight line.

Anne knew that look and it worried her.

"What aren't you telling me?" she asked nervously.

Trasker sighed. "It's about Nora."

Anne watched her cousin stride down the street with the dog. Nora hadn't stayed in touch as much during the past year. But Anne felt close to her all the same. *Sisters under the skin*, they used to say.

Anne felt her chest tighten again. "What about Nora?"

Trasker hesitated. For a split second, Anne wondered if Trasker were attracted to her cousin. Had they bonded on the phone, arranging Anne's visit? Did they like each other?

"She's under investigation by the Florida Attorney General for embezzling millions of dollars from her advertising company. It's a public company and there's a good chance that she's defrauded hundreds of stockholders."

"B-but . . ." Anne stammered. "How could that be? Her company's getting all this new business. We even passed a billboard they did on the way to Seaside Heights yesterday."

"Maybe the agency had a good cash flow, but also has lots of outstanding debt. Or maybe the investors were getting antsy. Or someone simply got overly greedy."

Anne was too stunned to answer. She felt lightheaded and anxious at the same time, as if she were stuck in a dentist's chair with a drill bearing in on her. Is that how Nora had gotten the collateral for the bail money? By embezzling it from a bunch of clueless stockholders?

Just at that moment, Nora looked up and saw Anne and Trasker on the deck. She waved and smiled as Bronte tugged at the leash. Anne stared at her cousin and wondered, for the first time in her life, if she knew Nora at all.

Chapter 12

> *Be specific in your commands to avoid confusion. Don't say "sit down" to your dog when what you really mean is "sit." Don't use "down" for "off," as in "get down from the sofa," or your dog may think you want her to lie down.*

"Why'd you do it?" yelled a voice in the crowd.

"Was it because of the money?" shouted another voice.

"Hey, Anne. What's your side of the story?"

About three dozen reporters and cameramen were camped out on Anne's front lawn, and when she stepped out of the Corvette, they charged her like defensive tackles rushing the quarterback.

Anne kept her head down as a phalanx of gray microphones were shoved in front of her face. How was she ever going to get inside her house, short of body checking the news media one by one? Nora had come around the car and was trying to shield her. Cece, whom they'd picked up on the way home, gave one buxom TV reporter the finger and told a newspaper reporter to go to hell. Bronte strained at her leash, barking furiously.

"No comment," Nora announced, in a loud, firm tone. "Please let us through."

She shouldered her way through the crowd, with Anne close behind and Cece bringing up the rear, as the reporters shouted their questions, drowning out one another in a volley of frantic words.

It's true what they say, Anne thought, as she finally slipped inside the door and walked into the living room. There's no place like home. As if to second the motion, Harry purred joyfully and rubbed against Anne's ankles, eyeing her with unbridled affection.

But his joy was short-lived. When he spied his nemesis, he arched his back and all the hair on his coat bristled.

"Where should I put the dog?" asked Nora.

"Anywhere Harry's not," Anne said, scooping her cat up in her arms and whispering endearments to him while rubbing one of his favorite spots behind his ears.

Cece went over to the window and yanked the drapes closed. "I'd keep Bronte in my room at the Gull, but Pat says absolutely, positively no pets."

On the sofa, Anne curled up with Harry. With the blinds drawn and the windows closed, the room was hot and airless. "What are they doing?" she asked.

Nora lifted a curtain and peeked out. "Milling around. Taking copious notes. That loudmouthed bimbo from Channel 12 is on the sidewalk with a cameraman, reporting her little heart out."

"Great." Anne sighed. "Just great."

Cece flicked on the overhead fan. "While I was waiting

for you guys to get back, I took a highly unscientific poll. About sixty percent think you did it, thirty percent say no way, and ten percent are undecided."

"Did you ask when they're going to lose interest?" Anne shot back.

"Not anytime soon," Cece said, smiling. "This is the biggest thing to hit the Heights since the nor'easter of '92."

Nora had deposited the dog in Anne's office from whence could be heard the sound of much scuffling and barking.

"Not counting the time we streaked on the beach and upset the Ladies' Auxiliary," Nora joked, looking more beautiful, Anne thought, than anyone had a right to on this lousy, reporter-infested day.

"What did you think of Trasker?" Anne asked her.

Nora smiled. "Oh, Annie, he seems terrific. Smart. Sexy. Funny." She smiled again. "Sexy."

"I can't believe I haven't met him yet," Cece complained. "Sounds like a great guy."

"Absolutely," Nora said. "And crazy about Anne. So, what can I get you guys to drink?"

Cece plopped down on the sofa next to Anne. "I'll have decaf tea with lemon and Sweet'n Low."

"Coffee, thanks," Anne said, as Nora headed to the kitchen and she realized belatedly that she should be the one playing hostess if she could muster up the energy. "Black. No sugar."

She had a terrible headache. Did coffee cure or cause headaches? She couldn't remember. On the way back from Trasker's she'd kept thinking of ways to talk to Nora about the embezzlement charges. But she didn't want to reveal that Trasker had been snooping. And she couldn't think of another way to broach the subject.

Instead she'd tried to draw Nora out about her advertising company. Was it hard owning your own business? How did they get new clients? How long did it take to turn a profit? Was there a lot of pressure to compete with other agencies for new business?

What she discovered, over the course of the drive, was how proficient Nora could be at lying. According to her cousin, the company was flush with cash and the heady allure of success. They had more clients than they could handle: banks, restaurants, hotels, health clubs.

In the middle of all this good news, Anne's mind had drifted back to senior year of high school. Their college acceptance letters had been received and it seemed that graduation day would never come. Most days Nora had decided to skip gym class in favor of hanging out at Friendly's or under the football bleachers, chain-smoking cigarettes and mapping out her future plans. When the third week of June finally rolled around and the ditzy gym teacher, Miss Gottenheimer, began tallying attendance records, she announced to the class, in a shocked and somewhat disappointed tone, that Nora Miller had racked up a total of thirty-six absences.

"Oh, goodness," Nora had exclaimed, looking oh-so-distraught. "I thought I told you I needed extra tutoring help in math and that fourth period was the only time Mr. Kress was available. Don't you remember, Miss Gottenheimer?"

A light bulb of comprehension shone above the gym teacher's doughy face. "Of course, dear," she had said, with a bemused smile. "Don't trouble yourself about it."

When what she really meant was: It is inconceivable that a stunningly attractive girl like you would concoct such a lie. Had it been anyone else, she would have checked with Marty Kress or handed out an incomplete, as she did to Susan Shaw and Jane Reilly, two girls with far fewer absences than Nora but also far less charm, beauty, and style.

But then lying was a necessary evil in the high-powered world of advertising, where products had to appear exceptional at all costs to succeed. Until today, Anne hadn't pegged her cousin as a liar; she'd merely admired Nora's cleverness.

"Earth to Anne," Cece was saying. "You're a million miles away."

The cat lay across Anne's stomach like a twenty-pound hot water bottle that purred. "I was wondering about something. Did you wind up asking Aunt Hannah for a loan Thursday night?"

"What?" said Cece, startled. Then: "No. I never got the chance."

"Why not?"

Cece got up and went over to the window. Pulling back the curtain, she peered outside. "When I called Auntie on the phone and told her I wanted to drop by for a chat, she practically hung up on me. She said she had no time for my 'shenanigans,' so I figured I'd back off until I caught her in a better mood."

"What time did you call?"

"A little after five, I think."

"And why'd you really need the money?"

"I told you already, for B-school."

The dog was yelping even louder now. Harry raised his head, ears flattened against his head in alarm, then spread out again on Anne's lap. His tail lashed back and forth uneasily.

Anne reached into her pocketbook and pulled out the one-page fax Trasker had given her. Without comment, she handed it out to Cece.

"Oh, my God," Cece whispered, horrified, once she'd scanned it. She crumpled the fax into a ball and stuffed it in the pocket of her shorts.

That had been Anne's first reaction. To get rid of the information; erase it.

"It's not what you think," Cece said shakily.

Anne wanted to get up and give her cousin a hug, to tell her everything would be okay, the way they all used to reassure one another when they were kids. No hurt was too big to be eased back then. Support and understanding came with the territory. But in the past twenty-four hours, everything had changed. The world as Anne knew it had been turned upside down, and she felt like she was riding the roller coaster in Seaside Heights, plummeting wildly through space, with solid ground a distant blur.

From the kitchen Nora sang out, "I think someone had better go get Bronte before she pees all over Anne's office."

"Please don't tell anyone," Cece begged. "Especially Nora."

Cece's hands hung limply by her sides. She looked ashamed, defeated. When she let herself out of the house she moved so silently that Anne didn't hear the door open or close.

"Bronte," Anne called. "You stop it this minute."

The pug had got hold of Anne's wallet and had secreted herself behind the sofa, where she was happily rooting through the contents. From his spot on the window seat, Harry stared at her quizzically as if to say, *What did you expect from a dog?* Then he turned his back on the scene.

"I know," Anne said aloud, as a credit card skittered across the floor. "It's all my fault. I shouldn't have let her out."

But the pug's obvious unhappiness had swayed her. After taking a shower and changing clothes, Anne had opened the door of her office only to find the pug gazing up at her, sitting squarely on her haunches, head cocked, barking in righteous indignation.

Anne had convinced Nora that she needed to get some sleep and her cousin had left, determined to find a lawyer to replace the "court-appointed doofus" Anne was saddled with now.

The truth of the matter was that Anne had no intention of sleeping, not until she got some answers. She'd made herself an early lunch—cream cheese and jelly on white bread, washed down with Diet Coke and a Twinkie. If she was going to wind up in jail, she'd better eat as much junk food as she could while she still had the chance.

But first there was the dog to deal with.

Spying the red crocodile trunk in a corner of the living room, Anne undid its silver clasps and peered inside. Bronte was certainly living the high life. Inside was a sterling silver dish, a cashmere blanket, a monogrammed sweater, a pillow trimmed with ribbons and lace, fancy chew toys with nubs that were designed to remove plaque and stimulate gums, and a traditional filigree collar decorated with dangling gold balls.

There was a bottle of homeopathic vitamins, dental floss and a toothbrush, a Gumabone Frisbee and some chewy dog treats. Oh, brother, Anne thought, eyeing the assortment, talk about your pampered pets! She took out a chew bone and offered it to Bronte, who immediately lost interest in the wallet and started gnawing on the treat. Harry, meanwhile, had resumed eyeing the entire procedure with a mixture of disdain and anger. His tongue flicked back and forth and his back was slightly arched. He looked like he was about to spit.

"It's okay, boy," she said to the cat. "Bronte's not staying with us for long."

Scooping the cat up in her arms, she went into her office and checked her e-mail, greatly relieved to find a note from Edie on the care and treatment of pugs. *Don't despair,* Edie had written at the bottom of her instructions.

Although some people find pugs unattractive, they make great pets and are extremely loyal. When it comes to grooming, they're pretty low-maintenance and fairly quiet, needing a minimum of exercise. You will find that pugs are social creatures who are fond of in-between meal snacks and who inspire extreme adoration in their owners. Though they can be obstinate and, yes, pugnacious (pugnus means "fist" in Latin), pugs are also bright and inquisitive, affectionate, and outgoing.

By the way, you are in good company. The Duke and Duchess of Windsor owned pugs, as did Marie Antoinette, Queen Victoria, Josephine Bonaparte, and Eloise, of children's book fame. If you find Bronte has a big sense of entitlement, she comes by it naturally. In ancient China, pugs were born to adorn the laps of emperors, who made sure the dogs had their own eunuchs to serve them and had them transported in custom-built carriages. Try a few simple commands on Bronte, such as down, stay, heel, come, wait, quiet, and don't touch. This should give you an idea of how well-trained she is. Or not. Good luck. E.

"Bronte," Anne called out. "Come."

The dog dropped the treat and trotted over to Anne. "Good girl," Anne said.

Out of the corner of her eye, she thought she saw Harry grimace.

"Bronte, stay," Anne commanded.

The pug dropped down to her belly, with her chin on the floor, staring up at Anne with her big plaintive brown eyes. "Stay," Anne repeated. "Stay."

She walked over to Harry and stroked the fur on his back,

trying to convey that she wasn't in the least playing favorites. She just needed to let their new houseguest know who was boss. Bronte remained on the floor, not moving while Harry snuggled beside Anne.

Well, this is progress, Anne thought. *At least they're in the same room and they're not trying to kill each other. But if I'm gone, who knows how long peace will prevail?*

She grabbed Bronte's leash and slipped it onto the dog's collar. "Come on, princess," she said. "We're going for a walk."

Bronte stayed put, her tail tightly curled and twisted over one plump hip.

"Come," Anne said. And Bronte followed her to the door.

Before going outside, Anne had donned a floppy, wide-brimmed hat and a big pair of sunglasses. Camouflage, of sorts. She wished she had one of Cece's wigs to help transform herself from murder suspect to carefree tourist. It would also have been easier if she didn't have Bronte. But although the dog made her more conspicuous, it was also comforting to have her around. If reporters started badgering her, maybe Bronte could serve as a buffer.

It didn't turn out to be necessary this time. A ramshackle fence stood between her property and the people who lived in back of her. It had been there ever since she could remember, though who erected it, owned it, and was responsible for repairing it was a matter of dispute. Over the years, storms had knocked out many of the wood posts, leaving gaping unsightly holes.

Anne scrambled through two of them now, thankful that she'd never had the money or the inclination to fix them. She managed to arrive at the Laughing Gull unnoticed and was relieved to find Pat herself behind the front desk and not one of the gossipy teenage girls Pat hired for the summer.

"Anne," Pat exclaimed, waving a delphinium in greeting. "It's all over the news. How are you? Do you need anything?"

Anne took off her sunglasses and glanced around the front parlor. Empty except for a fatigued-looking guest who was wiping ice cream off her toddler's hands, face, and hair, and Chase Merritt, who had put down his newspaper to glare at Anne malevolently.

Did she need anything? Well, an alibi and a topnotch lawyer would be nice.

Aloud, she said, "I'm looking for my cousin Kim. Is she around?"

"Kim and her husband went over to the beach about an hour ago. I sold them the passes myself. It's a dollar cheaper than if you buy them on the boardwalk."

"And the rest of my relatives?"

Pat shrugged. "Out somewhere. Alex is with Heather Vance. She came over bright and early this morning, all dolled up. Some folks think she's attractive, but I never have. Hey, is that dog chewing the fringe on my rug?"

Anne tugged at Bronte's leash. "Sit," she commanded, and was gratified when the pug promptly obeyed.

Anne noticed that Pat looked even more harried than usual. Her shirt was buttoned wrong, her hair was disheveled, and she was trying to balance the books, work the phones, and finish a flower arrangement at the same time.

"What's going on with you?" Anne asked.

"Oh, the usual. One girl quit, one's out sick. The upstairs toilet is overflowing. And I can't find a plumber to fix it."

"Well, good luck. If you see Kim before I do, could you please tell her to call me right away?"

"Sure. And if there's anything I can do to help you out—"

But before Pat could finish, Chase Merritt had bounded

across the room and planted himself squarely in front of Anne, so close she could smell garlic on his breath and see the day-old stubble on his chin.

"Why bother to help the woman who killed my darling Hannah?" Merritt broke in. "As far as I'm concerned, Miss Hardaway belongs in jail."

A low growl came from Bronte's throat and Merritt hastily stepped back a few paces.

Anne smiled and said, "You're probably just peeved because you're not mentioned in the will. All that sweet talk up in smoke."

"That's preposterous," Merritt sputtered, waving his hands.

"I see you're not wearing the ring my aunt gave you," Anne said. "Is it still in your possession?"

Chase Merritt glared at her angrily. "Not that it's any of your business," he huffed. "But I feel that an ostentatious display of jewelry is inappropriate in times of mourning."

Bronte began growling again. The dog was looking at Merritt like she wanted to jump up and knock him down. Anne wondered how much Bronte had seen the night of the murder and why the pug hadn't growled and barked, alerting the neighbors. Was it because the killer was familiar, someone Bronte knew?

"The other day at my house," Anne said to Merritt, "you must have been in and out of the kitchen three or four times, waiting on my aunt, bringing her fresh bread or a clean napkin or more ice for her tea. I thought your attentiveness was designed to impress her at the time, but now I realize you could easily have stolen my chef's knife."

Pat was studying Merritt intently and the dog was still growling, crouching as if poised to spring.

"How absurd," Merritt exclaimed. "Someone would have

noticed if I'd marched out of your kitchen brandishing an eight-inch knife."

"I thought so, too, at first. It's hard to conceal a knife that size. But you brought a book bag to lunch. And at least once you brought the bag into the kitchen with you. I remember seeing you do it."

Merritt took another step back, eyeing Anne and the dog with distaste. "Don't try to pin your crime on me. I had nothing to gain from your aunt's demise, unlike you and your cousins."

"But you couldn't have known that. Aunt Hannah was always talking about leaving us money in her will. Maybe she did the same to you."

The phone rang and for a moment no one moved. It felt to Anne as though the three of them had been holding their breath. Then Pat picked up the phone.

"Laughing Gull. How can I help you?"

Chase Merritt was watching Anne with unconcealed hatred. He looked as mean as a bull who'd been taunted with a red flag.

"Yes, Joe," Pat said into the phone. "Thanks for calling back so soon. I've got a toilet that's backed up from here to Trenton."

Anne started for the door. "Come," she said to Bronte.

The pug bounded to her feet and lunged left, nipping at Merritt's ankles.

"Bronte doesn't like you very much," Anne said, as Merritt scurried back to the safety of his chair. "Now why do you suppose that could be?"

Chapter 13

Don't let the dog days of summer get your pooch down. Allow your dog access to cooler rooms of the house, such as the basement, the garage, or a screened porch where there's a breeze. Place an ice pack under your dog's bedding to cool your pooch off as he snoozes. Buy a child's swimming pool and fill it with water for your dog to wade in. Place ice cubes in his water dish during the hottest times of the day.

Because of the cloudy weather, the beach was only about half-full. But the clouds didn't stop the tourists. People were unpacking food from their coolers and settling down to lunch. At the snack shack, they stood in long lines waiting to buy hamburgers, hot dogs, so-das, and chips. Kids built elaborate sand castles and splashed each other merrily. Dueling radios competed for air time, their music flaring up only to be swallowed by the wind.

The sky was a slate-gray, stretching moodily over the grayish-green ocean, like a watercolor painting by a sullen child. The salt air and suntan lotion and the hot, dry wind rustling the dune grass brought Anne back to her own child-hood, when she and her cousins would play on the beach for hours, inventing games and stories, fishing off the pier, get-ting sand between their toes, behind their knees, and in their scalps, so when they finally crawled into their beds at the end of the day, even after baths and showers, tiny grains of sand followed them to sleep.

Now Anne scanned the beach, hoping to spot Larry and Kim. When they were teenagers, her cousins had congre-gated at the south end of the beach, not far from Anne's house, in a spot between a lifeguard's stand and a jetty of mossy rocks that jutted into the ocean like a slick jagged path. At low tide you could walk on the rocks and it was al-most like walking on water. They called it The Place. It was their turf, their unofficial hangout. On hot summer days they'd gather on this patch of sand and stake their claim with towels and radios.

It was to that spot that Anne headed now, carrying Bronte in her arms because the dog didn't seem to like the hot weather. Did lap dogs mind the heat? Was it okay to take Bronte to the beach, even though there was no sign of sun?

She picked her way through a sea of half-naked bodies, feeling oddly conspicuous in her T-shirt, denim miniskirt, and sandals. Most of the sunbathers were out-of-towners, there for the day or the weekend down the shore. It was un-likely they'd recognize her from the paper or the TV newscasts. Who had time to follow a local murder when the beach beckoned? Still, as she tried to avoid stepping on towels and limbs, she couldn't shake the feeling that people were watching her, pointing her out to one another, eyes trained on her and Bronte beneath mirrored sunglasses.

"It's okay," she said into Bronte's pink ear. "Don't worry about a thing."

The pug was surprisingly heavy for a lap dog. How had the Chinese eunuchs managed it?

She almost didn't see Larry and Kim at first. They were about twenty yards away from where the cousins usually congregated. It was their beach umbrella that gave them away. Blue-and-green plaid. Pure Kim.

"Hi guys," Anne said, ducking under the large umbrella, which was totally unnecessary on this cloudy gray day.

"Annie," Kim exclaimed, putting down her novel, a hard-cover thriller by Jonathan Kellerman that was standard beach reading that summer. "And Bronte. Hi, sweet dog. Have you been behaving yourself?"

Larry grunted and flopped over onto his stomach. He was wearing a pair of black bathing trunks and dark sunglasses.

Anne sat cross-legged on Kim's blanket, with Bronte stretched out beside her, panting from the heat. Taking an Evian bottle out of her bag, Anne sprinkled some water on Bronte's head to cool the dog off.

"How are you feeling?" Anne asked Kim.

"Much better thanks," Kim said, petting Bronte's coat. "Larry found me some Sinutabs and my head has finally stopped throbbing."

Anne studied Kim. Despite her cousin's outwardly cheery demeanor, Kim didn't look better. In fact, she looked downright awful. Without makeup, her skin appeared washed out and pale. Her hair was stringy, her eyes red and swollen, as though she'd been crying.

As if guessing Anne's thoughts, Kim said, "My allergies have been acting up. Grass fever. Hay fever. You name it."

Somehow Anne didn't buy the allergy bit.

She took a doggie treat out of her pocketbook and set it in front of Bronte, hoping to cheer up the pug. But Bronte merely crinkled her flat nose, ignoring the offering.

"You know," Anne began, "we never did talk about what happened yesterday morning, when you were at Aunt Hannah's house."

Kim laughed nervously. "Oh, Annie. Let's not. I'm trying to forget about everything for a little while, at least until the funeral."

"Well, I can't exactly do that. Considering I'm facing a murder charge."

Kim dug her manicured toes into the sand. Her hands were manicured, too, but Anne noticed the polish was chipping off and the nails were raggedy, the skin around them red from where Kim had picked at it.

"You didn't do it, so I'm sure you'll get off," Kim said brightly.

Anne stared at her cousin in surprise. That was going to be it then. No expressions of concern or sympathy. No offer to help. Kim was acting as though a murder charge were a minor annoyance, no more serious than a lost ATM card or a bad blind date.

The surreal feeling had returned with a vengeance. The heat seemed to make the air thick and soupy. Colors were off-kilter. Even the ocean had changed, becoming more turbulent and alive. It hurt her eyes to look at it.

"Look," Anne said, feeling suddenly desperate to make Kim understand. "I need your help here. Anything you can tell me about yesterday morning may prove helpful, anything at all. So let's go over it again. Please?"

Kim hesitated. Her eyes flicked to Larry, then shifted to

the horizon where two small white boats were etched against the dreary sky. A gull shrieked overhead. "Sure," Kim said. "Okay."

Anne realized she'd been holding her breath and she felt herself exhale. "Great. First off, why were you at Dovecote yesterday?"

Kim bit down on her lower lip, then extricated her toes from the sand, brushing the grains off gently, like a waitress removing crumbs from a tablecloth. "I wanted to borrow some of Auntie's jewelry for a benefit party I'm chairing next week. It's going to be a black-tie affair, held at the Franklin Park Zoo, to benefit children with cerebral palsy. I dreamed about the party and when I woke up, I just knew I had to have Auntie's double strand of pearls. I thought it would look stunning with the gown I'm planning to wear."

Then why not wait until you all got home to Boston? Anne thought. Aloud, she said, "When I was talking to Pat, she told me she saw you leave shortly after seven. What time did you get to Dovecote?"

"Um, not till about a quarter to nine. I walked around the Heights for a while first."

"For two hours, in the pouring rain?"

Kim laughed uneasily. "It was refreshing, actually. I've always loved the beach during a storm."

Anne looked over at Larry. Though his face was turned away from her, she saw that he wasn't sleeping. He seemed tense, on the alert, listening to every word Kim uttered.

"What happened when you arrived at Dovecote?"

"I rang the bell, waited a few minutes. When Auntie didn't answer, I tried the knob. The door was unlocked, so I went in. I called Auntie's name. I walked through the house and then . . . " Kim's voice was quavering. "I found her lying there."

Anne tried to imagine Kim stumbling upon the body.

Squeamish Kim, who had refused to dissect her frog in biology class, who fainted while donating blood, who had to be given a mild sedative when her daughter Leigh fell off a jungle gym and needed fourteen stitches in her forehead. Kim had probably freaked out.

Aloud, she said, "What about the dog? Where was Bronte?"

Kim reached over and rubbed the pug gently between the ears. "Bronte was in the kitchen. I think I must have woken her up. She followed me into the study and became very agitated when she saw Auntie."

"And then you ran outside and bumped into me?"

"Uh huh."

"Why didn't you call the police?"

A shadow passed across Kim's face. "I didn't think of it. I just wanted to get out of there as fast as I could."

"So you figure you were in the house for about fifteen minutes then? Because I arrived at nine sharp and saw you running out of—"

"Enough," Larry interrupted. He'd sat up and was pulling a T-shirt on over his bathing suit. "Kim's told you all she knows and I won't have you upsetting her further." He stood up and held out his hand to his wife. "Come on, honey. Let's go for a walk."

Kim scrambled to her feet. "I'd like that." To Anne, she said, "We'll talk later. After the funeral."

Anne watched them make their way down to the water, past towels and blankets laid out on the sand like patches of a giant quilt. The clouds had edged a little higher in the sky, diminishing the threat of rain. Even under the umbrella, Anne felt like she was slowly baking. She surveyed the noisy throng of sunbathers, the teenagers showing off buff, tan bodies, the children screaming and frolicking at the water's edge, until her eyes came to rest on Kim and Larry. They were still holding hands, and Anne realized it was the first time she'd seen them exhibit the slightest trace of affection.

Petting Bronte's coat absentmindedly, she said, "Wow. What's wrong with this picture?"

Point Pleasant Beach was the seafood capital of New Jersey, with the best seafood restaurants, clam bars, and fish markets in the state. It was situated some fifteen miles south of the Heights, between the Manasquan Inlet and the Metedeconk River at the head of Barnegat Bay, and was home to one of the four commercial fishing fleets in the state.

Fishing trawlers and charter boats dotted the inlet. The markets sold fish that were caught only hours before being filleted and arrayed on ice. Some party boats specialized in weakfish or fluke, others concentrated on bluefish.

After crossing the drawbridge that led to the town, Anne turned right, onto Broadway, a road along the inlet lined with motels and restaurants. She and Trasker had eaten there several times—at Tesauro's, where they'd shared flounder formaggio and shrimp scampi, and at Spike's Fish Market, where the shrimp cocktails and steamers were out of this world.

Not content just to mine the seafood sobriquet, Point Pleasant Beach regularly dreamed up events to draw more tourists. The aquarium had hosted Penguin Appreciation Day, and if you showed up dressed as the King on Elvis Day, you could get into the fun house on the boardwalk for free. The Fourth of July brought the Classic Car Cruise, and in August you could enter the Giant Sand Castle Building Contest. Every Monday night there was a kiddie beach show, with magic tricks and pony rides. And there were weekly fireworks displays and laser-light shows. Once a year, the town sponsored a Festival of the Sea Weekend, which included a seafood festival, a five-mile run, and an inner tube race. Compared to Point Pleasant Beach, the Heights, with its fish and chips dinners and ice cream socials, looked positively somnambular.

Heading further inland, Anne came to Arnold Avenue, Point Pleasant's old-fashioned main street. She passed a string of antiques and curio shops: Fond Memories, Snow Goose, Point Pavilion Antique Center, the Time Machine. She'd been to all of them at one time or another, in search of the vintage 1950s glass and chrome cocktail shakers her mother used to collect. She remembered one shaker in particular, decorated with images of antique cars and instructions for making Manhattans, Gibsons, and highballs that she'd bought as a birthday gift two years before her mother had died, when Evelyn was so ill with Alzheimer's that she neither recognized Anne nor remembered that the shakers held any special significance.

Anne glanced at the card she'd found in Aunt Hannah's desk. When she'd called the phone number on the Greeley House card, a computerized voice had told her it was no longer in service. The address didn't sound like an antiques emporium. But when she pulled up in front of number 672 that's exactly what she saw. A two-story wood building with big plate-glass windows that looked like a cross between a barn and a general store. The sign out front said *Sea Isle Antiques*. Anne parked the Mustang and went around to let Bronte out. The dog had been pretty good on the ride down. For the most part, Bronte had stayed quiet and thankfully never seemed to get car sick.

"Come," Anne said, prompting the pug to trot obediently at her heels.

Commands were a wonderful thing, Anne decided. Too bad they didn't work on cats.

She led Bronte through the double front doors, into a vast space filled from floor to rafters with antique furniture, jewelry, mirrors, and what quite frankly looked like junk. There were Howdy Doody dolls, Partridge Family lunch boxes, pink hula hoops, Slinkies, Flinstones jelly glasses, lava lamps, mood rings, and a trove of other pop culture relics. This was the type of antiquing Anne loved. Forget Hepple-white chairs and art nouveau lamps. She'd rather sift through old Lawrence Welk records any day. Kitsch was in-finitely more fun than expensive, serious stuff.

The Sea Isle was empty, save for a couple of tourists. Anne had kept her beach disguise on to avoid being recognized and she wandered down the aisles, peering into the various stalls and trying to make sure Bronte didn't knock anything over. *You Break It, You Buy It* signs were posted all over the place.

Anne paused next to a cabinet containing a couple dozen Nancy Drew mysteries. As a child she'd owned the first fifty, but had donated them to the Ladies' Auxiliary book sale years ago. These had the same covers as the ones she'd read in the 1960s. She picked up *The Secret of Shadow Ranch*, one of her favorites, and set off to find the owner, with Bronte in tow.

She found him dusting a bone china lamp shaped like a shepherdess in a stall filled with Depression glass, mis-matched teacups, Bakelite radios, and shoe boxes brimming with old pictures of New Jersey from the days when women wore bloomers on the beach and diners were a newly minted novelty.

His name was Ralph Raunft and he was in his mid-thir-ties, tall and skinny, with sad eyes and cheeks that drooped, reminding Anne of a basset hound. Since she'd inherited Bronte, she'd begun noticing how many people resembled different breeds of dogs. On the beach that morning, she'd spotted dachshunds, poodles, collies, and Great Danes—in human form.

Handing Ralph Raunft the Greeley House card, she asked if the Sea Isle had ever gone by another name.

"It was the Hope Chest before my wife and I bought it three years ago," Ralph said. "The previous owner retired and moved to Arizona, but I think he ran the place for thirty or forty years. I couldn't say what it was before that."

He'd never heard of Aunt Hannah and had never set foot in the Heights. The phone number on the card bore no relation to the one assigned to the Sea Isle.

Another dead end, Anne thought glumly.

Thanking him, she took her book to the register, paid for it, and left. Walking outside was like stepping into a sauna. If the sun had been out, it would have been unbearable.

"What now?" she asked Bronte, pulling a doggy treat out of her bag.

That was another thing. She'd been talking to the pug more than she ever talked to Harry. On the drive down the shore, she'd chatted with Bronte about everything and nothing. Her thoughts, her fears, her hopes. It had to be because of the stress she was under.

Or maybe most dog owners held one-sided conversations with their pets. She supposed it was only bad when the dogs started talking back.

Chapter 14

The stress of being without the person they're accustomed to or being in a strange environment can cause dogs to lose their appetites. When a pet-sitter is around, leave some tempting treats, such as chicken or turkey, in the refrigerator. Instruct the sitter to hand-feed your dog if she rejects her meals. Or have the sitter take your dog's meals along on her walks. Pour gravy or other tasty liquids over dry dog food to make it more appetizing.

 On the way home, Anne stopped off in Landsdown Park. Landsdown was directly north of the Heights, but the two towns couldn't have been more different. At the turn of the century Landsdown had been a flourishing seaside resort. But in the 1960s race riots had torn the town apart, leaving a skeletal, impoverished shell. Dilapidated houses with boarded-up windows and trash-strewn front yards lined the streets. The boardwalk was largely deserted, save for Madame Mona, who told fortunes in a tiny shack with a giant, heavily lined eye on the front.

Anne drove through the main part of town, passing a few bars, a small grocery store, a thrift shop, a restaurant supply company, and lots of abandoned buildings. Teenage boys congregated on corners, riding children's bicycles three sizes too small for them and listening to loud rap music.

On one of the side streets stood a cluster of pawnshops, crammed with castoffs: electric guitars, pastel sweater sets, costume jewelry, wind-up toys, faded linens. The assorted detritus of a hundred different lives. Every so often you could find a treasure amid the junk—a genuine diamond pin shaped like a butterfly, a blazer so many years out of style it was suddenly "in" again, a framed photograph of such beauty and grace it deserved to hang in a gallery.

She went in and out of each shop, inquiring about the jeweled Easter egg. But no one had seen anything like what she described. At one of the shops, a man gave her the name and number of a pawnbroker in Manasquan who specialized in rare collectibles. At the last shop, she bought a water dish for Harry decorated with pictures of bells and ribbons.

She had to admit she felt guilty about spending so much time with Bronte when Harry was home alone. But Harry couldn't stand going into his carrier and she couldn't exactly lug him from place to place in her arms. She felt like she had two unruly siblings vying for her affections. Bronte was even starting to grow on her a little. The pug was still the ugliest creature Anne had ever seen, but Bronte's eyes were bright and inquisitive, and for a small dog she had a lot of energy and spirit.

She called the Tip Top Pawn Shop from her cell phone in the car, but was told the owner wouldn't be in until four and that he was the only one authorized to handle inquiries. She left her name and number and drove back to the Heights along the ocean road. The beach had thinned out, but it wouldn't completely empty until five-thirty P.M., when it officially closed for the day.

When she got home, she was hit with a distinctly unpleasant odor. "Harry," she called out. "Come here this minute."

She refilled Bronte's sterling silver water dish and set out in search of the cat, finding him amid a pile of clawed-up stockings she'd put in the bathroom, intending to wash them by hand.

"Oh, Harry." She sighed. "What's gotten into you?"

The cat stared at her unrepentantly and continued shredding stockings. Truth to tell, he looked as if he were the injured party and she the big bad human intent on spoiling his fun. She scooped up the stockings and turned to scold him, but he'd darted from the room, probably planning his next act of mayhem.

Great. A feline insurrection. She went to get the Resolve spray bottle, scrubbing those patches of the carpet where Harry had made his presence known. Bronte bounded between her ankles, frolicking playfully, sniffing the spray, like they were playing a new game: deodorize the house.

After she'd scrubbed the stains as much as she could, Anne went into her office, turned on the computer, and e-mailed Edie Mintzler. *My cat is acting out big time*, Anne wrote, *and I'm caught in the middle of a tug of war. Please advise ASAP.*

Hopefully, there was a solution to her odd couple pet

problem, she thought, as she immersed herself in sketching out "Chapter Five, Raising a Pet to Have Good Self-Esteem." Unlike her own situation, which was looking bleaker by the minute. Adoption, Greeley House, the stolen chef's knife, her cousins' financial troubles. "What did any of it have to do with Aunt Hannah's death?" she said aloud to Bronte, who was lying under the computer table.

At a quarter to five she called the pawnshop again, but the owner still hadn't returned. Then she took her second shower of the day and changed into the only black summer dress she owned, a sleeveless cotton jersey knit that she'd always thought looked a little too much like a long, tight sweater.

Harry had pulled another disappearing act. She put more food in his dish, which was placed as far from Bronte's as possible. The dog accompanied her to the door and waited expectantly for the leash.

"Sorry, not this time," Anne said. "I'll be back soon."

She felt a little nervous about leaving the two of them alone together. But what choice did she have? A funeral was no place for a pet, even though Bronte had as much right as anyone to attend. Hannah had loved and valued the pug more than any person in her life. Feeling guilty, Anne went down to the basement and brought up an old baby gate she'd used when she'd first gotten Harry and was trying to ensure he wreaked as little havoc as possible on his new home. She fastened the gate to the living room entryway, confining the dog to this one area and letting Harry have the run of the house.

Anne was just about to depart when she heard noises outside. Going to the window, she saw reporters and cameramen beginning to cluster on the sidewalk, preparing for another stakeout. The dog started to bark.

Good, she thought, as she slipped out the back door. Maybe Bronte will distract them for a few minutes. She slipped through the hole in the fence and cut through two more backyards, feeling like an overdressed thief, her high heels sinking into the grass, which was still muddy in places from the rain.

Emerging onto Pitman Avenue, she briskly walked north, keeping her head down, her eyes fixed on the sidewalk. She'd once dated an architect from New York City named Jack Mills, who'd told her this was the perfect way to walk in Manhattan. It helped make you invisible, he'd said, less of a target for muggers and perverts.

She thought she'd gotten the walk down pat. But the invisibility thing wasn't working. People kept calling out her name and coming up to her, some offering condolences, others clearly interested in learning more about the murder and the part she might have played in it. Tourists stopped to gape, recognizing her from the news. One middle-aged woman with a Southern accent even pulled out pen and paper and asked her for an autograph.

Anne shooed them all away. "Sorry," she mumbled. "Can't talk now." Then she stopped acknowledging or answering peoples' greetings entirely, darting out of the way and dashing across streets. Maybe murder suspects could afford to be rude. After all, she had bigger problems than offending and alienating her overly curious neighbors.

Two blocks from the Church by the Sea she pulled up short, sweating profusely. Her feet were killing her. Her heart was beating a mile a minute. And she could hardly believe what she was seeing. The news media gathered in front of her house had been nothing compared to this throng. News vans from all the major networks were double-parked on Ocean Avenue and there must have been close to sixty members of the press armed with cameras, microphones, tape recorders, headsets, and notepads.

Breathe, she told herself. Keep breathing. Have to get

away. Run away and keep running until this whole thing is over. *You mean until they arrest you and lock you in a cell for good.* She felt like she had a bull's-eye plastered onto her chest. All that was missing was a SWAT team.

"Unbelievable, isn't it?" said a voice behind her.

Anne spun around to find Cece dressed in the same black skirt she'd worn to the reunion lunch, paired with the same yellowed cotton blouse. She had on the platinum wig and was holding a small plastic bag.

"The vultures smell blood," Cece said.

"And I'm pretty sure it's mine."

Cece opened the bag and pulled out a chestnut-brown wig cut in a short bob. "That's why I brought this. I thought it might come in handy. Come on. Let's go."

They ducked behind the side of a peach-colored Victorian cottage, which was hidden from the street by a row of hedges, and Cece proceeded to pin Anne's red hair up under the wig.

"How many of these do you own?" Anne asked.

The wig felt uncomfortable and hot. It made her scalp itch.

"Nearly a dozen. I guess you could call them tools of the trade," Cece said wryly.

"About this morning, I'm sorry if I—"

"Don't be," Cece cut her off. "I should have told you the truth before now. But I guess I was too ashamed. When I lost my job at the restaurant it came at the end of a string of jobs I'd been fired from or quit. I was desperate and broke. A friend of mine who was an out-of-work actress had been turning tricks, and she was raking money in hand over fist. She had a few steady customers and I saw how well she did. So I decided to give it a try. It was only supposed to be for a little while, till I got back on my feet."

"When did you . . . how long ago was that?"

Cece gave a deprecating shrug. "Nearly three years ago."

Her cheeks had turned bright pink though her gaze was steady. "Then something happened that I never expected." A small smile formed at the corners of her mouth. "I got pregnant."

Anne smiled, too, then threw her arms around her cousin and gave her a hug. "Wow, that's fantastic."

"Yeah, it kind of is, actually. Julia is so beautiful, Annie. And one of these days you'll get to meet her."

"Was that a picture of her we saw in your wallet?"

"Uh huh."

Cece opened her bag, took out her wallet, and removed the photo. Anne studied the baby girl. She didn't look like her mother, except maybe a little around the eyes.

"She's beautiful."

"Thanks," Cece said. "She's almost two now." Cece's face darkened. "The only problem is she's not with me anymore."

"What do you mean?"

Cece wrapped her arms around herself like she'd suddenly gotten cold. "Social services took her away. They're trying to find her a foster home. And I'm trying to stop them."

Anne suddenly saw the whole picture clearly. "That's why you wanted money from Aunt Hannah. To help get Julia back."

Cece nodded. "If I could get my hands on some cash, I could get an apartment with a room for Julia, buy a suit or two so I could interview for a decent job, show social services I'm a damn good mother."

Anne thought a moment. "Did you tell Aunt Hannah the real reason you needed the money?"

Cece laughed. "Are you kidding? The minute she found out she'd probably make sure I never saw Julia again. I mean, let's face it, Annie. There's no way she could understand or forgive what I did."

Anne imagined Hannah's shock and disappointment, her aunt's righteous indignation. What if Auntie had somehow found out? Would she try to take Cece's baby away? Maybe give it up for adoption?

Cece pulled out a pair of dark glasses and handed them to Anne. "Let the dead rest in peace. Let's concentrate on you," she said, proceeding to unzip her skirt. "We have to switch clothes."

"Right here?"

"If any of those reporters spotted you on the way over, they might recognize your dress."

Anne looked around nervously to see whether anyone was watching, then quickly followed Cece's lead. Her cousin's clothes were a little tight on her, but otherwise she felt like the disguise was pretty effective.

"I think this just might work," Cece said, looking Anne over from head to toe.

"Thanks."

They exchanged another quick hug, then carefully emerged from behind the hedges. Back out on the street, Anne saw that there were even more news types than before, plus a cadre of police cars. A news helicopter hovered overhead. *America's Most Wanted*, eat your heart out.

"Let's go," she said to Cece.

"You first. You'll attract less attention if you're by yourself."

Anne hesitated. What if she was recognized? What if the hive of buzzing reporters swarmed her?

But then Cece gave her a gentle push and she found herself crossing Ocean Avenue undetected and slipping into the cool, airy confines of the church.

It was a huge, cavernous building, decorated with stained glass panels and crowned with a twelve-foot-high cross that glowed neon white at night and could be seen from thirty miles offshore. The ocean was visible through soaring windows, a tangible reminder of God's majesty on earth, or at least that's what Anne had thought as a child, watching the waves break on the beach as the minister delivered his sermon. Gulls nested in the rafters. The sand formed a tawny gold carpet leading straight to God's house. You could almost believe that heaven was just beyond the horizon, where the sea kissed the sky.

The building itself was handsome, yet plain, with burnished oak walls and hand-carved pews divided down the middle by a bright red carpet. At the front was a stage containing the pulpit, a large organ console, and rows of high-backed chairs. An electric flag hung above the stage. During concerts, the flag's lights blinked sequentially as though it were waving in an ocean breeze.

Anne headed down a side aisle and took a seat in about the tenth row of pews. From there, she could see her relatives seated up front. As much as she longed to sit with them, she didn't want to risk attracting the attention of reporters, who had already started to position themselves inside the church and were scanning the doors, probably awaiting her arrival.

She could just imagine the headlines in tomorrow's paper if she were spotted: KNIFE-WIELDING NIECE PAYS LAST RESPECTS. WIGGED-OUT WACKO ATTENDS FUNERAL. REDHEADED KILLER BIDS HER VICTIM ADIOS. Having worked for several years at a tabloid newspaper, she felt she had a pretty good idea of the way editors' minds worked.

She watched Henry approach her cousins, his face drawn, his gaze unfocused, like a man who had recently switched time zones and was having trouble making the adjustment. Behind him came Molly and Doris, Hannah's only surviving sisters, who had flown in from their retirement community outside Tuscon, Arizona.

Several more of her relatives filed in: Uncle Edward, who owned a car dealership in Parsippany and was given to wearing buttons with funny slogans on them; Edward's wife, Candy, who had once represented the state of New Jersey in the Mrs. America pageant and had reportedly had her breasts surgically enhanced; Nora and Alex's parents; Alex himself, on the arm of Heather Vance, who gazed at him so adoringly and walked so jauntily beside him that they could have been on their way to the altar instead of attending a funeral.

A parade of aunts, uncles, and third cousins followed. Anne didn't think any of them had seen Hannah very often. But death changed things, made people more forgiving and compassionate, more likely to do the "right" thing.

It occurred to her that she'd finally gotten her wish—the big reunion she'd hoped for. Only leavened with death and pain, a family forced together by a violent, senseless crime of passion.

Passion. Funny how she hadn't thought of it that way until now. But why else stab someone so many times? *Passion.* It was the last word she would have associated with Aunt Hannah, who'd always struck her as cold and bloodless, removed from life's baser pleasures. She caught sight of Chase Merritt, who sat apart from her family, staring fixedly at the stage. Merritt's passion was money, she felt sure of it. How far would he go to obtain his heart's desire?

The minister stepped onstage. He was new to the church, and as far as Anne knew, had never met her great-aunt. "We are here today," he intoned solemnly, "to bid farewell to our dearly departed sister, Hannah Rutter."

The coffin sat squarely at the center of the stage. An ornate mahogany box with gold hardware, surrounded by lavish displays of white lilies and gladiolas. Aunt Hannah would have approved. Maybe she'd picked it out herself months or even years before. Hannah had believed in advance planning, whether it pertained to planting annuals in her garden or choosing which necklace to wear to one of the many charity events she was forever getting invited to.

Why was Hannah interested in adoption? Why had she sounded so worried when speaking to Sherry Marcus at Hanley-Britt? Anne realized with a sinking feeling that she was no closer to knowing the truth than she'd been thirty-six hours ago. The minister was talking about faith and loss and the healing power of God. Anne looked past him out to the Atlantic, where the water was a deep blue-green, pushing rhythmically toward the shoreline. She could try to run, take every cent she owned and hop on a plane. Start someplace else under an assumed name.

She envisioned a one-bedroom cottage within walking distance of the sea, eating solitary meals, Harry basking in a square of sunlight by the window, taking long walks with Bronte, her life diminished but still satisfying, filled with good books and simple stews and the sound of rain drumming companionably against the roof during thunderstorms.

Oh, please, she told herself. How very Jane Austen. Get a grip. What about Trasker and her house and the book contract? Not to mention the fact that they'd find her and drag her back. And she'd look even guiltier in the end.

"We will now read from the Twenty-second Psalm," the minister intoned, "on the bottom of page 119."

People rustled the pages of their Bibles.

My God, my God, why hast thou forsaken me? Why art thou so far from helping me, and from the words of my roaring? Oh, my God, I cry in the daytime, but thou hearest not; and in the night season and am not silent.

Two clouds with the density and mass of packed cotton had drifted into sight above the ocean. Identical in shape, they looked as if they had once been part of the same cloud before being torn or cut in two. A sudden image of the chef's knife flashed before Anne's eyes. The spadelike pointy blade, its handsome wood handle. Something about the knife nagged at her, but she couldn't put her finger on what it was.

Save me from the lion's mouth, for thou hast heard me from the horns of the unicorns.

The manufacturer, some German company she'd never heard of before? No. The cutlery department at Linens 'n Things? No. The strawberries she'd sliced to test it out, not as ripe as they'd first appeared in their stiff supermarket plastic? No. No. No. It was no use. She couldn't remember.

All they that be fat upon earth shall eat and worship: all they that go down to the dust shall bow before him: and none can keep alive his own soul.

She tried to focus on the rest of the minister's sermon, on the words of comfort and prayer that floated through the church like mist. But her eyes kept drifting to the mahogany coffin and she couldn't shake the feeling that if she were to open the polished brass hinges and tear away the shroud, she would find herself inside the velvet-lined box, her own pale, stiff corpse, cold and dead.

Chapter 15

Does your dog steal scraps from the table? Chew on your shoes? Dig up your garden so it looks like a dust bowl? And then turn to you with the most innocent, irresistible expression, as if to say, "Who me?" Face it. At times like these it's tough to discipline your darling.

Before today, Anne had only been in a pawnshop once in her life. It was the summer she turned fourteen. The Alzheimer's had her mother firmly in its grip by then, although at the time, the doctors didn't have a name for the mysterious malady that was making Evelyn Hardaway sick. People in town thought Evelyn had gone crazy and Anne agreed. Evelyn had trouble remembering things, like where the frying pan was stored and how to get home from the Mini-Mart and what she'd named her only child.

Her behavior had grown disturbing, too. She'd dragged the good damask sofa down the front steps on garbage day and left it next to cans overflowing with books and china and linens. She became paranoid, fearing that Martha Cox, who lived next door, was plotting to steal her Midol, her car, her husband. She paraded up and down Ocean Avenue, clad only in a black lace bra, matching panties, and high heels, railing against seagulls and Jesus Christ.

At school Anne was taunted mercilessly. Eventually not even her cousins could protect her from the name-calling and pranks and obscene notes she was subjected to. So Anne decided her only hope was to run away. She'd taken her most valuable possession, a gold necklace given to her by her Grandma Betty, and walked over the bridge that separated the Heights from Landsdown Park.

The pawnshop, which had later become a liquor store and was now boarded up and vacant, was situated on Cookson Street. The man behind the counter had examined her necklace with a glass eyepiece, then had reached under a counter and extracted $55 from a rusty metal box. She'd expected to receive more, but was in no position to argue the point.

She'd pocketed the money and slipped it into a zipper compartment of the small vinyl suitcase she was carrying. Then she'd gone to the bus station and bought a ticket to Penn Station, New York. From there she'd planned to head west. California, maybe. Or Montana. Someplace where no one had heard of her or the Crazy Lady.

But Nora had ratted her out to her father, and before she could even board the bus, he had dragged her back home, making all kinds of extravagant promises he'd never be able to keep concerning how much better things would be.

Ironic, in light of the fact that he himself had already moved out.

She'd kept the necklace money, doling it out in dribs and drabs for ice cream and school supplies and the frozen dinners she'd cooked and tried to force Evelyn to eat.

The memory came rushing back to her as she walked into the Tip Top Pawn Shop, on Fisk Avenue in Manasquan, which was a little more upscale than the ones in Landsdown and definitely a cut above that long-ago storefront where she'd pawned her necklace. Along with sets of once-fashionable china, vintage dresses, and porcelain dolls, the Tip Top sold finer, more expensive merchandise: majolica soup tureens, embroidered linen tablecloths, glass perfume bottles with cunning silver tops, leather-bound books, art nouveau–style vases, mirrors encased in lavish gold frames that looked ornate enough to hang in a museum.

When she'd gotten home from the funeral (sticking to the side streets and miraculously avoiding running into reporters), she discovered that the owner, a man by the name of Walter Krzyzanowski had returned her call, but refused to discuss "the object in question" over the phone.

She found him sitting behind a glass display case, a red-haired man with a handlebar mustache and heavy-lidded eyes, the color of chestnuts. "What can I do for you?" asked Krzyzanowski after she'd introduced herself.

She gave a brief description of the egg.

Krzyzanowski cleared his throat discreetly and flashed Anne a broad smile. "And may I ask why you are interested in this particular item?"

"It was stolen two nights ago from my great-aunt's home in Oceanside Heights. As executor of her estate"—here Anne paused, trying to appear grave and serious-minded, befitting a representative of the court—"I wanted to locate the missing egg without attracting undue attention and in-volving the police."

At the mention of the police, Krzyzanowski stopped smil-ing. "Your aunt is . . . ?"

"Deceased. Perhaps you read about her death or saw it on the news?"

"I don't own a television," he said proudly. "There's really nothing worth watching anymore, including PBS."

He reached behind him and with an elaborate flourish brought forth a small lavender box, setting it carefully on the glass counter.

"Please," he said. "Open it."

But Anne's eyes had drifted across the shop to another display case where a gorgeous ruby necklace gleamed bril-liantly against a black velvet backdrop. Aunt Hannah's Fourth of July necklace!

Anne walked over to the display and pointed to the piece. "How long have you had this?"

"Since yesterday." Now Krzyzanowski looked alarmed. He ran his index finger along the top of his mustache ner-vously.

"I see."

She strode back to the other case and lifted the top off the lavender box. Peeling away layers of tissue paper, she re-moved the jewel-encrusted rabbit egg she'd last seen years ago, safe in Aunt Hannah's vitrine.

"The person who brought this egg in, did he or she also bring you the ruby necklace?"

"Yes," Krzyzanowski stammered. He had started to per-spire.

"Anything else?"

He stepped over to a vitrine at the side of the shop, which Anne had barely noticed before. Now she examined its contents more closely. "The gold bracelets, right? And the diamond earrings? And the double strand of pearls," she said, remembering that Aunt Hannah had worn them at lunch on Thursday.

Krzyzanowski gave an almost imperceptible nod. He looked as nervous as Harry did whenever Bronte was in the room. Anne turned back to the vitrine, picking out pieces she remembered seeing on Aunt Hannah over the years. "The coral bracelet. Those onyx earrings. The heart on the long silver chain. The emerald peacock pin."

She glanced up at Krzyzanowski. He didn't have to answer. She could see in his eyes that she'd guessed right.

Anne dug into her pocketbook and pulled out one of the photos that she'd taken outside her house on Thursday with Alex's camera. "Did one of these people bring all this stuff in?" she asked.

Krzyzanowski placed a stubby finger on the shiny surface of the picture.

"It was him," Krzyzanowski said, relieved to hoist the blame onto someone else.

He jabbed at Alex's handsome, grinning face. "I should have known something was fishy from the way the guy was acting. He was real skittish. Kept looking out the window like he thought he was being followed."

"How much did you pay him?"

"Six grand. The stuff he brought in is worth more than that. But he wouldn't take a check and that's all I had in cash." Krzyzanowski mopped his brow with a handkerchief. "You're not going to report this to the cops, are you? I let my insurance lapse, plus the negative publicity wouldn't be good for business."

He shoved the box toward her. "Take it," he said. "The jewelry, too. I run an honest business. I won't have stolen merchandise in my shop. If you can get my $6,000 back, I'd appreciate it. Maybe this fellow will ante up now that he's been found out."

But Anne wasn't listening. She felt dazed, drained. Could Hannah have given Alex the egg and the jewels before she died? No. It didn't add up. Anne was sure Alex had visited Dovecote the day Hannah died. Anne herself had heard his voice over the phone, had heard Hannah ordering him out of the house. Alex could deny it from here to Christmas. He had been in Hannah's house. He had stolen her property. Had he also killed her?

The sun was setting as Anne drove back to the Heights. On summer nights the dark sneaked up on you in increments, the sky changing from pink to iridescent blue to black within the space of several minutes. It was blue as Anne drove, a deep azure blue that backlit the Victorian cottages on Ocean Avenue, giving them the weird appearance of gigantic still life in a surrealist play.

Fireflies glowed yellowish-green, then disappeared. The lifeguard stands, illuminated by wrought-iron turn-of-the-century streetlights, cast spidery shadows on the sand. Anne was lost in the twilight of remembrance. She'd watched the sun go down hundreds, no, probably thousands of times, on hot summer nights when all you wanted was to feel salt water stinging your ankles or to lie down on the beach and count the beads of tiny stars strung across the sky or to share a kiss under the boardwalk, your heart beating in time to the rhythmic crashing of the waves.

She remembered how one night Alex had dared her to go skinny-dipping on a sunset swim. They'd waited until this same ghostly blue light suffused the sky and then they'd stripped off their bathing suits and dove headfirst into the water, Anne too numbed by the icy shock of the ocean to feel self-conscious or foolish or much of anything else besides an exhilarating sense of freedom.

Amazing how much more at ease one could be without that modest piece of cloth covering your anatomy. She'd felt like a fish, no, a mermaid, frolicking and swimming near Alex—though not too near, not near enough to shake the aura of fantasy wrapped like tissue paper around the memory of that faraway night.

Growing up, Alex had been part brother, part object of adoration. If she could, she would have hung a poster of him on her bedroom wall, the way other girls hung pictures of David Cassidy or Bobby Sherman or Donny Osmond. The room always seemed a little brighter when Alex was in it, the mood a little lighter. He had a talent for drawing people in; her cousins and the kids at school orbited around him like planets revolving around a fiery sun.

Aunt Hannah was one of the few who could resist him, Anne realized now. *Charm boy*, she used to call him, with a hint of derision. *The heartbreak kid*. Anne's mother once speculated it was because of a failed romance Hannah had had as a girl with a man named Jasper Reed, who jilted her a week before their wedding day and two years before she met and married the uniform king, Arnold Rutter.

Hannah and Arnold were happy together, her mother had said. But Jasper was the great love of Hannah's life, and few women experience that kind of passion twice.

Anne wondered if this were true. When it came to love and romance, her mother had been a cynic. Even before Alzheimer's struck, the marriage to Anne's father had been a troubled one. *We are temperamentally unsuited*, her mother used to say. *Like needs like*.

And in the end, Anne had heeded the advice. She and Trasker liked the same music, the same food, the same sports. Their views of work, relationships, politics, and religion were perfectly in synch. They had passion in spades. But it wasn't the first time she'd fallen hard for a man, and since she couldn't predict the future, she couldn't say whether it would be the last.

As Anne pulled up in front of Heather Vance's condo, she pondered what Heather would have to say on the subject. Heather and Alex had gone out briefly in high school. But when their relationship ended, she hadn't been bitter or tearful or tried desperately hard to win him back, like most of his other ex-girlfriends. Instead they became friends, allies, teammates in an unspoken popularity contest that crowned them king and queen of Oceanside High.

Heather was royalty in her own right. A tousled-hair blond with a buxom figure and bee-stung lips, Heather never lacked for dates. Being seen on her arm caused a boy's popularity rating to be ratcheted up several notches. Not that Heather was undiscriminating. You had to have displayed achievement or ability to win a date with Heather Vance—like being captain of the swim team or president of the debate club or editor of the school newspaper.

She was one of those girls of whom Anne had been in awe back then and half-pitied now when high school exploits were long gone, reduced to a string of stories told over a bowl of chips and a beer in a dark, smoky bar, with the Phillies game blaring in the background, muffling the slow song on the jukebox.

Heather had dropped out of college after two years and now, with a string of dead-end jobs behind her, worked for her father, who owned Advance Pharmacy. She stocked shelves and filled prescriptions and sometimes helped out behind the counter, making egg creams and flipping burgers. Not the most scintillating form of employment for an ex-cheerleader/prom queen. But the pay wasn't bad and if she

took too many sick days or three-hour lunch breaks her boss
was forgiving.

Anne had always expected Heather to be married by now,
with three kids, a Queen Anne cottage, and a well-behaved
dog. But Heather's life hadn't worked out according to plan.
She lived in the Bay Crest Arms, the only apartment building
in town, and was still unhappily (or so Anne heard) single.

In keeping with the historic character of the Heights, the
Bay Crest was designed to look like it had been there forever. Painted lilac with deep purple trim, the condominium
complex featured elaborate shingles, spindles, lavish mold-
ings, and finials galore. Spooled columns flanked the double
front doors and tiny balconies protruded from the facade,
like lips on a cheerful spinster. Add a couple of turrets and a
few panes of stained glass and the Bay Crest Arms would
appear to have been built in the nineteenth century, instead
of the mid-1970s.

Heather lived on the fourth floor. If she was at all surprised to see Anne on her doorstep at nine-thirty at night, she
didn't show it.

"Oh, you poor thing," she said, flinging her arms around
Anne's shoulders and enveloping her in a cloud of cheap
perfume. "What a time of it you've had."

Anne resisted the impulse to slip out of Heather's gooey
embrace and gag on the musky odor. She and Heather had
never been friends. In fact, every time Anne was around
Heather, she felt like she was watching the feminist movement being set back fifty years. Heather fancied herself a
Venus flytrap, her every move defined and regulated by the
actions and reactions of men.

She seemed to exist for the sole purpose of delighting
the male species, from the ten-year-old boys who stared in
unabashed joy at the ample cleavage she displayed, to the

seventy-year-old men who lingered for hours over cups of cold coffee at the pharmacy's soda fountain, only to brighten when she poured fresh refills.

When Heather stepped back, Anne was struck by the resemblance to a Bedtime Barbie doll she'd once owned. Pink mules. Pink nightie held up with spaghetti straps. Filmy see-through pink robe exposing plenty of curves and creamy powdered skin. There was hot pink lipstick on Heather's Kewpie-doll lips and bright blue shadow on her eyelids. Her streaked blond ringlets were swept in an updo, held fast by barrettes and a sheer pink scarf. She looked tousled and flushed.

Glancing past Heather to where Alex reclined on a sofa with his shirt unbuttoned, Anne figured she'd interrupted Heather mid-seduction.

"Hey, cuz," Alex called out. "Come on in."

Anne followed Heather into the L-shaped living room. Heather had redecorated since the last time Anne had been there, going from country casual to mainstream modern. The couch Alex lay on was made of a burgundy leather, flanking an oversize matching leather armchair and a Formica taupe-colored console table, on which were displayed chrome candlesticks of various shapes and sizes. The glass coffee table had a shiny metal base, echoed in the silver vertical blinds at the windows.

There were lots of gleaming surfaces, hard edges, sleek metallics. The entire wall in the dining area was mirrored, reflecting the remains of a Vic's pizza supper and a nearly empty bottle of Cabernet.

"We couldn't find you at the funeral or the cemetery," Alex said, sitting up and buttoning his shirt.

Anyone else might have been embarrassed at the intrusion, but Alex was cool as glass.

Anne explained about the disguise, which she'd left in the car. She'd skipped the cemetery and planned to pay her respects in private.

"How awful for you to have to hide like a criminal," Heather exclaimed. She was perched next to Alex on the sofa, with one hand resting protectively on his knee.

Anne wasn't in the mood for small talk or pity parties.

"Do you think I could speak to my cousin alone?" she asked Heather.

"Whatever for?" Heather said sweetly.

Up close, Anne saw that the foundation makeup Heather had applied didn't completely mask the fine lines around her eyes. Her hair looked dried out and brittle, as if years of bleach and sun had finally taken their toll.

"It's a family matter," Anne replied, matching Heather's saccharine tone. "I'm sure you understand."

"Why don't you wait in the bedroom, babe?" Alex put in helpfully.

Heather kissed him on the mouth—a quick, breathy kiss, but it said a lot—*I love you. I own you*—and reluctantly retreated to her boudoir.

When the door had closed behind her, Alex turned to Anne. "What's up?"

She opened her pocketbook and took out the jewelry and the egg, placing them carefully in the middle of the coffee table.

At the sight of the objects, Alex visibly started. Anne heard him suck in his breath. His hands gripped the sofa tightly and his whole body seemed to go on red alert. She realized it was the first time she'd ever seen him rattled.

"H-how . . . ," he stammered. "How did you . . . ?"

Anne waved the question away. "Not important. I need to know the truth, Alex. I mean it. If you lie to me, I'll go straight to the cops."

Alex got up and began to pace the room, moving behind the sofa, around the ottoman, over to the window, like a silver ball careening through a pinball game, his worried, anxious face reflected in the mirror. "It's not what you think," he began.

"Then enlighten me."

"I . . . I went over there to ask for money. I *need* money, Anne. Very badly."

"This is after you dropped by Dovecote earlier in the day to demand money, right? When I heard Aunt Hannah tell you to leave."

"Yes."

He sat on the arm of the sofa, then jumped up and strode to the dining room table, where he poured himself the last of the wine and drank it quickly, nearly choking.

Anne said, "Why did you lie when I asked you about it?"

"I don't know."

"Alex," she said flatly.

He threw up his hands and some of the wine spilled, staining his powder-blue shirt and Heather's beige high-pile carpet. "I didn't want anyone to know I'd been there that day, okay?" he said defensively.

"But you *were* there. And then you came back."

She felt as if she were standing outside herself, watching the two of them recite lines from a script. Her emotions were adrift, like a runaway kite sailing up, up, up into a cloudless sky.

Out of the corner of her eye, Anne saw that the bedroom door was ajar. Heather was probably eavesdropping. Anne wondered if Heather knew Alex had used her as an alibi. Was Heather in on this, too?

"After Auntie refused to help me, I got desperate," Alex continued. He'd knelt down on the carpet and was trying to scrub the stain out with a napkin. His motions were manic, frantic. "I went back around midnight. I figured Auntie would be sound asleep. She has so many trinkets she wouldn't notice a few had gone missing."

"You used the key in the bug spray, right?"

Alex stared at her in surprise, then nodded. He'd made the stain worse. It bloomed across the carpet like a bright magenta flower. He sank back, looking dazed.

"I took the egg from the vitrine and some jewelry from the wall safe," he said, sounding defeated.

"How'd you know the combination?"

"Lucky guess. After a few tries, I remember she got that hideous pug on the Fourth of July, four years ago. That's the combination: 07–04–96."

"What happened next?" she asked.

Although part of her didn't want to know. Part of her wanted to walk out the door and pretend none of this was happening, for things to return to the way they'd been before the reunion.

She pictured Aunt Hannah hearing a noise, waking up, padding downstairs to investigate. The knife descending again and again, piercing Auntie's back, shoulder blades, torso.

Alex was looking at her with alarm. In an instant he had crossed the room and was sitting beside her, taking hold of her hands.

Auntie screaming and screaming. Chairs overturning. The coppery smell of blood.

"Annie," he gasped. "You can't think . . . You don't think I killed her?"

His fingers dug into her skin. He was so close she could smell wine on his breath, mingling with his aftershave. His clear blue eyes were trained on her.

"She was already dead when I got there. Already dead. Please," he begged. "You have to believe me."

Anne slipped out of his grasp and shrank back against the sofa cushions. She could feel her heart thudding against the wall of her chest. "How did you know Hannah was dead?"

"I went into the study."

"Why?"

Alex looked confused. He raked his hand through his thick black hair. "What?"

Anne's mouth was dry, but she forced herself to continue. "You'd just stolen from Aunt Hannah. Jewelry. Cash. The safe was cleaned out. Why bother with the study? Why not get out before you were spotted?"

"I thought I heard a noise."

"You mean the dog?"

"No. I never saw the dog. I heard something. A rustling type noise."

Anne got up from the sofa, moving quickly. With one careless motion, she swept the egg and the jewelry back into her bag. "What was it?"

"I don't know," Alex said softly. "I got to the study and saw the body. She was just . . . she was lying there. Oh, God, it was awful."

"But not so awful that you couldn't resist helping yourself to some more of her jewelry?"

Alex looked taken aback. "I didn't steal anything else."

"What about the three rings she was wearing and her cameo necklace? You know, the stuff the police found in my house. She was already dead. So what did it matter?"

Alex's eyes blazed angrily. "I never realized you thought so little of me."

"I'm only trying to get at the truth," Anne shot back. "If you were in my shoes, you'd be doing the same thing."

"I suppose," he admitted reluctantly.

"So you won't mind telling the police what happened?"

A horrified expression clouded Alex's handsome features.

"Are you kidding? Theft is a crime. And I'm not going to jail."

"No, that's my department, right?"

She felt so furious with Alex she could barely stand to look at him. All the years she'd spent admiring, idealizing, worshipping him—shattered. She saw now that his charm and smooth manner were only tricked-out veneers, hiding a core of self-interest. He'd needed money. He'd seized his opportunity. And to hell with whoever got in the way.

She slung her handbag over her shoulder, causing the jewels to rattle. "I can go to the police myself, remember? I have all the evidence I need right here."

Alex glared at her. "I wouldn't, if I were you. I wouldn't tell a soul."

Anne strode to the door. She'd expected remorse, excuses. But threats? Never.

She felt flushed and lightheaded, like she'd been deprived of air. As she walked out into the hallway, she heard the clatter of heels and Heather's high-pitched voice. The door slammed shut behind her before she could make out exactly what Heather was saying. But the tone was clear. Soothing. Seductive. Make no mistake about it. Heather was definitely standing by her man.

Chapter 16

Boston ivy, hyacinth, tulips, cacti, geraniums, daisies, poinsettia, daffodils, iris, and wisteria are among the plants and flowers that may prove poisonous to your cat. Keep toxic plants out of kitty's reach. Trim hanging plants so they aren't a temptation and spray the leaves with a bitter-tasting antichew spray that will discourage your cat from munching on them.

Bronte was waiting for her when she got home, sitting patiently by the baby gate.

"Good dog," Anne said.

She went into her office and checked her voice mail. The tape had run out, but not before seventeen members of the

news media had left messages. Most wanted a comment on
the murder charge. Nine requested an interview, and one
promised that if she agreed to appear on his station's six
o'clock news broadcast, the station would not only send a
Town Car to pick her up, it would have someone available to
do her hair and makeup. Wow, Anne thought. A murder
makeover. Next they'd be offering to provide her with a
tasteful prison regulation pants suit and trendy accessories.

She checked her e-mail. Thank God. Edie had gotten back
to her with some cat versus dog advice:

> *Safeguard Harry's territory by moving his food bowl
> from the floor to higher ground. By creating an ele-
> vated feeding area that's off-limits to Bronte, meal-
> times will be less stressful. Prevent the dog from
> having access to Harry's litter bin. And consider in-
> vesting in a cat tree, so Harry can have a place to
> climb to for an undisturbed nap.*
>
> *When Bronte chases Harry, correct her and ask her
> to "sit." Use the "down stay" command while you pet
> and massage Harry so that he knows he's still loved
> and the dog understands that no matter what she
> thinks, the cat is to be left alone because you say so.
> Although it doesn't seem fair, Harry may prefer to
> spend the adjustment period sequestered in a small
> room with food, water, toys, a litter box, and a scratch-
> ing post. Let Harry choose how much or how little in-
> teraction he wants to have with his new roommate.*

Anne turned off the computer. Okay, she thought, it's a
start. At least now she wasn't flying blind. Rummaging
through her pocketbook, she found the business card that
Sherry Marcus had given her. Maybe Sherry had remembered something else, some new information that would

clear up the adoption piece of the puzzle. She dialed Sherry's home number.

"Hi," she said, when Sherry picked up. "This is Lynnette Quigley with the Neptune Township Sheriff's Office. I came to see you yesterday. I was wondering if—"

"I know exactly who you are, Miss Hardaway," Sherry interrupted, in a frosty tone. "But then impersonating a police officer is minor compared to murder, wouldn't you agree?"

"I didn't murder anyone," Anne said hotly. "But I'm trying to find out who killed my great-aunt and why she called your agency."

"I have nothing more to say to you or any other member of your 'family.'"

"What do you mean?" Anne asked, confused.

"A Mrs. Kim Ryerson came to see me this morning, also claiming to be Mrs. Rutter's niece, and asking the very same questions you did."

Kim? Anne was shocked. What would have led Kim to Hanley-Britt?

"Did she tell you why she'd come? Did she ask if—?"

"I have nothing more to say to you," Sherry cut her off. "If you contact me or any member of my staff again, I'll notify the police."

Anne heard a click and then silence as Sherry hung up the phone.

Her mind was reeling. What did Kim know? What was Kim after?

She picked up the phone and called the Laughing Gull, only to be told by the teenage girl who answered that Mr. and Mrs. Ryerson were out at present.

Kim had seemed so cool and nonchalant at the beach. Had she stumbled on something important? Why else was she snooping around? To cover her own tracks? Or Larry's?

Anne called Bronte over and fastened the leash to the dog's collar.

No sign of Harry. *God*, she thought. *I am the world's biggest traitor. I wouldn't blame Harry if he went out to dig around in the garden and never came back.*

She closed the front door behind her, and she and Bronte walked north along the boardwalk. It was a hot summer night. The waves slapped the shoreline with a gentle shush. The sand formed a smooth velvety carpet fading to black. Fog rolled off the ocean, obscuring the water, the lifeguard stands, the fog. Wisps of clouds drifted across the face of the moon, like black gauze hemmed onto a circle of white tulle.

She rarely walked along the beach at night. By the time eleven o'clock rolled around, she was usually in her pajamas, curled up with a novel or watching reruns of *Seinfeld* on TV. It felt good to be out at this time of night. The boardwalk was practically deserted and it was as if she had the whole town to herself.

Besides, there was something Zen about walking a dog. Bronte never traveled in a straight line, preferring instead to zigzag and wander as objects caught her interest. Were it not for Bronte, Anne never would have noticed the clump of dune grass shaped like a mushroom or the way a smashed and runny Popsicle glistened under the boardwalk lights.

No matter how hot and humid the air, it always felt cooler by the water. The breeze lifted her hair, brushing against her skin, like a promise. She felt rejuvenated, as though she could walk from there to Bay Head and back.

She passed a teenage couple making out on a bench, an elderly man smoking a pipe, two middle-aged tourists (probably from the South by their accents) discussing the pros and cons of the town's ban on serving alcohol. When she got to the fishing pier, she left the boardwalk and went all the way out to the end of the pier. Leaning over the railing and looking out to sea was like being on board ship. A gull flew down and alighted on a wooden post nearby. Spotting the bird, Bronte let out a series of rapid-fire barks and the gull immediately took off.

Anne leaned down and rubbed the top of Bronte's head. "Now why didn't you bark like that the night Hannah died?" Anne mused aloud.

Alex had said he never saw the dog. Although at that point, who could believe anything Alex said?

Ever since she'd left Heather's apartment, Anne had been pondering her next move. She could go to the police, show them the stolen objects, point her finger at Alex. But all the evidence was circumstantial. She needed tangible proof that Aunt Hannah had interrupted a robbery and Alex had lashed out in panic.

Now she let the cool ocean air wash over her, regulating her body temperature, which she was sure had risen in the last hour. Her cheeks still felt warm, she was running on pure adrenaline. Alex had set her up, stolen her knife, betrayed her trust.

"Is it true?" Anne whispered to Bronte.

The dog cocked her head sympathetically. Far out on the ocean two cabin cruisers were reduced to specks of white against the vast darkness of the sky.

"Do you think he killed your mistress? Can you believe they think I did it, and I'm out here in the middle of the night talking to a dog?" Anne tugged on the leash and turned her back to the Atlantic. "Come on," she said. "Let's go home."

Harry was waiting in the kitchen. When Anne flicked on the light, she saw him sitting on the kitchen table, calmly picking apart the leaves of a begonia plant that had been doing quite nicely in spite of her black thumb. Harry's one eye widened reproachfully as if Anne had been responsible for the damage.

Bronte rushed at the cat, then veered away at the last minute without making actual contact. Harry's eye widened. Anne could swear she saw his pupil dilate. But instead of fleeing, he let out an angry hiss and his tail lashed back and forth as if to say, *Don't mess with me.*

Moving warily, with her eyes on the two combatants, Anne picked up the remains of the bedraggled begonia and dumped it in the trash. "Poor kitty," she said, stroking Harry's back. "You've had a tough time of it."

Bronte yipped in what sounded like disgust.

"Oh, get over it," Anne teased.

She fixed herself a late-night snack: American cheese on a toasted English muffin and a cup of orange pekoe tea. While she ate, Harry lay by the refrigerator and Bronte stayed across the room, with her back to the stove. Two enemy camps, Anne thought. And not a cease-fire in sight.

Aloud, she said, "Come on, you two. How about a truce? Just for tonight."

The foes didn't budge from the territory they'd staked out. Oh, well. At least they had tacitly agreed to be in the same room without tearing it apart and terrorizing each other. Maybe that was progress of sorts.

The phone rang, interrupting her reverie. She debated whether to answer. The last thing she was in the mood for was more questions from reporters. But curiosity won out. Who could be calling this late at night?

"Hey, babe," said Trasker, when she finally picked up. "How are you feeling?"

"Not as low as this morning."

She filled him in on the events of her day.

"Looks like cousin Alex has some explaining to do," Trasker said, when she'd finished. "Turns out he mysteriously left his job a couple of days ago. But here's what's really interesting. The place where he worked is a company called Ace Plumbing Supplies that's owned and operated by the mob. The Feds have been trying for years to get something on the guys who own it: tax evasion, illegal carting, bribing contractors, anything that'll stick. But so far, no go. My guess is that Alex either stole from them or is into them big time for a nice chunk of change. Is he a gambler?"

Anne thought a moment. She'd never known Alex to gamble, outside of a few road trips to Atlantic City. But it wouldn't surprise her. Alex enjoyed taking risks and living large. He was a big spender. Before this, Anne had never really asked herself where he got the money to pay for his expensive toys.

"Could be," she told Trasker. "He's always liked being on the edge."

On the other end of the line, she heard the sound of papers rustling and the faint tones of Nat King Cole emanating from Trasker's stereo. She wished she was with him right now, eating takeout egg rolls on the living room rug or better yet, lying safe in his arms, feeling his fingers caress her skin, the sweet taste of his kisses on her mouth.

"There's something else," Trasker was saying. "I drove up to Bergen County this morning, did some nosing around. Turns out Henry's been a bad boy. He was arrested on May second on a DWI and a reckless endangerment charge. Apparently he ran a red light and hit a Honda Accord containing a thirty-two-year-old West Orange woman and her five-month-old infant daughter."

"Oh, my God. Were they okay?"

"The baby was strapped into a car seat in the back and didn't get a scratch. But the mother wasn't so lucky. She suffered massive internal bleeding, a broken jaw, seven broken ribs, a sprained wrist, a punctured lung, and worst of all, severe nerve damage to her spine. The doctors believe it's highly unlikely that she'll ever walk again."

"How awful," Anne gasped.

"Yes," Trasker replied. "Needless to say, she's suing Henry for every last dime and there's a good chance she'll win. Your second cousin had let his car insurance lapse, which means he's personally liable from a financial standpoint. He'd been begging his mother to help him, which she was apparently prepared to do, if only to avoid a public scandal."

Anne lifted the phone cord away from Harry, who'd been batting it with his paws. "Wait a minute. I'm confused. Did Hannah bail Henry out or not?"

"Yes and no. Privately she was in the process of having her lawyers settle the matter out of court. But she hadn't informed her son of her plans, so he thought she was letting him twist in the wind."

Anne pictured the satisfaction that would have given her great-aunt. Hannah had always been disappointed in her son, for no discernible reason. Now, in a drunken accident, he'd handed Hannah the greatest I-told-you-so of all.

"Annie," Trasker said. "You still there?"

"Yeah. I was just thinking how dysfunctional my family is."

Trasker chuckled. "Isn't everyone's? You never got to meet my folks. Moving to North Carolina was the best thing they ever did for me. In fact, it was probably the *only* good thing they did for me. Some people are not cut out to be parents, not by a long shot."

Anne sighed. "I miss you."

"Me, too, honey. It's getting kind of late, but how about you stay at my place tomorrow night?"

"That sounds great."

"Listen, get some sleep. I think we're a little closer to

cracking this thing. I'll be at the office most of the day, working on the Hughes case. But I'll check in when I can. Promise me you'll try not to worry."

"I'll try," Anne said, knowing how impossible that was going to be.

Bronte raised her perpetually worried-looking face and cocked her head inquisitively.

"I love you," Trasker said.

"I love you too, T."

"I won't let anything bad happen to you," he said, his voice softening.

"I know."

After she hung up, Anne rinsed the dishes and headed upstairs. Harry and Bronte followed, careful to leave several feet of space between them at all times.

When she reached the second floor, Anne grabbed a metal hook and used it to pull down the short flight of stairs that led to the attic. It was a narrow airless space, with wide plank floors and a low ceiling, cluttered with cardboard boxes, old toys, musty books, and broken appliances.

Anne's mother had been a hoarder all her life and after she died, Anne couldn't bring herself to throw her mother's things away. She'd briefly considered holding a tag sale, but who would be interested in buying clown figurines, a rusty child's bicycle, lamps with missing shades, dozens of school essays and papers?

Anne switched on the light, a bare bulb hanging from the ceiling. It cast a harsh glow on the jumble of stuff crammed into the small dusty space. Harry paused in the doorway. The cat had never been crazy about the attic, and usually steered clear, except for one time, when squirrels had gotten in through a hole in the roof and Harry took up sentry duty below the stairs, gazing wistfully up at the patter of little feet.

Bronte, however, bounded joyfully into the room, sniffing the mildew smell like it was Chanel No. 5 and batting every object she came in contact with. In lieu of selling the assorted piles of junk, Anne had long ago organized it according to her own system. Clothes off to one side, books arranged alphabetically before being tossed into boxes, her own childhood mementos in a back corner, placed in see-through plastic bins she'd bought at Linens 'n Things.

One bin was reserved for photos, which were stacked in albums, packed in shoe boxes, and sometimes left in the paper packets they'd been placed after developing.

Anne sat cross-legged on the floor, making a mental note to come back next week with a broom, dustpan, detergent, and air freshener.

The attic needed a good thorough cleaning. Bronte sneezed, seemingly in assent. The pug had found an old partially deflated rubber ball and was nosing it across the floor, then swatting it into out-of-the-way corners. Harry had retreated back downstairs.

Anne turned her attention to the photo bin, sorting through the contents until she found a thick album with a faded crimson cover. Some of the pictures had yellowed with age. But others were in remarkably good condition, considering the fact that they were thirty years old. Here were her aunts and uncles sitting under beach umbrellas, surrounded by plastic toys and picnic lunches; her mother holding a large stuffed panda she'd won at a traveling fair; Aunt Hannah looking regal under a white parasol edged with fringe; her cousins posed in Halloween costumes, at birthday parties, splashing in the ocean, displaying bugs they'd captured in jars, building elaborate sand castles; Alex laughing; Anne and Nora dressed as cowgirls; Kim standing by a fence bedecked with climbing roses; Cece and Alex making silly faces; more aunts; Anne and her cousins sitting in a row on the front steps of this very house, with their arms draped around each other's shoulders.

We had so much fun, Anne thought. The Fabulous Five. Together forever. How had they drifted so far apart? When did the split begin, the process that sent them spinning in different directions, into people she couldn't begin to understand?

She wondered if this happened in all families, if it was somehow inevitable as childhood ended and jobs, spouses, and circumstance conspired to sever what once had been unbreakable bonds. Still . . . a connection existed, fragile as gossamer wings, but there nonetheless. She felt it whenever she encountered her cousins. The sharing of a common past. The way they didn't have to fill the spaces between conversations. A comfort level of sorts. An acknowledgment of what they had shared.

She shut the album and was surprised to find herself on the verge of tears.

"Do you believe this, Bronte?" she asked the dog. "One trip down memory lane and I'm getting all sentimental on you."

Bronte knocked the ball in Anne's direction, but it hit a cardboard carton and skittered away.

She opened several more photo albums and noticed there were hardly any pictures of Henry to be found. Was he away at school or simply camera shy? She examined the shoe boxes, which contained older photos, from before she was born. These were black-and-white shots, formally posed. Her mother in graduation cap and gown. Her great-aunts wearing garden party dresses, with full skirts and demure necklines. A young, vibrant Aunt Hannah waving from a parade float shaped like a giant sea horse.

Anne couldn't tell who had taken the pictures. Her mother? Her grandmother? One of her great-aunts? Each photo was carefully labeled on the back: *Evelyn playing the piano, June 1965. Doris with baked goods at the Ladies' Auxiliary Fair, July 1955. Molly on the beach, September, 1952.*

Aaah. Here was Henry at last, sitting in a tall wicker chair on the front porch of Dovecote. He looked to be in his late teens, with his hair combed into a cowlick, wearing a V-necked polo shirt and dark trousers. A fat book was spread out on his lap, and the camera had caught him glancing up from it, momentarily surprised. His face was thinner, more carelessly handsome, but Anne saw traces of the same wariness he exhibited now.

A tightness around the jaw, those blue, close-set eyes. Anne wondered what it was like to be forced to enter a profession in which you had absolutely no interest. Did it make you feel helpless, dead inside? Did the accumulated days and weeks of work grow heavier each year like a millstone tied around your neck, dragging you under the waves? Was a bottle of scotch your only refuge, numbing you to boredom and thoughts of what might have been?

Anne picked up another picture. A blond teenager in a flowing white dress, with two curved wings rising from her shoulder blades, holding a long-stemmed rose. This time Anne recognized the face. The almond-shaped eyes, the snub nose, the frightened, almost tremulous expression.

Behind Jennie was a Christmas tree and a mantel hung with stockings. There was a piano off to the left. In the back of the room—a parlor, an entrance hall?—Anne could barely make out a formal-looking wing chair and a floor lamp with a pleated shade. Another person (it appeared to be a woman) was in the far corner of the frame, half in, half out of the picture, but time and the camera angle had reduced this figure to a blur of white.

She turned the picture over. *Jennie in the Christmas pageant at Greeley House, 1956.*

Greeley House again. Could it be a school? A theater? A church of some sort? Why else would she be dressed as a dime-store angel?

Anne stared at the photo of Jennie. The dress was too big, hanging awkwardly, the sleeves ending well below the wrists. The wings seemed to be giving Jennie trouble, and she'd thrust both arms out, as if to help balance herself. Instead of the intended cherubic effect, Jennie looked as though she were about to be devoured by a huge, angry insect.

Help me, Jennie's eyes seemed to beg. *Save me*. Once again Anne was struck by the familiarity of the image. She'd seen Jennie before.

The clock downstairs struck midnight, chiming out the hours. Bronte sneezed and stopped batting the ball.

No, not Jennie herself. Someone like her.

Anne's mind flew to the photos on the adoption agency's walls. Was it there, amid the blank dull eyes of the children, that she'd caught a glimpse of Jennie? This woman-child, this unhappy angel would have been Anne's second cousin, too. If she could talk, what secrets would she tell?

Chapter 17

Dogs, like people, have no control over snoring. Breeds with flat, pushed-in faces have a natural tendency to breathe loudly, snort, and snore. Since this is a physical and not a behavioral problem, your best bet is to have your pooch sleep as far from your bedroom as possible.

During the night, Anne woke to find Bronte's face inches from hers. The pug was curled on her stomach, snoring like a sailor. Anne propped herself up on one elbow and instinctively looked around for Harry. She always left a light on in the hall bathroom so the bedroom wouldn't be pitch-black and now this faint illumination revealed the cat's silhouette on top of the bureau. Harry's yellow eye gleamed like topaz.

"Come here, boy," Anne said into the darkness. "Come here, Harry."

In answer, the cat leaped from his perch and padded noiselessly out of the room. Harry usually slept at the foot of the bed, sometimes resting on Anne's feet, which in winter made for a pleasant hot water bottle.

The curtains lifted with the summer breeze, revealing a picturesque crescent moon. Anne turned on her side. It was a hot night. She tried to concentrate on the rhythmic crash of the waves, but her mind kept bobbing from one thought to the next.

When she finally drifted off, her sleep was troubled. She dreamed she was walking on the moss-covered rocks by the fishing pier. Low tide. A school of brightly colored fish swam beside her. The sun beat down on her head, coating the water with a metallic silver glaze.

"Annie."

She spun around. It was one of the fish, an orange-and-black fluke with a huge blue eye and the face of Alex Miller.

"Help me," Alex implored. "Save me before it's too late."

She walked faster, nearly slipping on the slick, wet rocks.

Her cousins thrashed about in the water, swimming after her in pursuit. Alex, Cece, Kim. Henry. Aunt Hannah's dead white face floating above the waves, Ophelia, aged and drowned.

"You said you'd help me," Hannah croaked. "You promised. Now see what you've done."

A cold bony hand grabbed Anne's ankle and she tumbled into the sea. Down, down, down. A ringing in her ears. Salt water flooding her eyes, mouth, nose. She fought the weight of the water, paddling frantically, trying to propel herself toward the surface. Panic electrified her limbs. She watched in horror as they jerked spastically, like a puppet. The ringing louder now. A brash *waaaah* puncturing the bubble of sleep.

She woke with a start to daylight and the shrill sound of a siren screaming its way down Ocean Avenue, as Bronte barked in unison. Throwing off the covers, she went to the window and peered out. An ambulance was just pulling up to the curb across the street, next to three black-and-white Neptune Township Sheriff's Office cars. Police officers milled about the boardwalk. A crowd had started to gather and a cop was pushing people off the boardwalk and onto the grass, penned behind a strip of yellow police tape.

It was Sunday. The beach didn't officially open until noon. Anne glanced at the clock on her nightstand: 8:37 A.M. She threw on a pair of shorts and a T-shirt and fumbled with the laces on her sneakers. Bronte wouldn't stop barking and jumping up and down in excitement. A chill crept up Anne's spine and the back of her neck began to tingle. Something bad had happened out there. She took the stairs two at a time, passing a startled Harry, who let out a screech.

As she stepped outside the house, a blast of humid air hit her squarely in the face. Hurrying down the porch steps, she ran toward the boardwalk. It was as though she were still half in dream sleep. The oppressive heat. The swell of the waves. The dark specter of death. Out of the corner of her eye, she saw several cops approaching, waving her back. But she ignored them. She reached the railing that separated beach from boardwalk and stopped short, staring at the black plastic body bag on the sand.

Two EMTs were zipping the bag shut. But before they finished the job, before Ed Burns sprinted over and dragged Anne behind the yellow police tape, before the horror settled in and she began screaming, unintelligibly at first, but then repeating one name again and again, she caught a glimpse of what lay inside. Blue-and-green-plaid dress, ashen skin, bangs, headband. And then the bag closed and Kim was gone.

She'd gone out for a walk. She'd needed some air. She'd had a migraine. She'd gotten some aspirin. She'd been depressed. Or mugged. Or mad. She'd had a fight with her husband. She'd had too much to drink. She'd lost her way. She'd planned to meet someone. She'd taken a lover. She'd been in the wrong place at the wrong time.

These theories and a dozen others were floating around town in an attempt to explain why Kim Ryerson, forty-four, from Newton, Massachusetts, was found dead of multiple stab wounds under the Oceanside Heights boardwalk. The body was discovered facedown in the sand by a group of eleven-year-old boys—friends vacationing from Delaware with their parents—who'd ignored the fact that the beach was closed until noon on Sundays and had begun to play a spirited game of touch football at about eight-fifteen A.M.

The woman they'd stumbled upon was covered with blood, the sand stained reddish-brown. Her pocketbook, an expensive navy leather Coach bag, rested not far from where she lay, its contents, including wallet, intact. There had been fourteen stab wounds in all, the deepest cut lacerating her heart so severely that the medical examiner reported it alone had been the probable cause of death, rendering the other wounds all but superfluous. There was no evidence of sexual assault and little indication of a struggle.

But Anne learned none of this at the time. All she knew was that Kim had been brutally murdered a mere two hundred yards from her house. Anne passed the morning in a sorrowful haze, interrupted by fits of crying and a smoldering anger that she felt slowly expanding inside her chest, each time she drew breath.

She and her cousins were holed up in a back parlor at the

Laughing Gull, alternately crying and reminiscing, instantly closing ranks, adopting an us-versus-them mentality toward the police, the news media, and outsiders in general. It was just like the old days, except now there were four instead of five.

Larry wandered in a couple of times between bouts of talking to the police, but he didn't say much or offer his own explanation. His grief (if you could call it that; Anne never saw him shed a tear or express any outward sign of sadness) was manifested by his subdued manner and by the fact that the anger he usually displayed in any and all situations had evaporated as quickly as mist blowing off the ocean. According to Larry, he'd gone to sleep at eleven P.M., as usual. Kim had been in bed reading. When he awoke at eight o'clock that morning she was gone. He'd called his daughters to break the news to them and had considered having Kim's body shipped back to Massachusetts as soon as the medical examiner would release it. But he decided she'd prefer to be buried near where she grew up, in the family plot at the cemetery outside of town. So he began the sad task of notifying friends and relatives. The funeral service was scheduled for Wednesday morning.

Bits of memories came back to Anne: Kim's collection of stray dolls, with their missing limbs and torn dresses. Kim teaching Anne to ride a bicycle. The day Kim broke her first pair of glasses and taped them back together rather than asking her parents to buy her a new pair. Kim styling Anne's hair for hours before the junior prom. Kim ripping open her SAT scores, ecstatic that she'd scored high enough to get into the University of Pennsylvania. Kim on her wedding day, pale and lovely in a Victorian-style satin gown with a high lace collar and puffy sleeves.

A single question echoed through Anne's mind: Why? Why? Why? Why would anyone want to hurt Kim? A kind, genteel, reliable woman who never had a bad word for anyone and who'd devoted her entire life to caring for her husband and children. It couldn't have been a mugging, Anne thought. No one had ever been mugged in Oceanside Heights for as long as she'd lived there. No, the only reason Kim was at The Place under the boardwalk was that she'd gone to meet someone and that person had killed her.

But no one besides the five of them knew about the spot under the boardwalk. Anne gazed at each of her cousins in turn. Nora's eyes were bloodshot from crying. Alex, who wore the sad, scared look of a lost boy, had his arm around Cece's shoulders. Cece was taking it the hardest of all. She appeared to be drowning in grief, so hysterical that she could barely speak without bursting into fits of sobbing. It was inconceivable that any of them could have laid a hand on Kim.

Then who? The same person who'd killed Aunt Hannah. Who'd lashed out with a knife, stabbing again and again and again, well past the point where the victim had drawn her final breath. She caught a glimpse of Larry speaking woodenly into his cell phone. Why had Larry married Kim in the first place? He never seemed to have loved her. And she hadn't brought a lot of income to the marriage. No, in Kim Larry had found a cook/maid/nanny who took care of his home life so he could run his business.

Larry took Kim for granted. He tolerated Kim. But he bore no great animosity toward her and had no motive for killing her. Unless . . .

Anne thought back to yesterday afternoon on the beach. (God, only yesterday Kim had been alive, petting Bronte and digging her toes into the hot sand.) Kim had been scared, Anne saw that now. But scared of what? Or whom? She remembered how Larry had taken hold of Kim's hand and how it had made Kim's face light up. Larry might not have loved Kim, but Kim loved her husband. She would have done anything for Larry—defend his faults, go begging to Aunt Hannah for money, lie or deny. *For better or worse. For richer or poorer, till death do us part.* Kim, on her wedding day, so innocent and trusting, so ready to forgive.

The answer came to Anne in a flash of insight: Kim was protecting Larry. That's why she'd been so scared. She was afraid Larry would get caught. Doing what? Killing Hannah? It could have happened that way. Larry, desperate to save his ailing company. Hannah refusing to help. The knife raining down blows in a flurry of anger.

That would explain why Kim had looked so terrified outside Dovecote the morning of the murder. Anyone would have been upset to discover a relative's dead body, but Kim had seemed panicked. Had she suspected Larry's involvement, noticed that he'd left the Laughing Gull in the middle of the night, maybe even spotted traces of blood on his clothes?

But then why would Larry kill his wife? He had nothing to fear from Kim. She would have protected him, no matter what.

Anne wiped more tears from her eyes with a balled-up napkin. Bronte gazed up at her plaintively with an expression of concern. Could dogs sense when people were grieving? Did they become sad in turn?

There was a sharp knock at the door and Pat poked her head in, bearing a tray laden with sandwiches and soft drinks.

"I made a light lunch. Turkey and chives with cranberry dressing," she said, setting the tray on a low coffee table cluttered with books, magazines, knickknacks, and mail.

The back parlor was part of Pat's private quarters and didn't look like it had been cleaned in some time. Old newspapers were piled on the floor, along with towels and sheets from the guests' rooms that had yet to be washed. The TV was so dusty you could have scrawled your name across the front. Small appliances that Pat had collected, but hadn't yet repaired, were strewn on chairs, bookshelves, the mantel, and the breakfront, making the parlor look like a cross between a fix-it shop and the sale aisle at Odd-Job.

"I don't think any of us are hungry," Alex replied.

Pat ignored him, setting the tray down with a thunk and causing a tower of magazines to topple against one of the glasses, spilling soda all over the place. Bronte let out a series of rapid barks.

"Damn it," Pat exclaimed. "My nerves are shot. There are all these reporters outside, sniffing around like a pack of wild dogs. My girls aren't getting a lick of work done because they're too preoccupied with being on TV."

Anne glanced up. "Maybe we should go back to my house."

"Don't you dare," Pat said quickly, wiping her hands on her dirty, food-stained apron. "You're welcome to camp out here as long as you like."

But Anne could see that the strain brought on by the jackal pack was affecting the innkeeper. Pat's right eye had started to twitch again. She looked tired and spent, like a washcloth that had been wrung dry. She probably wished that Anne's relatives had chosen another B&B for their ill-fated family reunion.

"Thanks, Patty," Alex said. "You're a sweetie."

Pat blushed to the roots of her hairline. She seemed flustered and self-conscious, as if realizing for the first time how disheveled she appeared. Turning to Anne, she said, "Detective Burns is out front. He said he needs to speak with you again."

Anne's stomach did a sudden flip-flop. That man wouldn't leave her alone. He'd already questioned her about

Kim's death that morning, at a time when she could barely speak coherently without bursting into tears.

"Don't talk to him, Annie," Nora advised. "You don't have to utter a word unless your lawyer is present."

"Nora's right," Alex put in. "You probably shouldn't have said anything to him earlier."

Anne considered her options. Since Kim's death, she and Alex had reached a sort of détente, bonding in grief. A part of her agreed with him. But another part wondered if Alex had a hidden agenda: The more she talked to the police, the greater the chance that she might implicate him in Aunt Hannah's murder.

Nora had hired a lawyer from Manhattan named Mike Callahan to represent Anne. But Mr. Callahan couldn't come to the Heights until the next day, leaving her stuck with the court-appointed lawyer in the interim.

"I'll see Burns," Anne said aloud. Turning to Bronte, she commanded the dog to "stay."

What was the point of postponing the inevitable? She felt a little stronger now. Anger had penetrated her sadness. Besides, maybe she could get a lead on how the investigation was proceeding.

She followed Pat into the breakfast nook, a sun-dappled, cheery space strewn with the remains of the Parmesan muffins and oregano and olive omelets that the guests had eaten that morning.

Ed Burns was sitting at the dining table, which had been painted seafoam-green and stenciled with images of seashells, crabs, and clams. He wore a gray pinstriped suit and a brightly patterned tie.

"Hello there, Miss Hardaway," he called out cheerily when Anne walked in.

Somehow this ebullient greeting chilled her more than if

he had presented his usual dour face. She sat down at the table, as far away from him as possible.

"Feeling any better?" Burns asked.

She threw a withering glance in his direction. *Sure, why not,* she felt like saying sarcastically. *It's been over three hours. Who cares that my cousin is dead?*

Instead she chose not to reply at all, studying a crack in the table that resembled the outline of a rabbit.

Burns turned toward Pat, who'd been hovering in the doorway. "Would you excuse us? I need to speak with Miss Hardaway in private."

"Oh, sure," Pat said, backing out of the room, her hands fluttering in the air like wayward moths. The door gave a sharp click when it closed.

"Now then," Burns said, smiling at Anne and revealing a set of stained, crooked teeth. "I'd like to review your whereabouts last night one more time."

She silently counted to ten, willing herself to stay calm and in control. They'd been over this earlier—how she'd strolled with Bronte on the boardwalk, gone home, been in bed by midnight. Now she repeated it, speaking slowly and carefully, aware that the detective had a personal ax to grind with Trasker and would like nothing better than to make her pay.

"So you're sticking to your story," Burns said when she'd finished. He'd been jotting things down in his notebook, although from the distance that separated them, Anne couldn't tell whether he was taking notes or just doodling.

"It's not a story," she replied curtly. "It's the truth."

"Is that so?"

Burns stood up and walked over to her, planting himself right in front of her chair. She resisted the urge to flee, to escape this man who'd become her chief tormentor.

"Some new information has come to light," Burns said, never taking his eyes off her.

"How interesting," Anne said coldly.

"We think so."

From this angle, Anne could see that whoever cut Burns's beard had done a sloppy job. The hair under his chin was uneven, longer on one side than the other.

"It seems that a neighbor of yours, a Mrs. Martha Cox . . ."

Here Burns paused, awaiting some sign of recognition.

Anne's expression didn't change. Sure, she knew Martha Cox. The meddlesome old biddy lived next door and was forever complaining about the sorry state of Anne's garden.

Burns said, "It seems that Mrs. Cox has a touch of insomnia. She was looking out her window at half-past twelve and chanced to see you crossing the street from the boardwalk and going up your front walk."

"Mrs. Cox wears bifocals," Anne shot back. "She wouldn't recognize her own mother coming toward her on a dark, foggy night."

"Nevertheless," Burns continued, "the lady's certain it was you. She's willing to swear to it in court."

Anne put her hand to her mouth so she was smelling her own skin instead of his sour coffee- and cigarette-laced breath.

She said, "You're implying that I had something to do with my own cousin's death. Why would that be?"

An oily, self-satisfied smile appeared on Burns's lips. "There are all kinds of animosities in families. Maybe she had something on you. She's been hiding something, acting weird." Burns was looming over her, so close she could see the pores of his skin and the faint shadows under his eyes. "Or maybe she just plain ticked you off."

Anne felt her body tighten in dislike and fear. *Don't panic,* she told herself. *That's what he wants.* "The knife," she managed to say. "Was it similar to the one used on Hannah?"

"Why, how perceptive of you." Burns smirked. "However did you guess?"

Anne had a sudden vision of Burns entering her kitchen and removing her knives, dropping them neatly into his police regulation plastic baggie.

She felt if she didn't get away from him soon, she'd suffocate.

When she spoke, her voice sounded thick and fuzzy. "If you think I did it, Kim must have been killed some time after midnight."

Burns laughed harshly and Anne recoiled further. "Honey," he chortled, "you need a better alibi." He leaned forward so that he was just inches away from her face, close enough to kiss her. "Are you sure you weren't with one of Neptune's finest? Your dark knight in shining armor, for instance?"

That's it, Anne thought. *This guy's got to be stopped.* She bolted from her chair, catching Burns off-balance, just as Bronte burst into the room, followed by Nora. The dog jumped up and put her front paws on Anne's legs, barking in delight. She almost looked adorable.

"Sorry for the interruption," said Nora, though she didn't appear to be, not in the least. She reminded Anne of a somber Madonna in a medieval altar panel, grieving yet lovely.

"We need to go over some final arrangements," she said to Anne. Then, turning to Burns, "You understand, I'm sure."

He nodded and fidgeted, flustered as most men were in the presence of Nora's beauty. "I'll be in touch," he said, and to Anne's amazement, made a half-bow in Nora's direction.

When he'd gone, Nora shut the door again and sank onto a chair. Bronte was still barking happily, so Anne picked up the dog and set her gently on her lap. The pug snuggled in as if she and Anne were old friends.

"Thanks for the rescue," Anne said.

"Please, please don't talk to the police again without your new lawyer present. There's no telling how the cops could twist things."

Anne shrugged. The morning had left her emotionally spent.

"I didn't do anything wrong," she said, "so there's nothing to be worried about."

The words were true, but even as she spoke, Anne could hear how hollow they sounded. Just as hollow as when Kim had said them the day before. If she were an outsider looking in, she'd consider herself a prime suspect, too.

"Have you seen Henry around?" she asked Nora.

"Not since yesterday. The police were looking for him this morning, but he's probably long gone. You know how good he is at disappearing," Nora said, arching her eyebrows. "Listen, I came in here to tell you something. Mark phoned just now and I spoke with him briefly. He has news for you. He wants you to call him right away."

Anne felt a stab of jealousy. In her pale pink silk blouse, white Capri pants, and designer spike heel sandals, Nora looked stunning, even in the face of tragedy. Anne remembered how in seventh grade, Nora had stolen away a boy she'd liked. Not intentionally. Just by being Nora—beautiful, poised, unattainable.

Oh, don't be such a ninny, Anne scolded herself. *Nora's leaving in a day or two. And she'd never interfere in your happiness, anyway.*

"What's wrong?" Nora asked. She was staring at Anne apprehensively, her cornflower-blue eyes assessing the situation. "Besides the obvious, I mean."

"Trasker told me about the problems you've been having with your company."

There, it was finally out in the open. No more skirting the issue and trying to draw Nora out. Although Anne realized she'd chosen this moment deliberately, when she was feeling threatened. She was closer to Nora than any of her other relatives, but sometimes, when you flew too close to Nora's flame, you got burned.

Nora waved her hand dismissively. "I don't know what you're talking about."

"The embezzlement charges. Trasker says there's a state investigation under way and you might owe your shareholders millions of dollars."

Drawing herself up to her full height, Nora assumed her classic modeling pose—aloof stance, chin tilted, expression haughty and cold. "Obviously, he's been misinformed," she said, in a clipped tone. "We had a slight problem with a couple of our investors, but it's all been taken care of."

She pivoted in one fluid motion and faced the door. Back in high school, Nora had shown Anne her modeling moves: the strut, the slouch, the way you never made eye contact on the runway or acknowledged anyone else was in the room. But Anne could never get the attitude down pat. She always felt too self-conscious, too ridiculous.

"Nora, wait," Anne called out, as her cousin reached the door. "Don't go like this."

Nora spun around, graceful as a gymnast atop a balance beam. "Why don't you worry about your own problems, Annie. The murder charge. Burns. The disappearing steak knife." Her eyes flashed angrily. "And as for that boyfriend of yours, maybe he shouldn't be poking his nose into Florida law."

"Nora, I just . . ."

"Save it," Nora snapped. "I've got to see about the funeral."

She slunk out of the room, and Anne was alone with the dog.

"What do you think?" Anne asked, stroking Bronte's head. "Is she telling the truth?"

A rhetorical question. Just like her brother, Nora lied as easily as she drew breath. People wanted to believe her, they wanted to be fooled, just as Anne wanted to believe right now.

What was the old saying? Truth is beauty and beauty truth. Except in Nora's case, where over the years, beauty had reclined like a princess on a rose-petal bed of tissue-thin lies.

Chapter 18

To correct your dog's behavior while walking him, jerk the leash quickly toward your right side and slightly upward. At the same time, give a firm verbal command: "No." Then quickly release your wrist and forearm, returning to your original position. Immediately following this, give your dog a great deal of enthusiastic praise, such as "Good girl," "Good dog," or "Attaboy."

Between Oceanside Heights and Landsdown Park sat a defunct amusement park that had once enlivened summer afternoons with colorful rides and games. Featuring ornate arches, gold minarets, twin towers, and colonnades, it was meant to re-create an Arabian fantasy.

This was back in the days when swan-shaped boats plied the lake that separated the two towns and red-and-white-striped bathing tents dotted the beaches.

Anne's mother had told her about some of the attractions at the Dreamland amusement park: the barrel rides, the spaceship that vibrated so furiously that couples were thrown against each other, the giant seesaw, the flea circus, the painted carts pulled by goats, the mineral cures.

Anne remembered one story her mother had told of a family who worked at Dreamland, returning year after year. The father sold tickets and was so strong he could lift two grown men over his head at once. The mother was known as the Lady Flame for her ability to swallow a fiery sword. The eldest son was so flexible he could bounce like a rubber ball, while the youngest gained fame by walking barefoot on a bed of nails. The daughter was supposedly so unsightly that if you looked at her in the daylight your eyes would hurt for days. She was called the Turtle Girl—a deformed creature, with scaly arms and a hard, spotted shell.

Anne wondered if when the family wasn't working they were able to lead normal lives. Maybe the sons did their homework at the kitchen table and the mother clipped coupons and did laundry. Maybe the girl slipped out of her shell and danced barefoot to the radio, pretending to be in love.

Dreamland had closed in 1965. Every so often, there'd be a fund-raising drive to restore the park to its former glory. But nothing concrete ever happened. The cost was too great; there was too much competition on the shore to the south.

Now the mint-colored walls of the pavilion rose up in front of her, plastered with faded advertisements for the Dreamland Museum. *Living Wonders of the World,* a sign promised. *Freaks of Wax. Spook House—Come One, Come All!*

Anne had been inside Dreamland only once, when a deranged killer had pushed her down a hole in the foundation and set the entire place on fire. That had been four years ago, and she had no desire to go back inside.

Instead she and Bronte skirted the building and slipped through a gaping hole in the chain-link fence surrounding the park. They walked west, away from the water, with Bronte stopping short or veering off course every time something interesting caught her attention. A small carousel stood next to a decrepit stand that had once sold deviled clams or plum pudding. The carousel had a domed mint-green roof, with a clown's face painted on the side. Weather and time had faded the picture so that an eye and part of his mouth had been erased. Even without the damage, it was clear that he'd been a melancholy clown, with a sad, down-cast expression and a tear languishing on one powdery white cheek.

Trasker was sitting near the clown, on the edge of the wooden platform that constituted the floor of the carousel. Instead of his usual suit, he wore khaki slacks, loafers, and a navy short-sleeved polo shirt, a concession to the fact that it was Sunday, as well as ninety degrees. A cooler sat beside him, from which he'd removed two cans of soda, a bag of Doritos, a couple of sandwiches, and a bunch of red grapes. He'd set the food on a checkered tablecloth next to the cooler, which Anne recognized from many picnics spent down the shore. He kept it in a wicker basket in the trunk of his car. You never know when you're going to want to eat outside, he liked to say.

He waved in greeting. "Hey, Annie," he called out. "This place is something else."

Anne smiled in acknowledgment. She'd been the one to choose the carousel as a rendezvous spot. She didn't feel up to braving the stares at a restaurant, and she couldn't face wading through the sea of reporters camped outside her house. The carousel was shielded from the road by the hulking remains of Dreamland and from the beach by a dilapidated brick building that had once housed penny arcades. It was about as private as you could get.

The moment he took her in his arms she felt better. Lighter. As if his mere presence reminded her there were other things in this world besides murder and death. He hugged her tight, rocking from side to side ever so slightly so that it would have seemed, to anyone watching, that they were slow dancing. Even in the midst of her grief, Anne could feel the sexual heat between them.

She pressed herself against him, aware of how strong and muscular his body felt, how he smelled clean and sweet as summer.

"I'm so sorry about Kim," he said, stroking her hair.

"I just can't believe it," she whispered, suddenly on the verge of tears again. "I can't believe she's dead."

"I know." His lips brushed against her cheek, forehead, lips. She felt desire break over her like a wave. She wished that they were back in his apartment, back in his bed making love. It was as though she'd ingested poison and his caresses were the antidote.

Reluctantly she let herself be led to the platform, where lunch awaited. Trasker was a terrific cook. He could take an ordinary can of tuna fish or a couple of eggs, and by the time he got done, you'd swear you were eating a dish that cost $24.99 at a fancy New York restaurant.

Now he held out one of his famous meat loaf sandwiches. But Anne had no appetite.

"I can't," she protested. "Maybe later."

Trasker nodded sympathetically. Taking another sandwich from the cooler, he removed the meat and offered it to Bronte, who chowed down with enthusiasm.

He and the dog ate in silence for a while. It was so hot that every movement seemed to require extra effort. Nothing moved. Even the birds appeared to be hiding.

Anne felt beads of perspiration trickle down her face and collect on the backs of her knees. She was incredibly tired, as though she'd run a marathon and still wasn't able to cool down or catch her breath. It felt like they were the only people in the world, three figures amid the hot desolate landscape. She'd seen a *Twilight Zone* episode like that once. In the aftermath of nuclear war, only one person survived. Burgess Meredith played a solitary man whose only joy in life was to read books. Delighted to be left alone in a library with no one to disturb him, he seemed untouched by the devastation—until his glasses broke.

"There's no blood on the knife," Trasker said, breaking the silence.

She turned toward him, startled. "What?"

He wiped his fingers on one of the cloth napkins he'd brought. "That's what I wanted to tell you. Only not at the office. And not over the phone. I'm not supposed to go within a hundred yards of this case, remember? But a buddy of mine in forensics over in the M.E.'s office in Newark owed me a favor. He pulled the report."

Anne sat up straighter. Bronte was nosing through the bag of chips.

"I'm not following you," Anne said.

"Okay. Here's the thing. Your fingerprints were on the knife that killed your Aunt Hannah. And the blade matched the type of stab wounds inflicted. But there wasn't one trace of blood on the weapon."

"Because the killer wiped the blood off before throwing the knife away."

Trasker shook his head. "Unlikely. If you were to wipe every trace of blood off a knife—run it under water, use a rag, whatever—you'd probably erase the prints along with the blood, or at the very least do so much damage to the prints that they'd be almost impossible to read. They're doing some DNA testing right now, but my guess is they'll only be able to match your DNA, not Hannah's."

Anne's mind was racing. "Which means that someone definitely set me up."

"Looks like." Trasker took the napkin and mopped his brow. "Where's the rest of your silverware?"

"In one of my kitchen drawers."

"When's the last time you took a good look at it?"

Anne had a sudden sick feeling in her stomach. "I don't know. Back in the spring, I guess, when I cleaned the entire kitchen on a whim."

"Well, a team of cops has probably confiscated the whole damn drawer by now."

The sickening feeling intensified. "There was nobody home this morning."

"Doesn't matter. It'd be easy to get a warrant. Probable cause and all."

Anne felt herself choke back panic. "But what you said before? About the blood."

Trasker shrugged. "They have to pursue every lead, baby. And I'm betting there's a knife in your silverware drawer whose blade and size correspond to the stab wounds on Kim's body."

"Because the killer took it."

"Maybe."

Bronte yawned and stretched out on the grass. The heat was starting to get to the pug. She looked tired and lethargic.

Anne surveyed the array of carousel horses behind her. Much of the paint had faded or been chipped off the wood, leaving them with bald patches here and there. But their poses were still expressive—nostrils flaring, legs prancing, necks straining, as though wanting to break loose from their stable of brass poles. They reminded Anne of her childhood, of riding the carousel all afternoon with her cousins, the music loud and brassy, the pleasure in picking a horse—the dappled bay, the white stallion?—the way it had felt like she was flying.

Oh, Kim. If only this hadn't happened to you . . .

"Who's been in your house the last couple of days?" Trasker asked.

"Nora and Cece. That's about it. Except for Detective Burns."

"Ed's a hardhead. And a bigot. He'd love to be able to pin something on me, get Internal Affairs involved. But I don't think he'd commit two murders just to end an interracial relationship."

Anne wasn't so sure. There was something menacing about Ed Burns. She knew he would like nothing better than to see her in jail for a murder she didn't commit.

Trasker started to pack up the picnic things. "What are you going to do for the rest of the day? I don't want you to be alone."

Anne had a sudden thought. "I want to get inside Kim's room. Could you help me?"

Trasker studied her face, then offered another handful of chips to the dog. "I don't see why not."

The back entrance to the Laughing Gull was located near a hose that Pat had hooked up for the sole purpose of encouraging guests to wash their feet before they came in from the beach. Most people were too lazy or in too much of a rush to use it, Pat had told Anne, resulting in sand clogging bathtub drains, lodging in cracks in the floorboards, and winding up trapped in people's bedclothes. But Pat left the back door ajar anyway, in the hope, as she put it, that some of the tourists would "grow some manners."

Anne and Trasker crept up the stairway, with Anne holding Bronte, who seemed grateful to be indoors and out of the heat. Anne knocked lightly on the door of Kim's room, in case Larry was inside. No response from within. She tried the knob. Locked. She heard a radio playing somewhere nearby, the sound of a door slamming, voices floating through the open window at the end of the hall, which faced the street.

Now what? she thought. She'd never considered exactly how they'd get in.

Trasker reached into his pocket, pulled out his wallet, and removed a three-inch-long piece of metal that curved at the top and looked a little like an oversize hairpin.

"Hey," yelled a voice. "Get away from there."

They wheeled around and saw a young police officer standing at the top of the stairs. Anne didn't recognize him. Trasker flashed his badge.

"Detective Mark Trasker," he said briskly. "Neptune Township Sheriff's Office. I need immediate access to this room."

The policeman hesitated, staring warily at Anne. He looked to be in his early twenties, with downy skin and pale gray eyes. The silver nameplate on his chest said *Reilly*.

"This area is off-limits to nonessential personnel," Reilly said.

"I realize that, Officer," Trasker said, using an authoritative voice that Anne had rarely heard. "But this woman is the victim's cousin and I need to ask her about some of the victim's belongings."

Reilly hesitated, thinking the matter over. "I don't know, Detective. I think I'd better clear it with the captain."

A man down the hall opened his door, took in the scene,

and then quickly closed it again. They'd gotten more than they'd bargained for on this vacation, Anne thought ruefully.

Trasker pulled out his cell phone. "I don't have time for this shit," he said brusquely. "What's your captain's number?"

A frightened expression appeared on Reilly's face. Anne could see him envisioning the consequences of angering a detective—a dressing-down, a demotion, or worse.

"There's no need, Detective." Reilly waved his hands like a white flag. "Just make it quick," he said with false bravado, trying to gain back some lost ground.

Trasker glared at Reilly until the cop turned away and headed back down the stairs. Then he took out what looked like a manicure set and inserted a nail file–type object into the lock, easing it gently up and down. Anne heard a click, Trasker turned the knob, and just like that, they were inside.

The room looked much as it had when Anne had seen it on Thursday. The bed was unmade, the curtains drawn. And everywhere were images of birds.

Pat had dubbed this her Foul-weather Room. If it rained, she was fond of saying, you could bird-watch indoors. Though smoking was prohibited, swan-shaped ashtrays adorned the nightstands. A nest with three tiny blue eggs in it sat on the dresser, next to a small statue of a heron made of glass and an *Audubon Field Guide to the Birds of North America*. One needlepoint pillow featured a flock of pelicans on a beach, another depicted Tweety Bird being gripped in the paw of an irate Sylvester the cat. Wallpaper showed the inn's namesake gulls diving, soaring, and executing loop-the-loops in the air.

"What are you looking for?" Trasker asked.

"I'm not sure. I guess something that explains why anyone would want to kill her."

She surveyed the personal belongings on the dresser: a

pair of sunglasses, a sun visor, a makeup case, a sewing basket, a couple of women's magazines, and a book on investment strategies, which probably belonged to Larry.

She began sifting through the magazines. There were the August issue of *House Beautiful, Martha Stewart Living, The New Yorker*, and *Good Housekeeping*. Anne thumbed through the last. It had stories titled "Slim Down! 30-Minute Menus," "Why Loving Parents *Shouldn't* Be Fair," and "Prettier Skin in 5 Minutes."

Tucked between the last two pages was a sheet of lined paper. In a lovely, flowing hand, the letters delicate yet precise, Kim had practiced her calligraphy. *Kim Ryerson*, Kim had written. *The Ryersons. Mr. and Mrs. Larry Ryerson*. All up and down the page. On the nightstand next to the bed sat the ink Kim had used. Jet-black India ink in a glass bottle with a silver stopper on top. And next to that, an old-fashioned pen to dip in the ink and a needlepoint pillow Kim had been sewing.

Trasker had gone to the window and was gazing out, making sure to conceal himself behind the green cheesecloth curtains. Bronte sat on the floor, idly chewing a loop of thread that had escaped from Kim's sewing basket.

"Stay," Anne commanded, though it was clear Bronte wasn't planning on going anywhere. The dog looked cool and content.

"I don't think we have much time," Trasker said. "Reilly might decide to call his commanding officer about us after all. Or any one of those cops milling around on the beach may get a hankering to play detective. You have no idea how many people sift through a victim's personal belongings after a murder has occurred."

"I'm almost done, I guess," Anne said, thinking that if Trasker lost his job because of her she'd never forgive herself.

She went over to the closet, opened the door, and was immediately hit with the scent of cheap perfume. Kim had packed too much for a weekend trip: more than a dozen skirts, dresses, blouses, and Bermuda shorts hung on padded pink hangers brought from home. Her shoes were lined up neatly on the floor—espadrilles, flat-soled sandals, demure pumps.

Anne gazed at Larry's side of the closet, which contained a blazer, a pair of khaki trousers, a light blue long-sleeved cotton shirt, and a straw hat. She leaned in and sniffed the collar of the shirt. Just as she suspected, the scent of perfume was strongest there. Only problem was, it was a brand Anne felt sure Kim never wore. For as long as Anne could remember, Kim had splashed Jean Naté on her wrists and earlobes. Anne picked up the sleeve of Kim's pink cotton sweater and held it to her nose. She smelled the light floral notes of Jean Naté. It made her sad.

Turning to Trasker, she said, "I think Larry might be having an affair."

She told him about the perfume discrepancy.

"Interesting," Trasker mused. "Do you think Kim knew about it?"

Anne pondered the question. Kim had looked so happy yesterday on the beach, not at all like a woman who suspected her husband was cheating on her. On the other hand, what would Kim have done if she *had* known? Anne couldn't picture Kim leaving Larry, getting a divorce, living on her own. Kim had been with Larry too long to start over. In a weird way, she needed him to need her. Maybe that's why the marriage had lasted so long.

"I don't know," Anne said finally.

"It raises some interesting questions. What's struck me about both these murders is the number of times the victims were stabbed. It indicates that the killer was probably enraged, as opposed to a random act of violence committed solely for the purpose of say, robbery."

Anne closed the closet door. She was feeling claustrophobic, edgy. She couldn't stand to look at Kim's belongings another minute. "Meaning?"

"What if you're right and Larry *was* having an affair? What if the woman wanted Larry to receive a share of Aunt Hannah's fortune and then wanted Kim out of the way?"

Anne's mind was reeling. "If that's true, what's our next move?"

Trasker went to the door, opened it a crack, and peered out. "We find out who the mystery woman is."

Chapter 19

To successfully house-break your dog, you need to work out a walking and feeding schedule and stick with it. Fifteen or twenty minutes of play is all the average puppy can handle before needing another outing. Initially, between outings, keep your pup in a wire crate. He'll want to keep his crate clean and dry. Over time, give him progressively longer periods of freedom after each walk and before he's confined to the crate again. After a few months, he should be down to three walks per day.

The library in Oceanside Heights was situated in a sky-blue Victorian cottage, with cheery white shutters, gingerbread trim, a wraparound porch, and a picket fence, also painted white.

Anne often found herself ensconced there, doing research for her books. It didn't hurt that one of Anne's closest friends was Delia Graustark, the seventy-five-year-old librarian, who was thrilled to find herself mentioned in the acknowledgment section of many of the books Anne had ghosted.

Though the library was closed on Sundays, Delia had long ago made Anne a spare key. This particular weekend, Delia was away on a bus trip to the Amish country in Pennsylvania. She'd promised to bring Anne back some handmade candles or jellies, whatever happened to catch her eye.

Opening the creaky blue door, Anne entered the front parlor, a cozy, walnut-paneled room with two window seats upholstered in a pastel brocade and several inviting floral-print armchairs. This was known as the reading room, a place to curl up with a good book and sample one of Delia's homemade fudge brownies or sugar cookies.

Anne passed Delia's big mahogany desk, which held a bouquet of wildflowers, and continued up the winding staircase to the second floor. Until recently the research section of the library had consisted of reams and reams of paper— old newspaper and magazine clippings, organized by subject matter and date—an arcane system, but one that Anne had found refreshingly helpful. Six months ago the entire research department was finally computerized, and Anne appreciated the change even more.

While researching Edie Mintzler's pet book, she'd had access to articles from all across the country on everything from housebreaking to car sickness. Anne walked into a room equipped with five computers, each one outfitted with its own small rag rug and office chairs that had dainty floral chintz slipcovers—touches Delia thought lent the room a homier air.

Anne eased into her favorite chair, the one farthest from the window so the sun's glare didn't affect the screen, and turned the computer on. This was probably a fool's errand. But she was out of ideas, out of clues, and out of time. Every passing hour brought her closer to being arrested again. Locked up for good this time, charged with double homicide. She had to do something, to fight back while she still could.

Something tugged at the corners of her mind. Something that had happened, right there in that room? What was it? She couldn't remember.

She turned her attention to the bookshelves above the computer. Delia had purchased a bunch of educational CD-ROMs for the kids and Anne idly looked at the titles on the shelf above her workstation: Sesame Street Search and Learn Adventures, JumpStart Kindergarten, School Zone Spelling. Whatever happened to learning your ABCs the old-fashioned way? With a workbook, ruled paper, and a sharpened number two pencil. Maybe the pundits were right. Maybe at some point computers would replace books and she'd be out of a job.

Punching several keys in a row, Anne entered the name and place she was interested in. The Greeley House, Point Pleasant Beach. She waited while the computer searched its enormous databank. Luckily, Greeley House wasn't a common name. When she'd typed in *dog* or *cat*, she got thousands of entries and it took a while to winnow the list down to what she needed.

Now there were a dozen or so entries in the *Oceanside Heights Press*, in the early and mid-1950s. She called them up on screen. Most read something like this:

The annual spring gala to benefit Greeley House will be held at the Palace Restaurant on April 13 at seven o'clock in the evening. Tickets are $10 apiece. Lamb, roast potatoes, a vegetable medley, and sherbet will be served. All interested parties are encouraged to call the Palace for reservations.

And this:

Attention crafts enthusiasts. The Greeley House in Point Pleasant Beach will hold a special crafts fair on August 26, from one to four o'clock in the afternoon. Among the objects on display are hand-stitched samplers, beaded bags, woven baskets, and paint-by-number drawings, suitable for framing.

It sounded like a school, Anne thought. She scrolled through the items, bringing up the same type of entries. Benefit parties, sales, an afternoon tea, an auction, nothing more concrete than that, until in 1956, she was rewarded with the following piece of information:

Fire Destroys Greeley House

A four-alarm fire swept through the Greeley House yesterday afternoon. No one knows what started the blaze, but Fire Commissioner Frank Schnitzer says he believes it might have been caused by a faulty electric heater. Three patients were injured trying to escape the flames, including Miss Doris Stouffer, who broke an ankle and had to be removed from the scene in an ambulance.

Fortunately, most of the occupants of the mental hospital were out of the building when the fire broke out, it being a Tuesday, when those who are able take a healthy promenade by the ocean, under the supervision of the staff.

"We are most distressed by this sad turn of events," said Miss Caroline Agate, the hospital's director. "The damage was so extensive that we will be forced to relocate our fine facility elsewhere, preferably at another site on the Jersey shore, where our girls can enjoy the sea air."

Founded by Dr. Sebastian Agate, the Greeley House has offered the latest technologies, cures, and therapies to mentally disturbed young ladies since 1933. All those interested in contributing to the new building fund are encouraged to call RE3-4551.

Anne stared at the screen. So Jennie was in a mental hospital. All those genteel auctions and teas supported a place that treated serious illnesses. She wondered what exactly had been wrong with Jennie. Whatever it was, it couldn't have pleased Aunt Hannah.

Anne was suddenly struck by an image of her mother running up and down Ocean Avenue, screaming at the top of her lungs that beetles were crawling inside her skin. But then Alzheimer's was a form of dementia and dementia seemed to run in her family. Did Jennie have Alzheimer's? Could you get it at such a young age?

There was only one way to find out.

All during Anne's childhood, the family could tell when Henry had been drinking. Not that anyone called it that. The doldrums, they'd say. The dark spells. Henry's troubled time.

The easiest way to tell was that Henry was suddenly around more. After staying secluded for weeks, he'd appear at a family picnic or a holiday meal, his eyes strangely bright, his cheeks feverish. He'd chatter away, his sentences running together like a sudden pile-up on the turnpike.

He was louder, funnier, looser, more charming. When Henry was on a bender—sometimes they lasted for days, sometimes as long as a week—he was nothing like the stereotypical drunk who falls down, slurs his speech, and makes a complete fool of himself. Far from it.

Anne remembered thinking as a child that when Henry had one of his "spells," he became his best self, the good-hearted, boisterous cousin she looked up to. When it was over, he retreated back into his shell, keeping to himself, withdrawing into the world of books. Aunt Hannah became slightly less tight-lipped and worried-looking, and things returned to normal, until the whole cycle started up again.

Henry could still hold his liquor well. Anne wondered if this was characteristic of a true alcoholic, the ability to carry on as if you weren't deeply inebriated. The ability to fake it, to glide across the surface of life and not take to your bed or spend half the day in the bathroom, retching into the toilet.

Her cousin drank alone, but he was also a social drinker, and Anne knew that when he was tanked, he craved the company of strangers. She'd watched him once holding court in a bar, and it had been something to see. Henry, surrounded by a dozen or so soused men and women, spinning some fabulous yarn and holding his audience as captive as he himself was to the bottle.

Since Oceanside Heights was a dry town, the best bars were next door in Landsdown Park. Anne went into several of them now. McSorley's, the Crazy Horse, Nick's, the Shady Lady. It was four o'clock on a Sunday afternoon. While the bars weren't full, they weren't empty, either. Hard-core drinkers, mostly men, nursed their drinks. Others sat in small groups watching the ball game on TV. The Phillies versus the Houston Astros.

Anne scanned each place for Henry. By the time she'd been to four of them, her clothes and hair reeked of smoke. Bronte didn't seem to mind. Anne had discovered that the pug liked new places. For a lap dog, she was pretty energetic.

In fact, it was Bronte who actually found Henry seated at a rickety corner table in the Blue Angel, a hole in the wall bar on Carver Street. He was with two older men and a middle-aged woman whose wild frizzy red hair and nose gave her a clownish appearance. They all looked as if they'd been drinking for hours. Bronte bounded over to Henry and put both paws in the air, begging to be fed the broken bits of pretzels and chips that sat in a bowl in the middle of the table. Instead, Henry stood up and with a deep bow, introduced his companions. He expressed no surprise that Anne had tracked him down.

Anne barely caught their names. She began steering Henry over to the bar, with Bronte bringing up the rear and Henry offering to buy another round for his new friends.

"What'll it be?" Henry said, when he'd gotten the bartender's attention. He spoke quickly, nearly tripping over the words. His eyes fairly glittered.

"Seltzer with lime."

"One seltzer and four scotch rocks, neat," Henry told the bartender. He parked himself on a stool to wait and his whole body seemed to sag. Anne sat down next to him. On the overhead screen, one of the Phillies struck out and Henry made a disgusted noise.

"I wanted to talk to you," Anne said. "About Jennie."

At the mention of his sister's name, Henry's features softened. "Jennie," he repeated dreamily. "Jennie Penny."

"What happened to her? Why was she in Greeley House?"

Henry's expression changed, becoming troubled and sad, as if remembering was too painful. "That place," he said disgustedly. "I went there once. They put on a good show, making the girls do needlepoint and serve afternoon tea. But do you know what went on there? They gave Jennie electric shock treatments. Electric shock!"

His voice had risen, but no one else in the bar seemed to care. The bartender came over with a tray of drinks. Henry plucked a scotch from the tray and knocked it back quickly. "For my friends," he said, waving in the direction of his table. The bartender set the glass of seltzer in front of Anne and took the tray of drinks over to where Henry's group was sitting.

"The doctors there were a bunch of quacks," Henry continued angrily. "They doped the girls up on all kinds of drugs to make them seem ladylike and genteel. That's why Mother liked the place. You could almost pretend they were normal at times."

"But why was Jennie there at all? What was wrong with her?"

Henry gulped down some more of his drink. Anne could see that his hands were shaking. The scotch sloshed against the sides of the glass.

"We didn't know. Jennie was eight years older than me. She was always nervous, even as a child. Hyper, I guess you'd call it now. She couldn't go to school because she couldn't sit still. She used to bounce from room to room at Dovecote, talking a blue streak. Jumping rope for hours or riding her bicycle up and down the street all day. She wouldn't even stop to eat. And then other times, Mother wouldn't be able to drag her out of bed. Jennie would stare into space, like a zombie. Mother had to get her dressed, feed her, bathe her, everything."

Anne thought of the pictures she'd taken from Aunt Hannah's bedroom. Jennie posed, through the years, as though someone had arranged her limbs just so, always staring vacantly into space.

"What did the doctors say?" she asked Henry.

"Oh, Mother got all kinds of diagnoses, from schizophrenia to a vitamin deficiency. Take your pick."

Schizophrenia. Alzheimer's. Madness seemed to bloom in Anne's family like orchids growing wild in the jungle.

"One time Jennie climbed up on the roof and started howling like a dog. Another time she went into the pharmacy and started throwing stuff off the shelves. Or there was the time she smeared black ink all over her body. You never knew what she'd do next. Hurricane Jennie, I used to call her."

Henry downed the rest of his drink and signaled for another. On TV, three muscular young men were ogling a buxom blond while enjoying the great taste of Miller beer. The bar had emptied out. There were just a few other men besides the group at Henry's table.

"After Greeley House burned down," Anne said, "then what happened?"

Henry sighed. His eyes had a glazed, filmy cast as if he were having trouble focusing. It occurred to Anne that it was probably harder to glide on the surface of his addiction now than when he was younger. Over the years alcohol had eaten away at him.

"Jennie moved in with us for a while, but that didn't work out. She refused to take her medication, acted crazy all the time."

Anne took a sip of her seltzer. It was flat. She looked down at Bronte, who probably needed a week's worth of baths to recover from lying on the dirty, grimy floor. This was another dead end. Jennie. Greeley House. It had nothing whatsoever to do with the murders.

"And then?" Anne prompted. Not so much because she really wanted to know but because she couldn't face the thought of climbing off her bar stool and going home. It required too much energy.

"Bartender," she called out. "I'd like a vodka tonic."

But what she really wanted was to be numb, to coast through the next twenty-four hours feeling no pain.

Henry waited until she got her drink. "To better days," he said, clinking the rims of their glasses together. "And to Kim. God rest her soul."

"Amen."

She took a long swallow and nearly gagged. The vodka burned her throat. It was like drinking carburetor fluid.

"Hey, Henry," the clownish woman yelled from the table. "How 'bout another round?"

"Sure thing," Henry said, ordering fresh drinks for his friends.

He was running up quite a tab. Anne wondered if he had enough money to pay the bill.

"If you could go back and change just one thing in your life," Henry suddenly asked, grasping her hand. "What would it be?"

He was staring at her as if his future depended on her answer. What would she change? Her mother's Alzheimer's? Her choice of career? Her decision to host a family reunion?

"I'd have Kim not be dead," she said simply, then realized she hadn't answered the question fairly. She was powerless to change what had happened, as much as she might wish it to be so.

But Henry seemed satisfied. "My life could have been so different," he said hoarsely. "If I'd left the house a minute earlier. Or a minute later. One minute." He was squeezing her hand so hard, it hurt. "That's all it took."

Anne thought of the car accident. A young woman's life destroyed forever. One turn in the road that could never be undone.

"Your mother was trying to help get the charges dropped," Anne said.

It was small comfort, but she had nothing else to offer him. "What?" he asked, stunned.

"Aunt Hannah's lawyers were trying to work out a settlement with the woman whose car you hit. I guess she didn't want you to know."

Henry let go of Anne's hand. His face looked as if it were about to crumple into pieces. His eyes got watery. "Mother did that . . . for me?"

Something in his voice made Anne shiver. She pushed her drink away. "What happened to Jennie?"

A tear slid down Henry's cheek. "Suicide," he said, nearly choking on the word. "They found her with her wrists slashed in some rundown motel. Blood all over the place. She'd been there for a couple of days. Her kid was too traumatized to get help. Oh, God." Henry was sobbing now, his face wet with tears. "Jennie begged Mother for money. She used to come to Dovecote and literally get down on her knees and beg. But Mother always threw her out. And look what came of it. Look," Henry yelled, bringing his fist down so hard on the bar that the glasses shook.

Out of the corner of her eye, Anne saw the bartender coming toward them. Impulsively, she threw her arms around Henry and hugged him. "It's okay," she whispered. "It's going to be okay."

They stayed like that for a few moments. Anne was conscious of the game blaring on TV, the low hum of conversation, the bartender watching over them. It was probably more acceptable to start a fight in a place like the Blue Angel than to break down in tears.

Henry pulled away first, mopping his face with a cocktail napkin. "Some family reunion, eh?" he said. Though his glass was empty, he didn't ask for a refill.

Anne said, "You mentioned that Jennie had a child. I didn't know about that."

"Nobody did. She met someone in Greeley House. An aide or an orderly I think it was. They had a brief affair, she got pregnant, and when Greeley burned down, he took off. My sister tried to find him, but I don't think she ever did. She was just a kid herself."

"And the child?"

"Jennie kept the child with her. God knows what the poor thing went through. Sleeping in welfare hotels, not eating for days, watching her mother sink into madness. Jennie used to drag the kid to Dovecote with her, begging Mother for money. But you know Hannah. She refused to help them unless Jennie signed some document relinquishing all parental rights. Jennie wouldn't do it. As sick as she was, she wanted her kid with her. She'd never let mother take away her only child."

"And then Jennie died." Anne leaned forward. "What became of the child?" she asked eagerly.

"I don't know. I asked Mother about it but she said there was no child. She said Jennie made the whole thing up. Mother forbid anyone in the family to mention Jennie again. It was like she never existed. I'm not even sure where she's buried."

Anne felt a surge of excitement. At last, she was getting somewhere. "The child. Did Jennie write you whether she gave birth to a girl or a boy?"

A wisp of a smile appeared on Henry's face. For a moment, Anne caught a glimpse of the old Henry, the man who hadn't been ruined by misfortune and alcohol.

"She had a girl. Rosalie Faith was her name because Jennie loved roses. Rosalie was three when Jennie died, if she ever existed at all."

Rosalie Faith. Rosalie Faith Rutter. Images flashed through Anne's mind in quick succession: the chef's knife, the poster at Hanley-Britt, a cube steak, a calligraphy pen, a bunch of pink roses.

"Oh, I think she exists all right," Anne said slowly. "I think she's been here all along."

Chapter 20

It's a dangerous myth to believe that a barking dog won't bite. Barking or growling can telegraph the intention to attack, which is why watching a dog's body language for signs of aggression is important.

It was hard to compete for tourists' dollars. Cape May had its annual Victorian fair. Point Pleasant Beach had fireworks over the boardwalk every Thursday night in July and August. Red Bank featured Riverfest, a jazz and blues extravaganza in Marine Park, overlooking the Navesink River, while at Ocean City there was the annual August Baby Parade, where dolled-up tots promenaded in gaily decorated carriages, strollers, wagons, and bicycles.

The tiny tourism office in Oceanside Heights sponsored the annual summer house tour, a couple of flea markets, a crafts fair, and an art show. In the fall, there was a Teddy

Bear Tea Party and at Christmas, a candlelight Victorian house tour. But the town was still lacking a blockbuster event that would generate excitement and create some elusive but longed-for buzz.

Enter the August regatta held the third Sunday of the month at the marina. Founded two years before, the regatta had already managed to attract an additional three thousand people to the Heights each time it was held. The premise was this: different types of races, involving sailboats, motorboats, canoes, yachts, even swimmers. Prizes involved restaurants and services in town, such as a free dinner for two at the Pelican Café or a free weekend at the Ocean Vista Hotel or a free set of vintage linens at Kitsch & Kaboodle on Main Street.

There was a $20 entrance fee for the races, and spectators had taken to bringing lawn chairs and picnic baskets down to the water, which lent the games a festive, friendly air. Anne had watched it each summer and had even considered taking part in the water-skiing competition, which rated entrants on speed, agility, and the difficulty of the tricks performed. But ultimately she'd decided the event made the perfect capstone to the reunion weekend. She'd planned to stake out a small patch of turf near the dock and had intended to pack a picnic supper for those of her relatives who wanted to watch the races.

Now as she drove through town, she passed all the decorations that had been put up to advertise the regatta. Small flags flew from storefronts and several blue-and-white banners arched over Main Street, flapping merrily in the breeze. The Heights was more crowded than usual, as camera-toting tourists and townspeople alike flocked to the marina. Anne pulled up to the curb outside her house and noticed, with annoyance, that every parking space on her street appeared to be taken.

"Sometimes," she said, aloud to Bronte. "I wish the tourists would take a hike."

But at least the reporters were gone for now. Hallelujah. Maybe her fifteen minutes of fame was history.

She made a right at the corner, then a left, continuing three more blocks to McClintock Street. Delia lived in a two-story putty-colored Victorian Eclectic house, which luckily had a small garage. Anne pulled into the driveway, thanking her lucky stars that some sunburned tourist hadn't decided to grab the space first and worry about the consequences later.

Walking back to Ocean Avenue with Bronte in tow, Anne saw that many people had dressed up to watch the regatta. Women in white linen dresses and stockings paraded by, wearing heels and makeup. Men had on blazers; a few even sported ties and straw boaters.

"Oh, brother," Anne muttered under her breath. "Next thing you know there'll be croquet."

She was in a peculiar mood, keyed up yet reflective, trying to understand the significance of the last piece of the puzzle. It was still beastly hot. The flat ribbon of clouds threading the sky over the Atlantic had darkened, promising more rain. Bronte trotted along behind her, too overheated or fatigued to do much exploring.

When they reached Anne's house, the pug bounded up the walk and skipped happily inside. It was a treat to be out of the heat, if only for a little while. Anne had left the fans on for Harry and the house was relatively cool.

She checked her messages. One from Cece, saying she, Alex, Nora, and Larry were going to the funeral home in Toms River to go over the final arrangements, followed by a trip to the mall to look for Kim's favorite music, Billie Holiday singing the blues. Could she come? Anne glanced at her

watch. By the time she got to the funeral parlor, they'd probably have left.

The second message was from Callahan, the New York
lawyer. He was driving down to the Heights tomorrow, first
thing in the morning. He'd be there by eleven, later if there
was traffic on the turnpike.

"Whoop-de-do," Anne said to Harry and Bronte, who had
followed her into the office and were eyeing each other warily from opposite corners of the room, ears flat and tails
twitching as if spoiling for a fight.

The third message was from Trasker. "Hey, Annie," he
said. "News flash. You know the guy we were talking about
at lunch? Turns out you were right. He *is* having a fling on
the side. I tracked down the lady and I'm on my way to see
her now. I'll call you when I get back. Love you."

So Larry was having an affair right under Kim's nose.
Anne hoped her cousin hadn't known. The betrayal would
have crushed poor Kimmie. She felt a surge of anger toward
Larry. Did he feel relieved now that Kim was gone and he
was free to take up with whomever he wished?

She thought about how Trasker had phrased his message.
No names. No specific information. Oh, God. The police.
Had they gotten a warrant and searched the house? She
raced from room to room, alert for signs of intruders, but
could find nothing out of place.

In the kitchen, she found what she was looking for. Someone had gone through the cabinets and drawers. They
looked . . . well, if truth be told, they looked neater than
usual, as if someone had taken care to replace the food, silverware, and pots just so. She felt a sliver of fear creep down
her spine. They were closing in. The next time they arrested
her, they'd put her in jail for good.

Moving mechanically, she put out fresh food and water

for the animals, taking care to keep their bowls as far apart as possible and to set Harry's on the counter, out of reach of inquisitive pugs. She poured herself a glass of iced tea and wolfed down a cream cheese and jelly sandwich. If she was right about the murders, she'd need proof. How to get it? How to get it?

Her eyes roamed around the kitchen, finally settling on the spot on the counter where the knife set had been. Of course. Why hadn't she thought of it before? There was still a chance.

Dumping the dishes in the sink, she turned the radio dial to a classical music channel. If music soothed the savage beast, maybe it would help the Fighting Foes calm down. She moved Bronte's food dish into the living room and locked the dog behind the baby gate.

"I'll be back in a little while," she told the pug. "Then we'll go for a walk, okay?"

Bronte gazed at her with reproach. As she grabbed her pocketbook and headed out the door, she could have sworn the dog looked hurt at being left behind.

Maybe there was some way she could take Harry, too, so he didn't feel so excluded. Pet sensitivity. Edie Mintzler was devoting half a chapter to it in the book.

Outside, Ocean Avenue was practically deserted. The beach had closed for the day; the sand was undisturbed save for a flock of seagulls picking through the trash. The sky had grown darker. Anne liked the Heights this way. Still, serene. It reminded her of the off-season, when the tourists had all left and the town quieted down.

It was still oppressively hot, but there was a pleasant breeze off the ocean, reminding her she was glad she lived by the water. When she got to the Laughing Gull, she went around the side of the building and entered through the side door, where you were supposed to rinse your feet with the hose. Moving as soundlessly as she could, she caught a glimpse of the front desk, which was empty. No teenage girl manning the phones or handing out messages. In fact, the whole B&B seemed eerily quiet. Great. All the better for what she had in mind.

She crept through the ground-floor hallway and entered the kitchen. Despite the messiness that pervaded the rest of her personal quarters, Pat always kept her kitchen spotless. She'd once told Anne you could tell good cooks by the appearance of their kitchens. A dirty sink and cluttered shelves indicated a sloppy chef. By the look of Pat's kitchen, Pat could have had her own gourmet cooking show on late-night cable TV. The tile floor had been swept clean, the sink looked like it had been freshly scrubbed, the countertops sparkled.

Anne took a brief inventory of what was on those countertops: a covered glass cake dome containing what looked to be half an orange layer cake, a coffeemaker, a microwave oven, a toaster, a spice rack, a ceramic cookie jar shaped like Little Red Riding Hood, and a knife set in a wood chopping block. She approached the knives, wondering why she'd never noticed them before. They were different from the ones she owned. The handles were slightly wider and there were two decorative circles on them, instead of three. Anne slid the eight-inch chef's knife out of its slip and held the blade up to the light. The word *Sabatier* was inscribed in tiny letters on the blade. The set looked new; the stainless steel fairly gleamed.

Had Pat bought it at the mall? In Linens 'n Things perhaps? Hard to say.

Anne studied the seafoam-green cabinets. Several had glass fronts revealing pretty Fiesta ware dishes in shades of green and pink. As striking as they appeared, Anne knew the look would never work at home. Her own dishes were jumbled together haphazardly. It was a blessing they were hidden behind solid wood.

She turned her attention to the cabinets underneath the countertop, opening each one in turn and examining the contents. There were lots of pots and pans, including the expensive no-stick kind with the iron-clad surface. Pat had stacked her glass nesting bowls neatly and had grouped her Tupperware together. There were all sorts of small appliances: blenders, choppers, peelers, mixers, and a collection of cake pans, muffin tins, roasting pans, and serving platters. The perfect tools for the perfect cook.

Anne stood up and glanced around the room, taking another quick inventory. Where could it be? Maybe the kitchen was too obvious a hiding place. She headed toward the dining room and then doubled back, remembering the pantry off the kitchen, a small three-by-eight-foot space, with a built-in cupboard, painted a soft cream color.

It was loaded with fancy dishes. Blue and white Delft china. Delicate Spode plates with gold rims. Teacups that had been painted with lifelike sprigs of lilac and clusters of lush peonies. Pat had also collected an array of glassware: pale green wine goblets, cut-crystal tumblers, slender champagne flutes.

In the lower left-hand cabinet, Anne found the good flatware, a five-piece set of silverplate for twelve, arranged in a tray lined with green velvet. There were damask tablecloths and napkins, several pairs of candlestick holders, a silver gravy boat. But none of them was what Anne was searching for.

She stood up and glanced at her watch. Six o'clock. In another half-hour or so, the regatta would end and the spectators would start drifting back toward the church for the concert. Maybe this was another wild-goose chase. Maybe she'd guessed wrong.

She stood still for a moment, listening. The Laughing Gull was quiet, so quiet that the only thing she heard was the sound of her own breathing. Then a thunderclap pierced the silence and Anne inadvertently jumped. She'd better hurry if she wanted to beat the storm.

Moving as noiselessly as she could, she walked down the hallway, past the sitting room she'd been in earlier in the day. At the end of the hall were three closed doors. She opened the nearest one. A bathroom with towels and cosmetics strewn on the sink. Opposite that was a linen closet, where sheets and towels had been jammed together helter-skelter.

Anne turned the knob of the third door and opened it to find Pat's bedroom. It was an even bigger mess than the sitting room. There were so many clothes, books, and shoes scattered on the ground that it was hard to make out the wood floor beneath. The bed was unmade, the shades drawn. Every surface, from the aqua-colored dresser stenciled with hopping frogs to the trunk covered with psychedelic stickers, was covered with stuff. It looked like a burglar had ransacked the place, but hadn't found anything worth stealing.

Closing the door behind her, Anne walked over to the closet and peered inside. It was in complete disarray. Dresses, blouses, and pants were piled on the floor in a heap, and every available inch of space was filled with objects jammed into bright plastic bins. Anne peered into the nearest one, which contained an old hairbrush, several *National Geographic* magazines, different-colored golf balls, a raggedy stuffed animal shaped like a sheep, theater playbills, a small American flag, and other assorted detritus.

It would take years to sort through this stuff, Anne thought grimly. Think, she urged herself. Where would a quasi-professional chef store her cooking implements? She glanced around the room. Not under the bed. Or in the dresser. Or in this messy pit of a closet.

When it came to her kitchen, Pat was immaculate. So where? Anne's gaze fell on the trunk. It was a chocolate-brown hue, with gold hardware, and Pat had covered the top with toile fabric depicting small birds flitting amid the underbrush. Anne folded the fabric back and threw open the lid.

Perhaps at one time Pat had intended to use the trunk as an occasional table. But now it was carefully packed with letters, cards, paperback books, a vintage toaster that was missing its dials, covered boxes, game boards, dolls, and a host of other unrelated objects.

She started to examine the contents, then suddenly froze. From somewhere in the inn, she thought she heard a noise. A soft thump, like a small package hitting the floor. She got up and went to the door. Had her cousins returned? Was one of the teenage girls manning the desk out front again? Or had Pat come home? She almost called out, then caught herself. This might be her only chance to search Pat's bedroom. She didn't want to lose it.

Another peal of thunder split the sky, nearer this time. Leaving the door open, she crept back to the trunk and began rummaging through it, pushing things aside, digging deeper, feeling like Bronte burrowing in the dirt, pursuing a succulent yet elusive bone. She wished the dog were there now, wished she could command Bronte to seek out the knife. Her hands touched cotton, metal, wood, wax. And then, plunging her hands deeper into the trunk, past a headless porcelain doll and a set of mismatched candles, she felt the outline of something smooth and long and sharp.

It was wrapped in a fleecy black angora sweater that had been folded into a small, compact bundle. Anne pulled at the sweater carefully, extricating it from the trunk as if it were a helpless newborn. Although the sweater looked old, it was soft and well laundered. Mother-of-pearl buttons were sewn onto the front. The sleeves had a slight hint of ribbing.

Anne swept away some of the clutter on the floor and lay the sweater down. She knew whose it was instinctively, though she'd never set eyes on it before. With trembling fingers she folded back the sleeves, unwrapping the sweater like a present. The knife lay inside a blood-stained rag. It was identical to the one she owned, the one the police had found in her dresser, with one small exception: Though the steel blade was shiny and clean, the wood handle was darker, as though patches had been stained a rust-colored brown. All that blood. You could rinse it off metal, but not off wood.

Anne stared at the knife, careful not to touch. If only she'd remembered about this earlier, the day Delia told her the knives were on sale. It was late April, still cool for spring. The forsythia had just started to bloom. She'd been sitting at one of the computer stations at the library, beginning to research *The Pet Connection*. And Pat . . . Pat had been there, too, at another computer, culling recipes from the *Landsdown Park Press*.

Pat must have gone to Linens 'n Things and bought herself the same knife set. Had she been plotting since then? Selecting her victims? When did she first suspect the truth?

Anne folded the knife back up in the sweater. Jennie's sweater. She tried to picture what Pat's early years had been like. The horrible scenes at Dovecote. Jennie begging Hannah for money. Screaming, crying. Hannah refusing, lashing out, threatening to take Pat away, the evil witch in a monstrous fairy tale gone wrong.

But then it was easy for her to imagine it. She, too, had had a mentally unstable mother. She, too, had been tempted to blame every bad thing that had ever happened to her on the madness that had seeped into her life without warning.

They had that much in common, she and Pat. The madness twisting and tormenting their mothers like an evil choking vine. But Anne had been thirteen when Alzheimer's struck her mother. How awful for Pat to have spent her most formative years trapped between Jennie's disease and Hannah's anger and indifference.

Anne felt tears sting her eyes. Poor innocent Kim and her endless string of hobbies. The family tree. The calligraphy practiced with painstaking care. The visit to the adoption agency. Kim had always been so detail-oriented and meticulous, so intent on getting things *right*. And where had it gotten her in the end? To the truth unveiled. To this last familial revelation. That dark smile. That bizarre twitch. This last hidden cousin.

Anne felt a white-hot surge of rage. Damn Pat Mooney and her tortured childhood. She had no right. No right.

Anne turned from the trunk and looked up to see Pat standing above her. For an instant, before something hard struck her on the head, before she blacked out and toppled to the floor, she saw the malice in Pat's gray eyes.

It was cool and dark. Rain drummed against the windowpane. The air smelled of damp earth and mildew. Anne's head throbbed. She was lying on her back, looking up at a wood plank ceiling laced with cobwebs. She couldn't move. And that thought filled her with a panic so intense that she tried to sit up and immediately sank back against the cold dirt floor. Pain exploded inside her head. She closed her eyes. But that was worse. Like being sealed alive inside a dirt tomb.

She opened her eyes and tried to scream. But there was something over her mouth. Something tight and immovable that kept her voice trapped inside her throat. She stared at the ceiling, where a spider was slowly descending from a silver gossamer thread.

Where is this place? Where am I?

Anne looked around, trying to take inventory without having to move her aching head. She squinted into the dark. Shelves. Lots of shelves. Filled with rows of cans and jars. Something floating in the jars? Bobbing darkly under cloudy glass? A bicycle with one wheel. A hula hoop. Hoses coiled tight as snakes. Boxes piled three and four high. Across the room, two rectangular windows, with cloudy, dust-streaked panes.

The basement. She was lying on the dirt floor of the basement at the Laughing Gull. In the jars, blueberries and strawberries were dissolving into jam. She wriggled her legs, only to realize they were bound at the ankles with thick, sturdy rope, as were her wrists.

She raised her arms carefully above her head and tried to read her watch, but it was too dark. Her fingers pulled at her bonds in vain. She'd been bound with her hands facing outward and she couldn't quite reach the ropes. She tried to sit up again so she could attempt to undo the ties binding her ankles, but the pain in her head brought her crashing back to the floor, in a flash of pain and nausea.

Rain pounded against the side of the house. From a distance, she heard other scattered sounds: the hushed trill of a telephone, the faint honking of cars, and above that a soft melody, snatches of music drifting beneath the house as if borne by the wind. The concert at the church. It had started.

Anne lifted her legs and brought them down heavily on the floor. But the dirt and the rain muffled any sound she might have made. Raising her arms over her head again, she inched backward, hands outstretched, searching for something she could throw or break, something that would make some noise.

Her hands brushed loose dirt, then bumped into something—a box, a carton?—too heavy to move. She wriggled backward at an angle, though each time she made the slight-est movement, she felt a burning, searing pain, like a brand-ing iron searing the inside of her head.

Her fingers touched cardboard again. This time the box seemed to be open or on its side. Anne felt something small and round and smooth. She cradled it in her palm and brought it forward. A Ping-Pong ball. With all the strength she could muster, she threw the ball at one of the windows on the far side of the room.

It landed short of the mark, just as the door swung open. Pat, after closing the heavy door behind her, skipped down the steps leading to the cellar. Anne felt her body tense up as Pat approached.

"Oh, good," Pat said softly. "You're awake."

In the half-dark, her eyes were flinty hollow orbs, her lips widening to form a polite, exaggerated smile. She sat down heavily on the dirt floor, with her knees tucked under her skirt. Her nearness made Anne wince.

"I was hoping I'd get a chance to talk to you before the end," Pat said, keeping her voice low. "So I could explain. So you'd know it had nothing to do with you. Nothing at all."

The end, Anne thought uneasily, feeling her heart skip a beat. Oh, Jesus.

"I've always liked your family," Pat continued. "Well, all except Cece. She's always been a little weird. Don't you think? But at least you *had* a family. Growing up, I used to wish I was adopted. Isn't that strange? But you knew it all along, didn't you, Annie? That's why you decided to hold the reunion here in town. You knew I was one of you." Pat sighed heavily. "I wish things had turned out differently, don't you? Imagine. We could have been like sisters. Wouldn't you have liked that? I'd have cooked you all my favorite foods. Borscht. And duck with papaya sauce. And tomatoes flambé. It could have been fabulous."

The rain was coming down harder now and Anne had to strain to hear the rest. The back of her head throbbed hotly and Pat's voice was thready and thin. She could barely make it out.

Aunt Hannah, Anne tried to say. But it came out sounding like *ahn na-na.* If she could just keep Pat talking a little longer. Until someone came. She shifted her weight, her skin chafing against the ropes. Her hands were still thrust over her head, like she was cooling down after an exercise class.

"But it's really worked out almost better this way," Pat said, nodding sagely. "Because otherwise you'd have had to spend the rest of your life in jail. And that wouldn't be any fun. I didn't want that for you. Honest, Annie. I just couldn't think what else to do. So I pulled a switcheroo." Pat giggled. "I bet you're wondering how I did it. Right? Well, it was easy. Remember Thursday morning, when you were helping me get the place ready? I just sneaked your house key out of your bag and made myself an extra copy. See, you thought I was in the garden, picking more flowers. But I was really at the locksmith. The guy makes up keys for me all the time on account of the guests keep losing them.

"On Friday morning, while you were at Dovecote, I hightailed it over to your place and planted your aunt's jewelry in your bureau drawer. Pretty smart of me, right? And I went back last night to hide the knife I used on Kim." Pat grinned proudly. "Have the cops found it yet? I buried it in your backyard, underneath the forsythia bush. And I made sure Martha Cox saw me heading up your walk. She's so nearsighted I knew she'd think I was you. Mother—I mean my adopted Mother, not my real mother—anyway, Mother always says how I'm not very bright, but I showed her, didn't I? I found those adoption papers when I was cleaning out her attic and it was like a light bulb clicked in my brain. Mother had insisted on knowing the birth mother's name and family background. I guess she was tickled to get Hannah Rutter's grandkid. Proved I had a good pedigree, good breeding. I wish I'd had the chance to know my real mother better. I bet we were a lot alike."

Anne shivered. It was pouring outside and the sky had grown so dark it looked like night had fallen. The tape over her mouth smelled of chemicals. She had to resist the urge to gag.

"Do you know what your aunt tried to do?" Pat demanded. "She wanted to buy me off. Get rid of me, like I was some sort of pest. But I could tell she was afraid of me. Even when I called and told her who I was and she got all high and mighty, I knew she was scared to death."

Pat scooped up a handful of dirt, then let it trickle slowly through her fingers. "I'm sorry about Kim," she said in a low conspiratorial tone. "She was always nice to me. But she figured things out. Just like you did. She would have told on me. She would have *told*."

Frantically, Anne threw Pat a beseeching look. She tried to send a message with her eyes: *Get a grip. Untie me. Be smart.*

But Pat was barely paying attention. She'd pulled something out of a pocket in her skirt. It gleamed silver, the blade sleek and metallic.

"Bye-bye, Annie," Pat said softly. "If you hold still, it won't hurt as much."

In horror, Anne watched the knife rise high above her body, then plunge down, down toward her chest. She rolled to her right, away from Pat, but not quick enough. A sharp pain tore through her left arm, just below the elbow.

Her hands scrabbled wildly for some kind of weapon, clawing at the contents of the cardboard box.

Help, she screamed, as loud as she could. *Help me*. But barely any sound escaped the tape.

The knife ascended again and Pat loomed above her, wild-eyed and determined. Anne rolled again. Once. Twice. The pain in her head and arm so terrible it felt like she were being set aflame. Dirt. Pain. Fire. The knife caught her left calf, slicing the skin open.

Anne was on her back, in agony. She'd rolled into a wall of boxes and found herself trapped. Flailing in panic, her fingers closed on something cold and round. She grabbed on to it and hurled it at Pat's head as the knife plunged down once more.

Pat uttered a soft "Oh" of surprise and fell backward, dropping the knife onto the dirt floor. With all the strength she had left, Anne swung herself up, the terrible pain crippling her movements worse than the rope bonds. She scrounged in the dirt for the knife but came up empty, bleeding profusely, woozy and hurting.

Pat had struggled to a sitting position and was pawing the dirt in a daze. Out of the corner of her eye, Anne saw the object she'd thrown, which had glanced off Pat's forehead. A small fire extinguisher. Bending at the waist, she snatched it up awkwardly and took aim. It sailed through the air and hit the target.

There was the sound of broken glass and then a loud, steady siren as the burglar alarm went off. Through a haze of pain, Anne thought it was the sweetest noise she'd ever heard.

Chapter 21

*Do cats have nine lives?
Kitties that fall out of windows two or three stories
high usually live to tell
the tale. Even falls of over
seven or eight floors are
sometimes not fatal. The
falling cat has enough
time to relax its body and
spread itself out, creating
enough aerodynamic drag
to slow himself down.*

"Her name is Elaine Dewitt," Trasker said, reaching for a toasted coconut donut. "She and Larry have been having an affair for the past eighteen months. She's divorced, in her early thirties, pursuing a career as an interior decorator, which is how she met Larry in the first place. He hired Elaine to redecorate his Boston office."

Anne nodded and took another sip of her iced tea. They were sitting on her front porch the following morning and she felt tolerably well, considering she'd spent the night at

he hospital, after receiving twenty-three stitches and being
reated for a concussion. Of course, the drugs helped a lot.
Thank God for Percodan.

"I wonder if Kim knew," Anne mused. "I doubt she did.
The way I figure, Kim thought Larry killed Aunt Hannah.
He was out with his mistress, this Elaine person, Thursday
night, but Kim believed he was over at Dovecote, robbing
Hannah, then stabbing her to death. That's why she was acting so strangely, wandering around in the rain for hours, being so brusque and uncommunicative. You know what else?
think Larry had pegged *Kim* as the murderer. It explains
why he was uncharacteristically protective of her at the
beach. He thought Kim killed Aunt Hannah to inherit her
money and help stem his business losses."

"Sounds like a marriage made in hell," Trasker said dryly.
"Meanwhile, Larry's facing criminal charges up in Massachusetts. Apparently the authorities have discovered that the
fire in the Newton house was deliberately set."

Anne stared at the ocean, which was calm today, a deep
royal-blue that looked deliciously inviting. Sunlight glinted
off the waves. After the storm had passed, the temperature
had dropped and the humidity had disappeared. It was shap-
ing up to be a perfect beach day.

"Your cousin Alex checked out of the Laughing Gull late
last night," Trasker said. "Packed his bag and split without
paying the bill."

Anne raised a questioning eyebrow.

"He must have realized he was off the hook for the murder," Trasker continued, "and it was an opportune time to
skip town. There were two men looking for him at the B&B
this morning. One of them has ties to organized crime, although the Feds have never been able to charge him with
anything."

"So it looks like Alex left in the nick of time."

Trasker nodded. "I hope for his sake those goons don't catch up with him."

"Poor Heather," Anne said, with a mock sigh. "Her knight in shining armor rode off without a backward glance."

"From what you've told me about her, she'll probably survive just fine. Incidentally, Chase Merritt has also left town. Burns spoke with the Boston PD and they're going to be keeping a close eye on Mr. Merritt, to make sure he doesn't prey on any more unsuspecting widows."

The cat sprang onto Anne's lap and leaned his head against her stomach. Anne broke off a piece of powdered donut and fed him some. From across the porch, Bronte began to yap and bark.

"Oh, shush," Anne scolded gently, tossing the rest of the donut onto the flowered rag rug. "There's plenty for both of you."

Bronte approached cautiously, her eyes trained warily on Harry.

"You think you'll keep her?" Trasker asked, gesturing toward the pug.

"Yeah, why not? She's beginning to grow on me. And maybe one of these days, she and Harry will start trusting one another. You know, Bronte's been through a lot—losing her owner, being drugged by Pat."

"At least Bronte probably didn't see Hannah get killed."

Anne nodded sadly and leaned her head back against the white wicker chair. The events of the last few days had left her emotionally and physically drained. It was just starting to sink in that she and Pat were related, that the madness in her family had surfaced again and her newest second cousin was probably going to be spending the rest of her life behind bars. Or in a mental institution. Pat's court-appointed lawyer intended to plead insanity. He was claiming Pat was bipolar and possibly psychotic. What if Anne had discovered the connection to Pat earlier? Could she have saved Aunt Hannah? Or Kim?

What if Jennie hadn't committed suicide, but had given Pat a stable, loving home? Would Pat have become like a sister to Anne? Would they have wound up being best friends?

Anne closed her eyes. There was no use wishing disease away. Anne knew from experience it didn't work. All the what-ifs in the world couldn't change what had happened. It would take more than reunions for her and her cousins to work through their grief, or look at each other the same way they did before, or sort through the upheaval, the lies and the mistrust.

"Annie, are you feeling okay?"

Anne's eyes snapped open and she saw Trasker studying her with concern. "I'll be all right."

"Good thing you've got a mean pitching arm."

Anne had to laugh. "Think the Phillies will sign me? I could use the dough, now that I'm no longer a millionaire."

Aunt Hannah's lawyer had called an hour ago with a financial update. It seemed that in a more recent will, Hannah Rutter had left her fortune to the Boston chapter of the Society for the Prevention of Cruelty to Animals. The cousins would receive $6,000 each a year. The will specified that Anne's portion of the inheritance go toward the care and feeding of Bronte.

Trasker reached across the wicker table and took hold of Anne's hand. "Annie, you're worth over a million to me. I don't know what I would have done if I'd lost you."

Anne's eyes inexplicably filled with tears. Taking one glance at her face, Trasker rose and came around to the back of her chair. He leaned forward and wrapped his arms gently around Anne's shoulders, showering her with kisses.

This is what mattered, she thought, feeling a glimmer of

joy penetrate her sad, pensive mood. He was her family now. Her heart. Her happiness.

She gazed again at the flat expanse of ocean before her, at the sunlight skimming the crest of the waves. The air smelled salty and newly washed.

She turned her head and saw Nora and Cece less than a block away, walking toward them on Ocean Avenue. Trasker saw them too and straightened up. Nora quickened her pace. Cece waved.

They'd have to figure out how Cece could get custody of little Julia again and how Nora was going to handle the embezzlement charges. Trasker would help. Anne was sure of it.

But for now, breakfast was waiting on the front porch, and it was time for another reunion of sorts, for both sides of her family to get acquainted.

Anne raised her glass of iced tea, as if to toast their arrival, and smiled.